Where the Cotton Once Grew

Stephen Harris

PAGE PUBLISHING, INC.
Conneaut Lake, PA

First originally published by Page Publishing 2021

ISBN 978-1-6624-5989-4 (pbk)
ISBN 978-1-6624-7572-6 (hc)
ISBN 978-1-6624-5990-0 (digital)

Printed in the United States of America

To the old marine and the Navy WAVE
that loved him so. Semper fi.

Acknowledgments

First and foremost, to my wonderful wife of many decades. Her love and devotion to our family stands tall among all women. She is beloved by everyone she touches.

I thank my daughters from the depths of my heart for being such daddy's girls and for loving baseball as much as I do.

To my friend Russell Roberts for his constant encouragement throughout many starts, stops, and constant failures and rewrites. He never lets me stay discouraged.

I would also like to thank Dr. Frank Gogan for watching over my health all these many years. He is a credit to his profession, and his bedside-manner approaches sainthood. There'll never be another like him.

My greatest thanks, though, is to the one who hung on the cruel cross of Calvary for a wretched sinner such as me.

Chapter 1

Early October 1938, Roxboro, South Alabama

Sara brushed a stray red hair from her face as she walked across the sandy loam of the peanut field. She watched her five-year-old son, Sam, efficiently pluck another green peanut from the stack, roll it between his hands to remove stray particles of sand, and then split it open with his front teeth.

She ducked her head and grimaced slightly as a warm south wind caused a dust devil to rise, buffeting her sunburned face with sand. Her denim overalls were heavy with sweat, and she tugged at the straps trying to find relief from the weight pulling against her shoulders.

The dust devil passed, and Sarah resumed walking toward Sam. She felt great relief as she dropped, knees first, into the soft dirt. Sam hadn't heard her approach. Her heart swelled as she looked at her son. "Sam, are you ready to eat lunch?"

Sam turned to face his mother. His skin shone a very healthy pink, though weeks ago, it was the pale pallor of white. His eyes were like hers, emerald green, but his hair was much lighter, a whisper from being white. Sara often wondered if Sam's small frame came from her or the sheer struggle to keep him fed since the day he was born.

Sara called Sam over and hugged him tightly, and she heard him grunt slightly from the embrace. The brutal rape that had produced her son had long since been pushed to the back of her mind. Her overwhelming love for Sam had given her the strength that she needed to survive.

She sat on the dirt, leaned against the peanut stack, not minding the pricking from the stiff stems, and reached for the burlap sack, which held their food and water jar. Sara opened the sack and pulled out a piece of fried catfish wrapped in old newspaper. She began feeding Sam the tender chunks of white meat.

"I'm full, Mama," he said, so she laid the fish on the bag and gave him a drink of water. Sara ate the rest while Sam watched a young orange-breasted robin swoop in, steal a peanut, and fly away. She felt her eyes well with tears and her body shudder as she watched her son. It had been such a desperate struggle to hold on to her boy. Of course, growing up a bastard child in Roxboro was no easy task. Sara had already lived that life, and now her son had to do the same.

Perhaps Lilly, her mother, had made it harder by being the way she was—a pretty, buxom woman with flaming-red hair who somehow supported her children without any visible means. Sara and her older brother, Stuart, had to endure the small-town whispers of, "There they are. Those children ain't got no daddy." They also had to ignore the talk of how their mother managed to pay the rent with no money coming in. Stuart and Sara tried their best to understand Lilly and her ways.

*****

They lived in a small settlement on the edge of town, at the end of a dusty, sometimes muddy dirt road. It was filled with little clapboard houses slapped together with wooden outhouses perched on the edge of dirt yards. On hot, muggy summer days, they would walk for miles and sit on the bank of the Pea River to escape the stench.

Most of the time, there was barely enough food, but Lilly insisted they were only one step away from living the comfortable life her family once lived. On the rare occasions that she spoke at length, she would tell how their family harkened from Harris County in Georgia. Before the war, they owned many slaves and worked hundreds of acres of land.

There were bountiful peach and pear orchards, catfish by the dozen on trotlines, smokehouses full of good sausages and hams, and hot summer evenings spent sitting on huge porches, fanning the night away. "One day, children, everything will be the same," Lilly would say with a flick of her head. "We'll have tea in fancy cups and take trips to Montgomery just to see a picture show."

Sara barely remembered the first time Stuart asked his mother the identity of their father. She had dismissed the question with a flighty wave of her hand. "Don't you worry, children," she said. "I'll tell you when the time's right." With confidence, Lilly strolled away as if the secret would be revealed tomorrow and they would be dining with the cream of society soon. But Stuart and Sara had to live with the reality of a pretty unwed mother whom other women feared losing their husbands to.

One summer day, Sara sat in the dirt, drawing, as Stuart leaned against the corner of the house, watching the other children of the settlement play tag. Leaving her drawing behind, she pushed to her feet, dusted off her breeches, and walked to her brother. The edges of his brown hair were wet with sweat, but he made no effort to hide from the sun as he followed the rhythm of the game.

"Why don't you play, brother?" she asked innocently, assuming he wanted to join the fun.

"Naw, don't want to," he said. Sara shrugged, then plopped down in the dirt beside him and resumed drawing. A few moments later, she looked up to find a boy a good head shorter than Stuart standing close by. She studied him curiously. A cowlick on his front hairline stood an inch high and traveled in two different directions.

"Y'all want to play?" he asked, revealing a blackened gumline, a common problem in the neighborhood.

"Yeah," Stuart said, suddenly changing his mind. "Come on, Sara," he urged, pulling her up by the arm. Soon, a knot of children circled, and Stuart acknowledged the familiar faces from school. "I'll be it," he announced, hitting his chest proudly. Dust flew with children ducking and weaving, trying to outrun Stuart. He almost caught Sara, but she changed directions quickly and escaped. Before he could chase down another child, a screen door opened, and a mother flew down the steps, yelling and flapping her apron.

"You children, stop this game! Joe!" she called harshly to her own son. "I've got some work you need to do. Git in that house! Now the rest of you, children, go home! I'm sure you've got work to do instead of running around this yard, making a racket! Git!" Sara and Stuart walked away. Their slumped shoulders showed the sting of rejection that was so hard to understand.

Christmas was always the worst. The missionary ladies of the town would show up in their poor settlement, dressed warmly against the winter chill, and deliver handmade baskets to those whose lives were less fortunate. Every year, as Sara and Stuart shivered on their rickety front porch, the brightly dressed ladies would turn up their noses and walk by them as though they weren't there. They would hear the cheery call of "Merry Christmas!" and then the same women would march back, averting their eyes. The children would huddle together, sharing the only thing they had: their own love and warmth.

On Sara's first day of school, Stuart held her back on the well-worn path to the schoolhouse. She thought her brother looked real nice. He had washed his hair and slicked it back, giving it a darker look that matched his brown eyes. "Let the other kids go," he said. "I'll walk you to your class the first day. Don't matter if I'm a little late, because I've got the same teacher as last year. She's moved up a grade, and she likes me okay. I'll explain how I wanted to get you settled.

"Sara," he said, "school's not so bad in some ways. But if you have any trouble on the playground, anybody makes fun of you or tries to hurt you, you call out nice and loud, and I'll come running. After a time or two, they'll leave you alone." She found her brother true to his word. After the first week, it was established that Sara was to be left alone, or Stuart's knuckles would be firmly planted on the offender's nose.

One day, Sara used the partial shade of a large hickory tree to hide from the hot fall sun. She sat on one of the large roots with her dress pulled over her knees, drawing pictures in the sand. In the background, children chanted, "Pocket full of posies, we all fall down." Enough leaves remained on the tree that blocked Trace Marion's shadow, but she felt a sense of danger before he spoke.

"Heard my daddy say your mama must be a whore," he said in a low, cruel voice. Sara drew her legs tightly together and shut her eyes, hoping he would go away. "Said she's got to be one, living in that old shack he owns and paying her rent without a job."

He walked around in front of her, planting his feet directly toe to toe with hers. She kept her head down and could only see his feet, which were clad in shiny black leather shoes. She wished Trace would go away. He was one year older than Stuart and the meanest boy on the playground.

Without looking up, Sara could imagine his bluish-gray eyes, which always carried a hue of spitefulness, and his red hair and tall stature, which gave him a fear-inducing presence. "Reckon you might look like her when you grow some more. I might just come and visit you one day."

The sneering voice was terrifying. Sara's lower lip trembled, and her eyes welled with tears. She wanted to scream for Stuart, but he had stayed home, sick. She was relieved when she saw the black shoes move away.

*****

The vivid memories brought Sara back to her son as he heaved a clod of dirt with all his might. This was their third day of working in the field. She chuckled to herself as Sam started a new conversation with his imaginary friend. He was always the sweetest child, never complaining. Even as a baby, he seldom cried.

At this time next year, he would have to start school, and she dreaded the cruelty and the questions that would come: "Who is my daddy, and where is he?" She breathed in a worried breath knowing the harsh words would hurt, but they couldn't take Sam away from her. But Milton Marion, Sam's grandfather, could; and he was waiting for any chance.

Sara heard the rumble of the tractor starting and pushed herself to her feet as she let out a low groan. She noticed the sky was robin's-egg blue. She stared for a second at the wisps of clouds passing by as if she was looking to heaven for answers to the questions and problems that would surely come.

Chapter 2

As Sara and Sam approached the shack on the Pea River, she stopped for a second to admire its simple beauty. It was just an old log cabin with a sagging front porch and a rusted tin roof, surrounded by large oak trees. Sara wished her brother could feel the cabin's comfort, smell the scent of the trees, and just spend one night listening as the water of the river slowly trickled south to the Gulf of Mexico. She untied her bandanna and held it to her mouth, muffling a low sob that threatened to escape anytime she thought of Stuart.

She couldn't help herself when it came to remembering that day even though it made her sick inside. It was not the violent attack, the ripping of her simple dress, or the feeling of Trace Marion crushing her with his weight while choking, violating, cursing, and threatening to kill her. The smell of him, of being tangled in saw briars, and his sweat dripping in her face didn't make her sick. What caused the bile to roll out of her stomach and choke her throat was that his actions made her lose Stuart forever.

Sara never breathed a word of the rape to Stuart. She knew well her brother's protective nature. She was fifteen at the time, and Stuart realized how the boys looked at Sara as prey because of their mother's reputation. But there was one thing Sara didn't count on after Trace raped her. She wouldn't talk, but Trace refused to keep it to himself. He bragged in the schoolyard how easily Sara had given in to him.

Within hours, another boy whispered the news in Stuart's ear; and that night, he asked Sara to tell him the truth.

*****

She sat staring at a book, pretending to read by the dim light of an oil lamp. The house felt cold and damp. Lilly rocked incessantly in the other room, humming, lost in a world only she knew. Lilly was slowly going crazy. Her behavior became more and more erratic each day as she gradually withdrew into herself.

Sara heard Stuart's feet scrape the front porch as he cleaned the soles of his shoes. Moments later, he knelt in front of her chair and rested his hand tenderly on her knee.

"Is it true, sister?" he asked.

"What?" she asked, pretending not to know.

"Did he do what he says he did?"

Sara averted her eyes, studying the flecks of corn dust in his hair, and lied. "I don't understand what you're asking, Stuart." Her composure sagged as she felt bile rise in her throat.

"I could barely believe it," he said, pulling her torn and stained dress from the back of his overalls. "You should have hidden this better."

Sara felt a weight crush her heart. "Stuart, please don't do anything. If you just walk me home from school, he can't do it again. Please?" she pleaded in a tiny, desperate voice. Sara finally looked him in the eye. "Please, brother. You're all I've got. Maybe we can go tell the sheriff what happened."

"Not in this town, Sara," Stuart said. "Not with Trace's daddy being Milton Marion. He controls most of the land and all of the people. Farmers have to borrow money from his bank to plant their crops, and if they cross him, there'll be no loan. They have no choice but to sell their crops through him too. We have to buy from his store, along with everyone else.

"Hell, Sara," he cursed bitterly, "we live in Mr. Marion's house and pay rent to him just like everyone else in this settlement. No, I

14

have to handle this because if I don't, he'll do it again. And as your brother, I'm bound before God to never let him hurt you again!"

Sara saw that his eyes were not full of rage or hate. They were dull and lifeless as if he were an old man in the throes of death. "Please, Stuart," she begged as he walked away.

Sara awoke the next morning from her fitful night of sleep hoping to convince Stuart that he could protect her. She was more than willing to take the chance of being attacked again if it meant keeping her brother. Above all, she loved him more than herself. Sara searched their home, but Stuart was already gone.

Cold drops of rain fell from a ragged gray sky as she walked to school. Sara prayed that Stuart's rage would relent and that she would find him standing outside after school, waiting to walk her home under his protective shield.

Her heart pounded as the teacher released the class for the day. She raced outside, looking desperately for Stuart among the throng of kids milling about. Relief flooded through her when she saw him standing next to the hedgerow that marked the edge of the school property.

"Stuart!" she called over the noise of the other children. Sara thought he didn't hear her as she saw him reach into the bushes and pull out an ax handle. She shoved the boy in front of her out of the way.

"Trace!" Stuart yelled as he swung the wooden handle with both hands. The first blow caught Trace across the flat of his nose, crushing it. Blood, snot, and pieces of small bone flew.

"Stuart!" Sara screamed, surging forward, clawing her way through the other children. Sara watched the second and third blow with horror as she struggled to reach him. Trace lay facedown on the ground, unconscious. Stuart raised the ax handle the final time, bringing it down hard and hitting Trace in the back of the head with all the strength he could muster. Sara reached Stuart as he dropped the blood-covered handle to the ground.

Stuart, his fury spent, calmly walked over and sat down under the old hickory tree, where Trace first threatened Sara when she was six. She sat beside him, not minding the cold rain. He put his arm around her shoulders, and she cried gentle tears into his chest until the sheriff came and took him away.

Trace spent two weeks in a hospital bed with drool running down his chin before succumbing to the injuries. The charges against Stuart were upgraded to murder.

Sara watched the dust dancing in the sunlight that shone through the courthouse windows as the judge sentenced her brother. New life moved inside her as she became mesmerized by the particles. At Stuart's request, she showed no emotion, not one tear, as the judge sentenced him to death. "Don't give the bastard the satisfaction," he had said.

The speed at which Stuart was charged, tried, and convicted came from the express orders of Milton Marion. The judge's gavel banged, and the sheriff pulled Stuart to his feet. He allowed Stuart a brief moment to speak to Sara. She saw a small half smile break on her brother's face, but his brown eyes were burning with fire and anger. "He'll want the child," he whispered fiercely. "But damn him to hell, Sara, before you let him have the baby."

One week later, Sara sat staring out the window while worry and loneliness ate at her soul. Stuart had already been taken to the state prison at Atmore to await his death in the electric chair. Lilly sat in the other room, rocking and humming as always. She hadn't spoken a word in days. The constant sound of the rocker grating against the wooden floor wore on Sara's nerves. She prayed Lilly would be normal when it was time to deliver the baby. The local doctor was out of the question even if they had the money.

Sara knew it couldn't be good news when the sheriff drove into the yard. She froze in place, praying he was going to someone else's house. When she heard his boots thump on their front porch, the blood drained from her face. She took a ragged breath, pushed herself up from the chair, and walked to the door. She opened it before he could knock. Sheriff Clinton Barnes looked at her through the missing wire of the old screen door.

"Sara, I need to talk to you and your mother," he said, much more gently than she expected.

"Please come in," she answered. Sara stepped back as the sheriff entered. She led him in and began to move a chair for him to sit.

"Sara, just take your seat," he said gently. "I can hear your mother. Would you like for me to get her?"

"Sheriff, she doesn't understand things sometimes. Later, I'll try to explain whatever it is you're going to tell me."

Clinton squatted down in front of her, leaned back on his heels, then rested his hands on the arms of the chair. He was tall enough to be at Sara's eye level even in that position. Sara could see where he had missed a spot on his chin when he shaved that morning, and even in the dim light, she could see gray specks in his blue eyes. More than that, she could see the deep crow's-feet around the corners of his eyes and knew his troubled face deepened them.

"Stuart's dead, isn't he?" she asked in a whisper.

Sheriff Barnes nodded. "Another prisoner killed him last night. I just got the wire."

"Mr. Marion wasn't satisfied that the state was going to kill him soon," Sara said calmly. She saw the sheriff grimace.

"Sara, that's not the case," he said. "Prison can be a violent place."

"If you'll leave me be, Sheriff, I'll try to explain this to my mother," she answered coldly but without any other emotion. Sheriff Barnes didn't take her eerie, frozen tone personally, nor did he doubt that Milton Marion was capable of paying a prisoner to take such revenge. He secretly admired Stuart for what he had done, knowing that young death often came to ones as evil as Trace.

He rose with a slight cracking of the knees and showed himself out. Sara sat silently, praying that her brother was now at a peaceful and beautiful place. She then moved slowly to the other room to try and explain to Lilly that Stuart was gone.

As Sheriff Barnes drove away, hot tenderness started to build behind his own eyes. He couldn't know how Sara would have reacted if he had given in to the unfamiliar impulse when he delivered the terrible news. He was overcome by a desperate desire to lift her small body out of the chair, hold her tightly against his chest, stroke her red hair, and feel the warmth of her breath against his neck. He wanted to whisper softly that she was the most beautiful creature he had ever seen and that he would protect her from his own father-in-law and love her, care for her, and die before letting anyone hurt her again.

Clinton Barnes shook his head, trying to drive the disturbing feeling away. Never before had he allowed his mind to wander so dangerously, but she came back again in the next moment and the next minute and the next hour. As he lay down that night, tired and unsettled with the worry of her fate on his mind, he slipped into an uncomfortable sleep. And then she entered his dreams.

Chapter 3

Sara removed the bandanna from her mouth and swallowed hard, her sadness contained for now. Walking toward the cabin, it seemed as though years had passed since Lilly's death instead of just a week. She found Sam in his usual position—his hands cupped and sitting on the weather-worn steps.

"What are you holding?" Sara asked, already knowing the answer. Every afternoon, he caught a green grasshopper and tried to scare her with it.

"Nothing, Mama," Sam replied, opening his hands and throwing the bug at her. Playing along, Sara shrieked and swooned and swatted and danced in fear to the delight of her child.

As she started up the steps, a fat catfish hanging from a rusted nail flopped, catching her attention. Lying on the floor below it was a flour sack. She picked up the sack and peered inside and saw four large sweet potatoes. The night before, there were two smaller catfish on the porch. She didn't know who brought the food, but she was grateful for the gifts.

Each time Sara entered the old cabin, she had a warm feeling. Its logs were cut closely and fitted together seamlessly. The bedroom had its own fireplace, which would serve them well come winter. The kitchen's woodburning stove heated quickly and worked well. But to Sara, the greatest gift was the hand pump for water, which sat directly over an old tub with a makeshift drain. Her house in the settlement didn't have an indoor pump.

Sara laid the potatoes on the kitchen table and dropped the flopping catfish in the sink. Unbuttoning the front pocket of her overalls, she took out Stuart's old pocketknife and used it to quickly skin and gut the fish. She would fry it tonight, and it would serve as the next day's lunch.

She picked up a bar of lye soap, then pushed the screen door open. She watched Sam chase a lizard around a lone nandina bush for a few moments. "Let's go, Sam. Time to take a bath." She relished the Indian summer and enjoyed bathing in the warm river.

"Mama, I had one yesterday." Sam wrinkled his nose as though he had just encountered an unpleasant smell. "Why can't I stay here and play?"

Sara couldn't help but chuckle. He had spent the day eating and playing and playing and eating. Dark streaks creased his face, and his arms were scratched from the peanut vines. Sara let him complain for a minute. Sam rarely fussed.

"Nope. You're going to get washed. Mama's rule." He started to complain again, but she shook her finger as if to say, "No more." Sam gave up and started walking to the river, dragging his feet as though on a death march. Looking down, Sara noticed a set of footprints in the sand.

Boots, she thought. Though the prints were small, she guessed they belonged to a man. *Must be my benefactor.* She wondered who in this county would be so kind. Reaching the river, she checked each bank carefully for unwanted eyes. Finding that they were alone, she stripped Sam naked and then herself.

She knew Sam was getting too old to bathe with her and would have to deal with it soon. His advancing age brought on another persistent worry: starting school. Milton Marion was not only on the school board. He was the school board. She had been so careful all these years to keep Sam within her sight, but next fall, he must start school, and every teacher was beholden to Milton Marion for their jobs. She knew the end was near, and they had to find a way to leave before then.

Sara washed Sam quickly and thoroughly, laughing at his resistance. "Go sit in the sun and dry," she commanded, pointing to a large rock. Sam obeyed with no further objections. She longed for another pair of overalls as she shook the pants to remove the dust and sand that had accumulated during the day's work. Then she could wash these. The denim material was just too heavy to dry overnight.

Lathering the bar of soap, she started first with her hands, scrubbing hard, wincing from the burning the lye caused. She rinsed them in the river, then took another look at her badly blistered palms. She picked at several of the sores to remove the dead skin. They would hurt tomorrow but also heal quicker. Sara finished her bath and, for a few minutes, sat on the sandy bottom, letting the water flow across her body. She squeezed the water from her hair and thought of the anguish and torture she had endured at the hands of Milton Marion.

Each time Mr. Marion came to the door for the rent, Sara would try so hard to hide her fear. His ruddy face would stare at her, mouth in a half jeer, and his eyes would say, "This time, you don't have the money." She despised him. Always so nattily dressed, he reeked of money, power, and the trappings that went along with being in control of so many lives.

Sara could always read his body language: "Whore. Trash. You cost my boy's life." She would match his look with angry eyes: "Your boy raped me, and you took my brother's life. I'll be damned if you'll get my son." But she also knew that if Lilly didn't rise from her catatonic humming and put the rent money in his greasy, sweaty palms, he'd have her boy.

Twice in her young life, she had witnessed the county welfare agent, Milton Marion's cousin, drag screaming children away after their parents were evicted and declared indigent by the welfare lady. "It was for the good of the children," she would quote to the paper. "At least this way, they won't starve to death in an orphanage." But Sara understood the real truth. Milton Marion loved wielding his power no matter how evil the intent. Those actions kept the rest of the county under his thumb.

When Lilly stood and walked to the door each month, Sara would will her knees stiff as Mr. Marion's face once again flashed an anger reserved only for her. Sara never knew the source of Lilly's money, but she dismissed the rumor they had endured all those years. She couldn't be selling her body, because Sara was with her night and day. Milton Marion unjustly increased the rent on their ramshackle home each year, but somehow, Lilly always managed to have the cash to pay.

Sara realized that she wasn't truly living, only existing. She fed and dressed Sam, held him and loved him, and put him to bed. She prayed each night that maybe someone in the church or in the town would be brave enough to help them, all the while knowing that it wouldn't happen.

She still remembered her brother's last words as the sheriff led him away: "He'll take your baby if he can. That'll be the way he can hurt you the most!" The same thought entered her mind each day as she awoke: "Endure, pray, and don't do anything to lose Sam."

Sara slipped quietly out of the water, trying not to disturb Sam. He had drifted off, tired from the day's activities. She sat on the overalls in the last vestige of light, waiting for her body to dry. Somewhere in the forest, a large limb crashed to the ground. Sara felt a creepy shiver, the sound forcing her to replay Lilly's departure. She put her head down, and for the first time, she began to cry over the death of her mother.

*****

That last night, Lilly moved her rocking chair and placed it in front of the door. Sara put Sam to bed and tried several times to talk to her, but as usual, Lilly ignored her words. When she awoke the next morning, Lilly was still in her chair, rocking and humming. Sometime in the night, she had put on her best dress and loosed her hair. It flowed gently back and forth.

Sara fed Sam and sent him outside to play, then knelt in front of her mother, placing both hands on her knees. "Mama, I love you. I need you," she said. Lilly gave no response, only the same vacant look. Sara couldn't help but admire Lilly's beauty. Her skin was fair and smooth. Not a single blemish had ever rested on her face. She had shining green eyes, which held dark flecks of gray, and a long, sculptured neck with not a hint of sagging skin. Her jawline was perfect, making her chin small and proud.

Sara stayed there, gently rubbing her mother's legs until the aches of her own became too painful. She stood, slowly feeling the blood returning to her cramped muscles, and wondered how anyone so beautiful could be left so alone. How could some man impregnate her and walk away?

There was not a relative, friend, or anyone whom she could ask about her mother's earlier life. It was as though her mother simply dropped onto earth in Roxboro with two bastard children. As Sam played, Sara sat on the steps and pondered all the questions she and Stuart had asked Lilly about their father. Putting all the evasive, noncommittal answers together still left her with so little information. There was never anyone to speculate about.

She heard Lilly stop rocking and drag the chair toward the bedroom. Sara rubbed her face with both hands and wondered why she had changed positions. Several minutes went by as Sara waited for the rocking to resume. She was just pushing herself off the steps when she heard the sound of the chair falling over and banging against the wooden floor. "Stay out here, Sam!" she commanded. "Do not come inside!"

She raced into the house and saw Lilly's body hanging from a piece of rope she had tied to a wooden trestle on the ceiling. Sara hurried to the small kitchen, grabbed a knife, and ran back to her mother. The cold fact hit her squarely. It would be of no use to cut her mother down. That realization drained Sara's body of strength as she stood watching Lilly's lifeless body gently swing back and forth. She took a painful breath, willing herself not to throw up, and turned away.

She opened the door and found Sam still drawing pictures in the dirt and talking to his imaginary friend. Sara looked around the settlement, wondering whom she could go to, which neighbor would help. She thought of Mr. Ewell, who had given Stuart work at times, but finally decided it would be no use. She took her child by the hand and walked into town to find the sheriff.

"Stay outside," Sheriff Barnes gently said. "Fred will be along shortly with the wagon." Sheriff Barnes took long strides up the steps, entered the house, and saw Lilly's body. Ignoring the screaming in his own head, he took the cover from the neatly made bed and laid it on the floor under her body. Clinton righted the fallen chair, using it as a stepladder, and with one sweep of his sharp knife, he cut the taut rope. Lilly fell with such a hard thud that it shook the dirt from the old slated ceiling. He grimaced regretfully knowing that Sara had heard the terrible sound.

During the process of wrapping the body, Clinton's deputy, Fred, entered the room, his face ashen. He helped the sheriff finish the grisly process, both taking care to hide Lilly's contorted face.

"You ready, Sheriff?" Fred asked queasily.

"Yeah, Fred," Clinton replied.

With great effort, they moved her dead body to the wagon. Fred quickly climbed aboard, grabbed the reins, and clucked for the mules to move. Clinton watched as the wagon rattled away, then turned to Sara.

"I'll see to it that the county pays for her burial, ma'am."

"Thank you," Sara whispered as her body began to sag. Clinton reached to support her.

"Can I get you something?" he asked, his face unsure.

"I just need to sit for a minute, Sheriff," she said, trying to hold back a thousand different emotions. Clinton held her upright and eased her to the steps.

Sara took a seat, then looked at his face. "I'm all right, Sheriff. Thank you again for your kindness." He hesitated for a moment, then walked away, not knowing what else to do.

Sara never had any dreams of a knight in shining armor coming to her rescue or being carried over the threshold by strong and loving arms. No, in her own practical mind, surviving each day and watching Sam grow up with the love of a mother, which she had been denied, was enough. But for the first time in her life, the strength of Clinton's hand sparked something she had never felt before. Despite his family ties, she knew there was a kind and gentle man beneath the uniform.

She took a deep breath, willed her strength back, and tore Lilly's bedroom apart, finding only three dollars and forty-two cents hidden in an old box. She counted it over and over again, each time hoping it would be more. She realized that the climax of the battle was now here and quickly made a hard and desperate decision. They came like vultures the next day when she opened the door to what little Lilly possessed.

Most of the time in death, people would come with food, offers of sympathy, a gentle hug, or encouragement. But they came as thieves in the night, smelling desperation. Sara wanted to hate them, to loathe, and to spit and curse as they offered a nickel for this or a penny for that, but she couldn't. Sara sold what she could. Most of them were only slightly better off than she.

The men worked for Mr. Marion in the cotton gin, turpentine forest, or the fields, doing hot, dirty labor, for which he paid them little. Then he took back what scarce dollars he invested in them through his store and bank. The economy was so ravaged that there was little choice but to remain, putting one foot in front of the other, while hoping and praying for a whisper of a job somewhere else.

They all longed for some stranger to come to town and say, "Looking for some men. We'll pay a dollar a day if you work really hard." It didn't happen, so they stayed in Roxboro, replaying this vicious cycle, knowing if they left and didn't find work, their worn, thin wives and undernourished children would starve.

The next day, with steely determination, Sara put her plan in place. She knew that soon, the county welfare agent would show up at her door, demanding Sam. The two of them would walk out after dark and try to make it several counties north, traveling at night to keep from being seen. She knew Marion's influence was strong everywhere in the southern part of the state, but if they made it far enough, she hoped to find a church that would help. Maybe the preacher wouldn't be in Mr. Marion's influence and would convince the congregation to give them a chance.

All that day, she watched Sam play while she sat restlessly on the steps. Time after time, she glanced at the sun, praying it would slip beneath the horizon. Her back tensed, and her mind ran hard, thinking so many thoughts at once. Doubts rang in her mind. Was she selfish? Should she just give Sam to Mr. Marion and walk away?

He would have the best of everything—a warm bed, plenty to eat, and nice clothes to wear—and he wouldn't have to bear the talk that she and Stuart had lived with. People wouldn't dare. Oh, they might say things behind his back, whispering in their own homes, but never in the street. *No, the way would be cleared*, she thought.

The people of the county would praise Mr. Marion for taking the child in. "Mama was a whore," they'd say. "Look at him now, such a pretty and polite child. His mama got pregnant when she was just fifteen and ran off and left him. Mr. Marion took him in— adopted him, mind you—and look how well he's done. That's what happens when you live by Christian principles."

Sara thought she would go mad if the sun didn't set soon. She looked west for the last time, and in the glare of the sun, she saw two men riding toward her in a Jersey wagon. She shaded her eyes, trying to get a better look. A minute later, the older of the two, Mr. Ewell, looked down.

"We're here to get you and your boy. I've got a place on the river for you to live and some work you can do."

"He'll hate you for this," Sara answered bluntly. She didn't have to explain who "he" was. She knew Mr. Ewell was one of the few farmers in the county who owned his land and remained clear of debt, but she also knew he had to sell to Mr. Marion at harvest time. He answered her words with a shrug.

Knowing that he alone would reach out, Sara and Sam climbed aboard after the two men loaded their few belongings. Sam giggled and Sara smiled as they swung their legs back and forth from the rear end of the wagon. By dark, everyone would know they were gone, and she felt the relief wash over her, flushing her face with warmth.

Even with Mr. Ewell's intervention, Sara realized Sam was still within Mr. Marion's grasp; but until next fall, the devil was at bay. For the first time in her life, Sara felt a taste of sweet freedom. When the wagon came to a stop, she pushed off with both hands, then turned to give Sam a lift.

"Danny and I will move your things in," said Mr. Ewell as he climbed from the seat. "Why don't you and the boy look around till we're done?"

"That'll be fine," Sara quickly replied, not trusting her voice to say anything more. She took Sam's hand and led him to where they could see the river.

The afternoon sun was in the perfect position to make the water sparkle. Sara turned away from the light to look around the back of the property. There was an old pole barn with the roof half collapsed where someone had once kept a mule. She peered inside and found that it still contained a fair amount of manure. *Maybe I can borrow some turnip seed so Sam can have something green to eat this winter.* There was also a chicken coop that appeared to be in better shape than the barn. With just a little work, it would be functional again.

In her mind, Sara went over what she owned, and she was still tallying her small number of worldly possessions when she heard Mr. Ewell cough. She turned to face him. She appreciated his wide, strong shoulders, which were covered with a blue denim shirt. The sleeves were rolled up to his elbows, not neatly but rather pushed up as though he wouldn't bother with such detail.

His overalls were new, still holding their deep-blue color. His hat showed more wear with many bends and creases and a dark circle around the headband, a combination of dirt and sweat. He wore it pushed up slightly on his forehead, and she could see where his once brown hair was turning gray. The black clip-on eyepatch that he wore made his good eye focus sharply.

"Ms. Sara," he started, "Danny's taking the wagon back to our house. He'll return directly with a few things you might need."

"That's kind of you, Mr. Ewell."

"It won't be much but should help you get on your feet. He's going to bring a couple of chickens so you and the boy can have eggs this winter. He'll come back another day and plow you a little spot for greens. I'll give you the seed, and you can work it off in the peanut field. I need a little help for the next month or so, and after that, we'll worry about something else to do."

"Mr. Ewell, I can't thank you enough for your kindness. But we both know that Mr. Marion will try to extract a price. He won't take this—"

"Ms. Sara, I'll deal with that when the time comes. This year's crop is already sold. Next year, maybe Danny and I will try to haul our loads across the flats and sell them in Meadville."

Sara knew that would be quite a gamble. The Pea River was normally twenty or thirty yards wide and too deep for a wagon. The flats were a strange-looking crossing where the river expanded to a hundred yards or so, and most times of the year, it was only one or two feet deep. But the unstable sandy bottom could cave in under a heavy load. At one time or another, most farmers had tried their luck for a better price than Mr. Marion offered; they attempted the crossing and lost their load when the sands shifted and the wagon sank. Their products—whether corn, peanuts, or cotton—were destroyed by the moving water.

"Ms. Sara, Danny will be back soon. I'm gonna head home, and early tomorrow morning, you just walk to my house. We'll be working in the south forty. You'll see the peanut stacks."

"Yes, sir."

"I wish I had something better—"

"It's quite all right, Mr. Ewell," Sara interrupted. "I thank you again for your generosity." She noticed he accepted the thank-you with a soft nod of his head as he turned and walked away.

After Mr. Ewell left, Sara and Sam explored up and down the river; and to her delight, she found a small patch of broom straw standing waist-high. After a few minutes, she had gathered enough to fashion a makeshift broom. After returning to the cabin, she attacked old spiderwebs, the dust in the windowsills, and rat droppings that cluttered the home.

As the sounds of the wagon approaching grew louder, she swept the last remains off the steps. Danny sprang from the seat and landed softly in the dirt. He walked quickly to the rear of the wagon and wrapped his arms around an old wooden chest. With a slight grunt, he carried it to the front porch.

"Ms. Sara," he said quickly, "these are some of Mama's things. After she died, I saved them. There are a few dresses and some other..." Sara wondered why he was stammering until she realized that "some other" meant undergarments.

"Thank you, Danny," Sara replied, trying to ease his discomfort. "I'll slide this in the door while you unload the rest of the wagon." She saw his relieved look and added, "If you will just put the things for the house on the porch, I'll move them in. I've probably got you behind on your chores—"

"No, ma'am, I've still got plenty of time," he replied quickly. "The old chicken coop," he said, changing the subject, "needs just a little bit of work, and I'll have it fixed in a jiffy." He dragged the roll of wire from the wagon, hefted it onto his shoulder, and marched away.

Sam, who had stopped his playing and had listened to the conversation, started walking behind Danny, mimicking his movements. Sara thought of calling him back but changed her mind. He'd spent his life without a man around, and she wouldn't deny him such a simple pleasure.

Chapter 4

Sheriff Clinton Barnes drove within sight of Uncle Hiram's house on the river and parked. He opened the door, swung his long legs out, and stood, closing the door behind him. He removed his cowboy hat, rubbed a hand over his closely cropped blond hair, then resettled the hat.

After leaning back on the patrol car, Clinton looked toward the house. No light was shining, but it was a nice night to wait. The south wind felt inviting, and the first hint of the harvest moon had broken the horizon. He wondered if Uncle Hiram had seen Sara since Mr. Ewell had taken her and the boy in. His land joined Mr. Ewell's on the south side.

Clinton tried to shake the thought of Sara away and focus on why he was there in the first place. There had been a killing in the Negro settlement on Saturday night, and he needed some information from the old bootlegger. Despite that unpleasant event, Clinton was glad he didn't have to go home to Ruth right away.

Ruth was much like her father—demanding, ill of temper, and spent most of her time looking down on the rest of the county as trash. And as she reminded Clinton daily, if it weren't for the grace of her father, he would be just another poor farmer begging to borrow money. In her caustic world, Milton Marion didn't deal harshly enough with the population.

It bothered Clinton that he had been fooled years ago. Looking back, he realized it wasn't Marion's generosity that led him to offer Clinton a job in the store after his father couldn't pay the mortgage on the farm that year. It wasn't kindness or any Christian value that caused the event. It was a well-thought-out plan. Milton Marion played the odds of human nature in order for Ruth to catch a husband.

Clinton had to give the man credit because no young man in his right mind would be attracted to Ruth. It wasn't so much her looks that were unappealing, though most men wouldn't give her a second glance. It was her attitude, which had much the same cruel nature as her brother, Trace, and Clinton knew that gene descended straight down the family tree from their father.

Looking back with a clear eye, he also knew his completion of high school played a part. Most boys his age dropped out because times were too hard for a pair of working hands to be away from the farm. If they weren't needed at home, they worked for Milton Marion in some way, making a quarter a day.

He finished school strictly because his father, for some strange reason, demanded he did so. He didn't understand his persistence, but then again, that wasn't the only thing that puzzled him about the deceased Mr. Barnes.

Milton Marion's store resided on the only paved road that ran north and south through the county. It was a large wooden building with multiple layers of high shelves filled with products from linens to house furnishings and a host of other things the poor people could little afford. The floor of the store was filled with tables containing sacks of flour, meal, salt and sugar, overalls, cotton shirts, socks, racks of cheaply made dresses, and all other staples of life.

Under the front counter was "the book," the bible of the store, in which every purchase made on credit was recorded. Each poor farmer had his own page. When the amount was entered on the right side of the page, the debtor was required to sign their name or make their mark. At the end of the month, the total was tabulated and transferred to the office at the bank.

Clinton knew that sometimes, the year, which Milton Marion handwrote at the top of each page, was added into the total. His father-in-law generally only used that trick for the Negroes, but he wasn't above applying it to certain people who were in danger of paying off their debt.

To Clinton's surprise, soon after he started at the store, Ruth also began to help each Saturday. It seemed strange to him that Marion would want his daughter to associate with the commoners. To him, she was much more suited to visit with the missionary ladies, the deacon's wives, and the cream of society in Roxboro.

There was a small contingency in town who didn't have to worry about making it through the winter without going hungry. The postal clerk and the people who were employed at the courthouse had steady paychecks. There were also a few with old money whom the carpetbaggers managed to miss. They lived on Main Street in white houses with yards full of azaleas tenderly cared for by gentle old Negro men.

Maybe I was just too naive, Clinton thought. He had heard the talk of the other boys in the schoolyard. They whispered which girl in the quarters would do it for a quarter and would dramatically retell the feat, but that chatter left him feeling ill and uneasy. He felt differently, but maybe that's why on late Saturday nights after the store closed, the brush of Ruth's hip started to arouse him.

He wanted to prove he was like the other boys, not weak or unmanly, and that he wasn't absent the physical yearnings of a young man. No, he knew that wasn't true. Many restless nights were caused by his own vivid dreams, but they were different from what had been described. His were gentler with hushed, loving words and warm embraces that caressed the skin and brought joy to the heart.

Soon, though, the brush of Ruth's hip turned to a soft pressing of breasts against his back, always an accident followed by a low, murmured apology. She seemed to smile more then, which softened the hard line of her mouth. It wasn't long before his beautiful dreams degenerated into quick, consummated passion among the flour sacks. Months later, he stood terrified in front of Milton Marion, paying for his sins.

"I give you a job, and this is what you do to me?" Marion shouted. Clinton stood with his shoulders slumped, staring at the wooden floor.

"I'm sorry, sir." Clinton knew the apology was a poor excuse for his actions and was bound to enrage Milton Marion that much more.

"Lift your damn head up and face me, you bastard!" he screamed. Clinton did as he demanded, finding a horrible sight. Spittle gathered in the corners of Milton Marion's mouth. His face was contorted in anger, flushing a deep red, and his intimidating blue eyes were piercing Clinton's soul. Satan with all his demons couldn't have scared Clinton more.

"You know, boy"—Marion's volume dropped a decibel but lost none of the seething hate—"what I should do is call in your folks' note."

Suddenly the room felt stuffy and stifling, causing beads of sweat to break out on Clinton's forehead. He realized it wasn't an idle threat. If Marion demanded the money owed, the land his parents worked so hard to hold on to, what they had slaved over and worshipped all these years, would be gone. Their only hope for a comfortable old age would evaporate all because of what he had done. They would end up in the turpentine forest or cotton fields and would be driven into early graves. He had already dug too many long, narrow holes for such people.

While enduring the ranting and raving, Clinton didn't realize that Clair Marion had slipped into the room. "Tell him what you have to offer," she said. "I mean it, Milton. Not another angry word to this boy!" The stern, commanding tone of her voice surprised Clinton. The change on Marion's face indicated that Clair surprised him also. They both turned to face her. Her feet were planted firmly as if she wasn't leaving anytime soon.

"I'm getting to it, dear." His tone sounded softer, and Clinton realized that there was one person Milton Marion couldn't bully. "Clinton, I assume you're planning on doing the right thing?" he asked evenly.

"Yes, sir. I plan to marry Ruth with your permission," Clinton replied, much calmer than he felt. He saw Marion's eyes dart to the back of the room, checking with Clair. He calmly removed his coat and walked around his desk, carelessly slinging it over the back of the chair.

"Sit," Marion half asked, half commanded, pointing to a straight-back chair. Only later did Clinton realize that the script had been planned beforehand. "Clinton, you and Ruth will take my car tomorrow and drive south to Kentland to get your marriage license. Get the probate judge, Harry Redstone, to marry you two. I've already spoken with him." He then reached into his pocket and pulled out a thick collection of bills. He snapped off a twenty and handed it across the desk to Clinton.

"This will cover the cost of the license and a place to stay. Check into Mary's Boarding House and spend the night there. The next day, you and Ruth will drive home and come to our house. We'll tell the town later in the evening how the two of you decided to elope. Oh, and you'll say I was fit to be tied, and I almost shot you before seeing the marriage license." Clinton could see a faint smile with the last statement.

"Next Monday, you and Ruth will be leaving for Auburn University. It will take me pulling a few strings to get you in, but I'll make it happen. Can't have my only daughter married to an uneducated man. Ruth will have the baby there, and by the time you finish college, most folks will forget the timeline."

The edgy statement turned scornful, but Clinton resisted the urge to smile. Many of the young girls of the First Baptist Church were known for having very healthy premature babies.

"We'll discuss more about your future after you get your degree in business." Clinton nodded in agreement. "I trust you will do well. It's a lot of money I'm spending on you, boy."

"Yes, sir." Clinton knew the emphasis on the word *boy* served to make sure he knew his balls were firmly grasped by Marion, who would squeeze them any damn time he liked.

"You're free to go," Marion said, dismissing Clinton with a wave of his hand.

"Mr. Marion," Clinton said timidly, "I don't know how to drive." Clinton saw the tyrant's face tinge a deeper red and start to scowl.

"Ruth will take care of that," he said exasperatedly. "These are simple instructions, but if you don't know what to do, just ask her!" Clinton turned from Mr. Marion and found Clair looking at him intently. Behind him, he could hear the man sitting down hard in his chair. She winked and smiled slightly as he passed. It left Clinton with more of an uneasy feeling than one of relief. Clair's attractive looks and the strange gesture made his anxious feelings grow.

Ruth lost the baby a few days shy of a month after moving to Auburn. Clinton couldn't understand why she treated the miscarriage as if it was just another body function to be ignored. While he grieved losing the child, Ruth not only acted as if she was happy but also berated him for his deep feelings. Clinton was astonished the day that she announced, with much malice, that she wasn't willing to try again, and their physical relationship was over.

Two days after he turned twenty-one, Clinton received a telegram summoning him home, because college wasn't important anymore. The night after arriving, he sat in Marion's office with new orders. "Clinton," he said with his usual calloused demeanor, "Bob Lawrence has suddenly decided to retire as sheriff. You need to run for the office, and with my endorsement, you'll win." The way his father-in-law sat perched behind his desk reminded Clinton of a buzzard sitting on a fence post. Only the occasional flaps of black wings were missing.

"I've got a lot of money invested in you," he said. "And I expect a lot in return."

"Yes," Clinton said, careful to keep contempt from his voice. "I owe you a great deal."

"Good. I'm glad you see it my way," he replied. "First order of business after the election is to catch that damn bootlegger Hiram and put his ass in jail. He's been a thorn in my side for years. That damn lazy-ass Bob Lawrence always has an excuse why he can't jail that nigger. You'd better try harder and succeed, understand?"

"Yes, sir," he replied, backing out of the room after being dismissed.

Clinton ran for sheriff not because Milton Marion demanded it and not because he wanted to be sheriff but for several other reasons. For one thing, his parents were still deeply in debt, and the country remained in financial chaos with little other work to be found. Mainly, though, he did it to learn how to run away.

The thought of spending the rest of his life with Ruth caused constant shivers and nightmares. He knew that a divorce would never be possible. Marion would take that embarrassment so personally that Clinton feared a trumped-up charge of great magnitude was a significant possibility. Marion had too many friends at the capital in Montgomery.

Three days after Clinton won the election, Bob Lawrence took him for a ride around the county for a briefing. He listened as they bounced down old, rutted dirt roads.

"Leave Uncle Hiram alone if you want to keep control of the crime," Bob said. "He'll be your greatest source of information when there's a cutting or killing in the county. Most folks look up to him, the only nigger in these parts that owns his land. Besides him being a shaman, most are just superstitious enough that they are afraid to cross him. He might put a spell on them, send a haint or something like that," the outgoing sheriff said. "Besides, he has a way of extracting information from all his customers.

"Couple of years ago," Bob explained, "there was a young buck that made a lot of noise about taking over from Uncle Hiram. He whispered around the settlement that he would come one night and kill him, rob him, and take over his business. My deputies found that young nigger floating in the river with his throat slashed. No," he advised, "best leave Uncle Hiram alone regardless of what your daddy-in-law says."

"How'd you manage to keep out of his way all these years?" Clinton watched as Bob gripped the steering wheel tighter, causing his hairy knuckles to grow a paler shade of white.

"I found my way, and you'll have to find yours. When I first came to office, I intended to treat everyone the same." Bob eased the car to the side of the road, careful not to slide off in the sandy ditch. "Everybody ain't the same," he said, looking across the car. "It's a fine line you'll walk. Your daddy-in-law will want you to do things you'd rather not do. No one can tell you what decision to make. I only know it's hard to live with yourself sometimes. You won't always do right. It's impossible. Just do the best you can and try not to think too much. You'll find it easier to sleep."

Chapter 5

Clinton took another glance at Uncle Hiram's house and saw that it remained dark. Determined never to catch the old man in his illegal business, he never walked up unexpectedly. Even if he put out maximum effort, Clinton realized that he wouldn't be the first to fail. In past years, scores of state and federal agents had visited Roxboro in an effort to arrest the old man, but not a one had ever succeeded.

Earlier in the day, Seth Walker, an agent for the Department of Revenue in Montgomery, stopped by Clinton's office for a visit.

*****

"Sheriff," he said, "just wanted you to know I was in town. My superiors have been getting complaints about Uncle Hiram again, and I'd guess you'd know the source. I'll poke around some," he said, "and write a few reports on all the investigating I've done. Take about two or three days," Seth said as he grinned broadly.

"Oh, by the way," he asked, "if you manage to lay hands on a gallon or two, I'd be quite pleased. I've got a special occasion in a few weeks, and there's no better way to celebrate than having a few drinks of Uncle Hiram's liquor."

"I'll see what I can do," Clinton answered, amused.

"Be checking in the hotel soon if you need me."

"If I come across anything, I'll bring it by, Seth," Clinton promised. Then in a more solemn tone, he said, "And thanks for always driving down after Milton calls his friends in the legislature. I know that pressure must roll down—"

"Sheriff," Seth interrupted, "that old bootlegger just makes me laugh. I don't know if it's his crafty nature or the fact that he tells the whole world to kiss his ass that compels me to run a little defense for him."

*****

Clinton saw the all-clear light appear in Uncle Hiram's window, and with it being such a pretty night, he decided to walk the hundred yards to his home. Uncle Hiram heard the sheriff's boots thumping on his front porch and hollered from the kitchen, "Come on in here, boy, and rest them long legs under Uncle Hiram's table."

Clinton opened the screen door and walked lazily across the wooden floor. The walls were covered with artifacts of Uncle Hiram's Creek ancestors: a wooden bow, a quiver of arrows, and a tomahawk that Uncle Hiram swore belonged to William Weatherford. The famous half Creek Indian masterminded the Fort Mims massacre and later surrendered to and was spared by Andrew Jackson.

Uncle Hiram claimed his mother was a full-blooded Creek and kin to the fierce warrior. Clinton didn't know if his stories were true, but it was good entertainment. He always tried to soak up as much of the home as he could. The exterior was made out of logs, but the interior walls were rough planks cut from heart pine that smelled faintly of turpentine.

The kitchen walls were lined with shelves that contained plates, coffee cups, mason jars for drinking, pot and pans, clear glass bowls full of smooth stones that had been polished by the river, and cans of flour, meal, and sugar. Uncle Hiram fathered seven children by four different women. His oldest, Johnny, left the county in September, headed to Tuskegee Institute for college. The youngest had just started at the one-room Negro school. They were an easy clan to spot—all well-dressed and small in size like their daddy. He took good care of them but chose to live alone.

Clinton pulled back the bench, slid his legs under the table, and listened as Uncle Hiram rustled around in his pantry. He had once stuck his head around the corner and saw it was full of canned pears and peaches and jars of dewberry jelly.

He always enjoyed these visits and wished this one was about something more pleasant. Before he could think any further, Uncle Hiram appeared and placed a mason jar on the table. Clinton took a drink and felt the slight burn of the whiskey as it slid down his throat.

"Thanks, Uncle Hiram. I needed a drink tonight," Clinton said.

"You could have used a touch the first time you came here, boy. Never seen a child so scared."

Clinton remembered the visit as if it were yesterday. Warts had slowly started appearing on his fingers as a small boy. His father took him to see Uncle Hiram, who was known for his ability to "look off warts." That phrase, in a child's mind, sounded as if they would be removed with a butcher knife.

It took a piece of stick candy to bribe Clinton into letting Uncle Hiram within reaching distance. "They'll be gone in a week or two," Uncle Hiram had proclaimed after giving his hands a good stare. Sure enough, one week later, they disappeared.

When Clinton became sheriff, his curiosity led him to the courthouse in an effort to find out the old man's real name. No one seemed to know. A search of the records revealed that his legal name was Hiram Tulare Macarthur, and much to Clinton's surprise, each document was signed in a very legible script. Most Negroes in the county, especially the ones as old as Uncle Hiram, couldn't read or write.

Clinton found Uncle Hiram watching him and realized he had drifted off. Hiram's eyes were deep forest in the middle of a moonless night—black. In this light, his weathered face could give the illusion of being a hundred, but his hair was just now showing a smattering of gray. The broad nose indicated Negro, but Clinton could see the high cheekbones, marking his Indian heritage.

It occurred to Clinton that if he didn't approach the task at hand, he would be here all night. "Uncle Hiram," he began, "you know we found Charlie Ed dead Saturday night." Uncle Hiram nodded in agreement. "Well, it first looked as though he'd done what he always did on Saturday night, got drunk and lain down wherever he got tired and slept it off."

It was a common occurrence in the county, but most ignored his habit if he wasn't drunkenly snoring on the sidewalks of town. This time, things happened differently. Rarely would Roxboro have any traffic at night, but one unfortunate man on his way to Montgomery ran over Charlie Ed as he took a drunken nap in the middle of the road. At least it seemed that way at first glance. When the local doctor, who doubled as the county coroner, examined the body, it became quite evident that Charlie Ed had been murdered.

"Any idea who killed him, Uncle Hiram?" Clinton shifted his weight on the bench as Hiram answered.

"That nigger got himself killed," Uncle Hiram stated in a matter-of-fact tone while tugging at his broad nose. "You know that light-skinned nigger Joe Marsh, the one with the bad scar on his arm?" Clinton nodded. "Well, he liked to walk across the flats and spend time with Carrie Hawkins. You know that mean-ass woman over in Roetown?"

That shanty enclave in Hover County was known for its trouble. Clinton also knew the prostitute by face and reputation. She carried herself proudly and would knife anyone who angered her.

"Well, Charlie Ed took a spark to her too, and Joe Marsh didn't like it, her sharing and all. I'd guess she was playing one against the other, trying to make each man pay a little more. They got into a fight, and Joe clubbed Charlie in the head with a crowbar. Charlie Ed should have known better than to fight that big nigger," Uncle Hiram declared. Then with a tilt of his head, he caught Clinton by surprise with more news. "Mr. Ewell's going to be asked to leave the church Sunday."

"Really!" Clinton exclaimed. Generally, Ruth would inform him when some change was coming in the Roxboro Baptist Church. Milton Marion remained the largest contributor and the leading deacon. Being asked to leave a church in South Alabama was akin to being branded for life. To most, it was a terrible punishment guaranteed to follow them even if they moved away.

"Your daddy-in-law is mad at Mr. Ewell for taking in that girl." Clinton was well-versed in how much Milton Marion hated Sara and how he wanted her boy without admitting that Trace raped her. He hoped Uncle Hiram couldn't read his face. Sara's troubles bothered him greatly. "You know that bastard girl—" Uncle Hiram started after the sheriff didn't respond.

"Uncle Hiram, I know who you're talking about," Clinton answered. This was one time, even though he cherished the company of Uncle Hiram, that he wished he wasn't here. With hard eyes and stern looks raining from the old man, he knew that Uncle Hiram was about to explain the differences in how the two races of the county viewed life.

"You know, Sheriff, you white people sure are funny," he pronounced with narrowed eyes.

"How's that?" Clinton asked.

"Y'all go to church on Sunday, and the preacher always hollering about drinking whiskey and the sin of flesh. The men in the pews are nodding their heads in agreement even though many have taken a drink of my liquor the night before."

Clinton chuckled and slowly relaxed his shoulders with a rolling motion, wondering why he was so tense. What Uncle Hiram said was true. Not only did the statement pertain to the men but also the women in town were just as guilty of hypocrisy. One of the main ingredients in their cakes and pies was a dash of Uncle Hiram's best.

"That's not counting how many men have given up at home and tip across the settlement looking for some dark flesh," Uncle Hiram said as he took a swat at a lone housefly.

Clinton cringed at the statement, knowing that Uncle Hiram knew the darkest secret of his life. But the words weren't meant to sting him or to bring up what his father had done. Of course, Uncle Hiram knew every dirty tidbit of darkness in the county. If he were to spill the secrets he kept, most men would be down front next Sunday, tail between their legs, rededicating their lives to Jesus. Probably a few women would make the journey too.

"You know, Sheriff," he said, tracking the fly, "us niggers don't call children without daddies bastards. To us, they're just another child. Now that Billie Ewell's got the girl in that shack on the river, Uncle Hiram carry her a little food and whatnot each day."

The statement didn't shock Clinton, and he could tell Uncle Hiram didn't intend it to. "You do too much," Clinton said trying seriously to give the old Negro a warning, "and some of the men around here will break out the white sheets." Clinton remembered too well Marion's rage when he learned the news of Mr. Ewell helping Sara. Clinton looked at Uncle Hiram again and saw narrowed black eyes that showed no fear.

"They ain't going to do that," he replied quickly. "Ain't been any of them around here for years, but if they do, I'll fill their asses full of buckshot! I ain't some poor ole nigger that hasn't got money for a gun."

That part, Clinton conceded, was true. You can't run rough-shod over men who are armed and willing to fight back.

"Sides," Uncle Hiram said, "she ain't never going to make a go-round here. Your daddy-in-law will see to that. Someone needs to give her more than just a little food and do something better than what Billie Ewell's doing." Clinton thought at first the old man was making a general statement about Sara, just stating the obvious, but then he recognized the mischievous look.

"No! No! Uncle Hiram." He leaned forward, wanting the old Negro to understand his message loud and clear. "You mix that girl up in your business; there'll be hell to pay. Just one damn whisper," he emphasized strongly, "that she's involved with you and it will all roll down on me. The preacher will be hollering from the pulpit, and Marion will camp at the door in Montgomery trying to bring agents down here to catch you. Never mind the pressure he'll put on me."

"Now, Sheriff," Uncle Hiram said lightly, "you worry too much; I ain't going to cause you any trouble. Be crazy of me to do such a thing. I just wonder how you white people can spend so much time on Sunday talking about Jesus while everyone is just waiting for her to lose that boy. It just ain't right that's all."

Not wanting to talk about Sara or people's hypocrisy anymore, Clinton moved to change the subject. Remembering Seth Walker's request, he said, "Uncle Hiram, if I were to find a couple of gallons in my car it wouldn't hurt anything."

"Sheriff, you sit right there and finish your drink. Uncle Hiram be back shortly," he said, rising from the table. "If you need more, it's in the pantry," he finished, already pushing the rear screen door open.

Clinton listened as Uncle Hiram's footsteps faded away. He lit a rare cigarette and leaned his back against the wall. He thought of what the old man had said. He might have denied planning to involve the girl, but Clinton knew that Uncle Hiram would do whatever he wanted. A moment later it dawned on him that Uncle Hiram revealed his plans on purpose. It was a challenge for him to resist any pressure from Milton Marion and to give Uncle Hiram time to help Sara. Clinton drained his glass, feeling the welcome heat, then rose to find more.

Chapter 6

Sara was grateful that Mr. Ewell called a halt to the work at noon on Saturday. She had casually mentioned to Danny that she needed to buy a few supplies. This would give her and Sam ample time to walk to town and back before dark. As she placed her pitchfork in the tool wagon, she heard the now-familiar grunt of Mr. Ewell.

"Danny's going to take you to town, Ms. Sara," Mr. Ewell volunteered. "And when he carries you home, he'll cut you some firewood."

"Thank you, Mr. Ewell," Sara replied as she hitched up her overalls. "I'm grateful for both offers."

"You'll be needing the wood sooner or later," he replied. "It's been right warm and dry, but that north wind could start blowing next week. I'd feel better knowing you and the boy had enough either way." He turned and walked away after their brief conversation.

"Sam," Sara called loudly, "come on. We've got to get going." Sara figured he was behind the remaining peanut stacks, chewing away. She looked across the dusty field and saw the empty stack poles fashioned as crosses, and a feeling of anxiety ran through her veins. She wondered about the future once the harvest was done. "Sam," she called again, "where are you?"

"He's right here, Ms. Sara," Danny hollered, getting her attention. "We were in the barn," he said, drawing nearer. "Hope you don't mind. Sam was helping me hitch the—"

"No, that's fine, Danny," she answered quickly, trying to show how much she approved of him taking time with Sam. "Glad he helped. He needs to learn how to do things."

*****

Mr. Ellis tried hard to concentrate and not let his eyes wander to the wide gap between Mrs. Robinson's front teeth as she prattled on about her son, the lawyer. "Got work at that firm a year ago," she said loudly, hoping others in the store would hear. Roger Ellis nodded his head on cue. She was friends with Mr. Marion, so in no uncertain terms, he had to be nice. Finally, she paid for her items and moved on.

Somehow, Roger Ellis missed Sara as she entered the store. He saw her working her way through a stack of bib overalls as her little boy stood close. Roger couldn't admit his affection for the girl, because he also bore the weight of Milton Marion's tyrannical power. Helping her in the store, which always caused him trouble, was his only way of resisting the man he hated so much.

He reached to his forehead and swept the few hairs that graced the top of his head back in place. As Roger approached Sara, he took the opportunity to admire her gentle and precious face. Sara felt his presence and looked up.

"May I help you, miss?" Roger asked.

Sara knew Mr. Ellis from previous trips, and he had always helped her while the others walked by as if she was an invisible ghost. "Yes, sir, please," she responded nervously, expecting Mr. Marion to walk in and demand that she leave. But Mr. Ellis's soft eyes seemed so anxious to help. Sara noticed how his black tie formed a perfect knot and how his white apron wrapped all the way around his thin body and tied at the front.

"If you will, Mr. Ellis, I need a pound of sugar, meal…" She found herself trailing off as he walked toward the table that held the bags of sugar. He placed the item on the counter, took her order for the next purchase, and moved through the store. Soon, all her supplies were gathered. Sara glanced down, watching as he added up her purchases, and then exhaled quietly in relief after seeing the final figure. She had enough money to pay, and there would be five dollars left over.

Sara unbuttoned the front pocket of her overalls, removed her red bandanna, and nervously tugged at the knot. She had placed every penny they had in the kerchief, so afraid that somehow she would lose the money. "That's the way old nigger women carry their cash," Hoxie Hill, a farm woman who was one degree from white trash, said from behind. "Except they always keeps theirs stuffed in their bosom."

Roger Ellis looked at Sara, his eyes speaking instead of his lips: "Don't pay any attention, dear. She has no class." Sara handed Mr. Ellis her money. "Let me have the rest," he said. "I'll give you back silver half dollars. Maybe you can save them for the boy." He gently placed the coins in Sara's outstretched hand and waited patiently as she tied the bandanna. "Did you walk here?" he asked. He seemed worried about how she and the boy could carry all the supplies to the river.

"No, sir," Sara answered. "Danny Ewell brought us in the wagon. It's right outside."

"Let me help you, then," he said.

Sara started to object, knowing that by nightfall, someone in the store would inform Mrs. Ellis and Mr. Marion of his activity. She didn't want to cause him any trouble, but to her surprise, he was already headed to the door with everything, except the overalls. Sara followed ten steps behind and caught up with him after he had placed her items in the rear of the wagon.

"Thank you, Mr. Ellis," Sara offered with deep gratitude.

"My pleasure, Ms. Sara," he replied softly. "Anytime."

The wagon faced north, parallel to the street, and Danny sat on the right side of the seat with his shoulders turned slightly to the road. As Sara walked around the end of the wagon, she saw that he was talking with Eugene Bryant.

Eugene stood on the county slag with his feet shoulder width apart. His powerful forearms, sprinkled lightly with dark hair, were locked across his chest. He was shirtless and only wore overalls, which looked as though they hadn't been washed in months. Eugene's hair—long, stringy, and pulled behind his ears—was slick and greasy. His feet were bare and blackened with dirt, adding to his unkempt look.

Instinctively, Sara pushed Sam behind her and back onto the sidewalk, knowing Eugene's presence was an unfortunate development. Dangerous would be the only way to describe the young man. The night after her mother died, he showed up at the door, waving cash around.

*****

"Two weeks' pay, Sara," Eugene crowed, flashing grossly crooked yellow teeth, "to let me up under your dress."

Sara's gut instinct caused her to worry that when she said, "No. Leave me alone, Eugene," he might force himself on her. She tightened her grip on the fireplace poker, determined that she would beat him to death if he tried. As he eyed her warily through the old screen door, she saw that he was making the calculation, wondering if it was worth the risk. She stood her ground, determined. Not again.

Eugene smiled wickedly and walked away until reaching the edge of the yard. In the darkened night, he yelled, "Whore! Slut! You think you're too good for me? Don't think you've seen the last of me."

*****

Sara felt a sudden shudder when Eugene looked from Danny and leered at her once again. "Here comes your whore, Danny," Eugene said loudly for everyone on the street to hear. In a flash, Danny leaped straight at Eugene, trying to catch him around the neck and take him down. Eugene, older, wiser, and already a full-grown man, spun sideways, caught Danny's overalls in the front, and twisted, slamming him into the road. Sara heard Danny's breath rush from his body.

With Danny pinned, Eugene caught his throat in a firm grip with his left hand and began viciously punching his face with his right. Sara felt her legs freeze momentarily, then realized that not a soul would help. The bystanders, whether they were townsfolk or farmers, were content to watch the fight.

Sara quickly unbuttoned her front pocket, removed the bandanna, and used it as a sling to hit the top of Eugene's head. With all her might, she swung again and again, grunting out loud each time. Finally, the weight of the silver coins opened a gash on Eugene's scalp. Sara aimed and slammed home another blow. This time, he rolled off Danny and scrambled to his feet.

She cocked her arm, intent on catching him on the nose with her makeshift weapon. Suddenly, as Eugene lunged forward, Sara saw a large arm come out of nowhere, catching him in the chest. He pushed him backward with such force that he stumbled and fell.

"Stand down, Eugene!" the deep voice commanded. So intent on defending herself against the rising man, Sara couldn't see who was talking. Eugene stood upright, his eyes locked in struggle with hers, and she knew at that moment that he was capable of murder. Sam's frightened voice cried from the background: "Mama!"

The sound of Eugene's cheekbone cracking widened Sara's vision. Sheriff Barnes had swung his sap, a piece of lead entrapped in a leather casing, and caught Eugene on his right cheek as he advanced. He dropped hard on his knees and brought his hands to his face.

Sara felt sweat trickling down her forehead and scalp as Danny pushed himself off the ground and Sheriff Barnes barked orders. "You!" he said sternly, pointing at another young man. "Take him to Doc Benson." The bystander obeyed, grabbing Eugene under his shoulders and helping him to his feet. "You," he said to Sara, "put your boy in the wagon and go home."

As Danny reached for the wagon, Sara could see blood running from both nostrils, staining the front of his shirt. The sheriff turned his attention to Danny, saying quietly but with a hint of admiration, "If you're going to fight someone like Eugene, you'd better bring a stronger weapon with you. Maybe a good hickory limb, piece of pipe, or ax handle. Something that will put you two on equal footing. Nice try, but he's a little much for you right now."

"Yes, sir," Danny answered, oblivious to the blood running over his lips and dripping off his chin. Clinton stood in the street and watched as Sara and Danny rolled away. He turned and, glaring at the gathered crowd, spat in the street before walking away in disgust. He regretted that Eugene dropped so easily. He truly wanted to beat the man to a bloody pulp.

*****

As Danny maneuvered the wagon off Main Street, his nose freely dripped blood.

"Stop the mule and let me help you," Sara said.

"Whoa," Danny commanded while pulling back on the reins.

Sara untied the bandanna and dropped the coins in her pocket. "Hold this to your nose and tilt your head back."

Danny took the kerchief and pinched both nostrils. Then he replied with a nasal twang, "Can't drive this way."

"I'll take the reins," Sara answered. "You keep your head back, and the bleeding will soon stop. Come up, mule," she hollered. The mule started walking and then, sensing they were on their way home, advanced into a comfortable trot.

*****

The blood had dried and caked around Danny's nostrils by the time they reached the river. After stepping down from the wagon, Sara insisted that he follow her into the kitchen so she could clean his face. Sam watched for a moment, then wandered away to play outside.

Danny sat in a chair, feeling the blood coagulate in his nose. His face stung as if he was being attacked by a hundred yellow jackets. In that unguarded moment, he did what he had wanted to do ever since the woman and child came to the cabin. He admired her beauty. Shy, stolen glances were all he dared risk before. Now with her attention taken with washing his blood out of the kerchief, he eyed her willfully. He watched her slim arms move the pump handle up and down. Gracefully she rinsed the soap away, and too soon, she turned her attention to him.

"This might hurt a little," Sara offered.

Danny avoided looking her in the eye. "Yes, Ms. Sara."

"You don't have to call me miss, Danny. Sara will be just fine."

"Yes, ma'am."

Sara decided to wait for another day to tell him to leave off *ma'am* also. She started working the small cuts on his face left by Eugene's knuckles. She wiped gently, trying not to cause any pain. When she finished, she turned her attention to his swollen nose.

Sara tenderly felt the bridge, finding the bone intact. Danny resisted closing his eyes and focused on the shelf above the sink. Her hands were warm even though she had washed the kerchief in the cold water of the well. She slowly started wiping away the blood caked around his nostrils. Twice she heard him stifle a grunt of pain.

"Sorry," she whispered.

"That's okay," he replied.

Sara placed her hand under Danny's chin and gently tilted his head back, gaining better light to review her work. "You'll look like a raccoon in the morning," she pronounced. She had cleaned Stuart's face more than once from his scrapes and knew what to expect.

"Yes, ma'am," he said with a slight smile.

Sara didn't release Danny's chin, wanting him to understand what she was about to say. "Danny, you don't need to fight over me. This county has been talking about my family for as long as I've been breathing."

"It ain't right," he answered, the words catching in his throat.

"Might not be, Danny, and I appreciate the effort more than you'll ever know." She felt moisture creeping into her eyes but willed the tears back. "But right now, this place and the kindness of your father are all I and Sam have. It'd be awful if we cause so much trouble that he has to ask us to leave."

"He wouldn't do that," he exclaimed. She could read hurt in his expression.

"Danny, we've got nowhere else to go." Her desperate statement chilled the room.

"I'll keep that in mind, Sara," he answered as she released his chin. "I'd better start cutting the firewood. Haven't got but about two hours of light left."

As he stood, Sara realized Danny changed at that moment on the street. She watched as he squared his shoulders and walked away, proud to have defended her honor. She also realized just how quiet, shy, and lonely he was.

Chapter 7

Mr. Ewell pushed his graying hair back and looked in the mirror. After donning his wire-rimmed glasses, he hollered loudly, "Danny, you got the mule hitched?"

"Yes, sir," Danny called from outside. He turned toward the sound of the screen door slamming. His father stopped on the last step after noticing his face.

"What happened?" Mr. Ewell asked. Danny briefly explained, and he wasn't surprised that his father's only reaction was a grunt.

As they rode away, Danny found the courage to ask, "Daddy, the peanuts are about picked, and there's not much work left to do. There's no way Sara and the boy can make it through the winter."

"I've been thinking about that," Mr. Ewell responded. "I'll pay her to clean the house a couple of days a week. That should be enough to keep her and the boy going till spring planting."

Danny clucked his tongue, urging the mule to a faster clip, and soon, the redbrick First Baptist Church of Roxboro came into view. The imposing white columns, four of them, greeted its members each Sunday. To the right of the main entrance was a separate building for Sunday school with a covered walkway that connected the two.

The back of the church contained a small low shed made of blocks that housed four woodburning stoves and a barbecue pit. Once a month, the congregation used it to serve dinner on the ground, a day-long church service interrupted only at noon by hog meat dripping with red sauce.

Most in the county belonged to Roxboro Baptist. No one would admit it, but everyone knew that it was dangerous not to. Milton Marion always found a way to punish those who didn't.

As Danny maneuvered the wagon to the parking area, the aroma of past meals wafted from the cooking pit. This morning, he saw Mr. Marion's new car surrounded by a crowd and heard his pompous voice explaining all the features. "Cadillac" drifted in the breeze countless times.

Danny followed his father to their seats: third row from the rear and at the end of the pew. It was their custom. Billie Ewell preferred to escape after the service with little conversation. Today, as people started filing in, several boys he knew from church and school nodded slightly as they passed but didn't speak.

Danny felt his face redden; he knew the story of the fight had already made its way around the county. Not a one stopped to tease him with the usual "Where'd you get that shiner?" or "What'd the other feller look like?" All the normal banter was missing, and people left them completely alone.

He tried to concentrate on the preacher's words, the usual sermon about the wrath of God, but found his mind always wandering back to Sara. The anticipation of seeing her again this afternoon made him appreciate his father's brief ways. Finally, the sermon wound down, and the call to the altar was announced. Mr. Houston, a cranky old man with a baritone voice, stood before the congregation and started leading the song of invitation.

Two verses later, the hymn ended with the preacher making no effort to drag someone down front and be saved. When Mr. Baluster gave a brief closing prayer, ending the service extraordinarily early, Danny knew something wasn't right.

*****

Just outside the church door, Mr. Ewell reached for John Tillie's hand. The reverend shook it. "Mr. Ewell, if you will stay for a few more minutes, Mr. Marion and I would like to discuss something with you." Danny knew the difference between a request and a demand, and this fell into the latter category. The preacher's eyelashes, which were long and almost white, fluttered like a woman's if she were tittering. He always thought the reverend carried himself with a feminine nature.

"That'll be fine," Mr. Ewell replied, giving no indication of what he was thinking. "We'll just take a seat till you're through."

"Danny doesn't have to stay, Mr. Ewell. I'm sure he would like to go visit with his friends."

"The boy will stay with me," Billy Ewell answered with a downward edge in his voice.

"Very well." The preacher looked slightly dour because his suggestion wasn't heeded. "We'll be with you shortly."

*****

As he spoke, John Tillie's words echoed slightly in the empty church. "Mr. Ewell, we appreciate that you've been such a faithful member all these years. But it has come to our attention that you've got that young girl with the illegitimate child living in your place. I'm afraid that sends the wrong message to the younger people of this church: that one can sin and not have earthly consequences."

Danny looked at his father, expecting a reply, but he just stared impassively into the man's face. John Tillie's long lashes fluttered nervously as he spoke again. "We're asking you to withdraw membership, but we would like for Danny to remain. We can't, as Christians, visit the sins of the father on the child."

"Billie," Milton Marion said, stepping in front of the reverend, "we've been doing business together for a long time, and our folks were much the same." The two men locked eyes, and Danny saw his father's bad eye sharpen its focus. "Get that girl to move on," Marion demanded. "And we'll forget this unpleasant business."

Mr. Ewell thundered his reply, filling the church with a loud bellow. "You little, fat, pompous ass! If you had one bit of Christian in you, you'd take the girl in yourself! That child was produced from the wickedness of your boy, and now you stand here and tell me to throw her out!" Milton Marion involuntarily stepped back as Mr. Ewell leaned closer. "You, sir, can go straight to hell!" he hollered, then turned to leave.

Danny stepped to follow, but Mr. Ewell stopped, turned again, and pointed with his finger. "As for you, preacher man, you might want to pull the shades down a little lower before you minister to the women of the town."

"I have never…" He trailed off.

Mr. Ewell glared as if he would snap his neck. "Before some husband comes and sticks a shotgun in your face."

*****

The two rode in silence for a few minutes before Danny spoke. "You knew it was coming, didn't you?"

"Yes," Mr. Ewell answered.

"How'd you know?"

"Hiram."

Danny would have guessed as much. The two neighbors were as close as he was with Uncle Hiram's oldest son, Johnny. Danny missed him now that he had gone away to college. He always thought that the relationship between his father and Uncle Hiram was a little strange.

Billie Ewell didn't drink, smoke, chew tobacco, or curse—only that had changed this morning—and he didn't tolerate those who did. Yet Uncle Hiram fell into a whole different category when it came to sinning. Not only should the whiskey taint him in his father's eyes, but so should the fact that four different women had his children out of wedlock.

Danny swatted at a deer fly and chuckled. "Didn't know you knew how to cuss."

"I'm sorry you heard me talk like that, son. I reckon we'll spend next fall hauling our crops across the flats."

Danny grunted at his father's remark as if there was nothing to the feat. "How'd you know the preacher was messing around?" he asked, hoping his father would elaborate because he would love to spread the news.

"I didn't," Mr. Ewell said with a rare laugh and a mischievous expression. "But he sure did look guilty, didn't he? He'll be worried for weeks that the town is talking about him. Never liked the man much. I'm sorry, son," Mr. Ewell apologized. "Ain't right to be talking this way, because we're all sinners falling short of the glory of God."

*****

That afternoon, Sara raked the sandy land smoothly, covering the seed, as Danny worked the last of the manure in. He wiped his face on his sleeve. "Sara, you might want to fashion a scarecrow to keep the birds away till the seed sprouts."

"I will," she answered, grateful for his help. "Could I get you some water?"

"Thank you, but I'm fine."

"I have a piece of pie left if you'd like," she offered.

"No," he answered politely. "I'd expect Sam would like to eat that. Besides, I'd better head toward home. I've got a few chores left, and Daddy's probably hungry too."

"You do the cooking?" Sara asked curiously.

"Yes, ma'am," he said quietly, slipping back into his shy nature. "Kinda had to since Mama died."

"How long has she been gone?"

"Long time."

"I know you miss her," she said, hotness creeping into her eyes as thoughts of Lilly arose.

"Yes." He could see her effort to hold back tears, and it saddened him. Danny watched her turn away, and he wondered if it was to hide her tears or if she had just realized his growing affection for her.

*****

Sara sat with Sam, playing, as Danny loaded the wagon. Soon, she heard the familiar jingle of the harness as he drove away. Suddenly a shadow startled her, and she looked up to find Uncle Hiram standing there, smiling.

"Sorry, miss. Didn't mean to scare you," he said gently.

"You didn't," she responded. "I just didn't hear you coming, that's all." Sam, so involved in playing in the sand, took several seconds to realize his mother wasn't talking to him. He looked curiously at the old man.

"I've been tipping around these woods for a long time, miss. I always move quiet-like. Never know who might be following."

Sara knew Uncle Hiram from reputation, but she wasn't alarmed. His small feet were clad in boots, which answered her question as to who had been leaving the food. He was smiling infectiously, and she returned it like a little girl.

"What ya doing with that fish basket?" she asked, a trace of hopefulness in her voice.

"Thought you could use it. And I brought some cottonseed cake for bait too. You and the boy might get tired of eating fish, but they'll keep you fed. Come on," he encouraged, holding his hand out and helping her up. "Let's go catch some." In one swoop, he picked Sam up and started walking to the river. Sara hustled along, trying to keep up with his pace, while Sam giggled, showing no fear of the man.

Uncle Hiram dropped the basket at the edge of the river, set Sam down gently, and reached into the pocket of his khakis, pulling out some twine. "Ms. Sara," he said, opening the trapdoor to the basket and dropping in the cottonseed cake, "check the basket every morning and night. When the cottonseed runs out, use the entrails instead."

He tied the twine to the basket and, in a swift motion, tossed it in the moving water. Sara watched as he tied the other end to a nearby tree. "Miss," he asked, "I got something else way's back. You mind if the boy goes with me?"

"No, I don't care," she answered.

"Good. The boy and me will be back in a few minutes. Why don't we meet on the porch?"

"That'll be fine," Sara agreed.

*****

Sara sat on the top step as Uncle Hiram and Sam arrived. Her son hugged his neck tightly as he took a seat on the second step. He carefully dropped another large cloth sack on the ground, then looked up at Sara.

"Ms. Sara, I brought you a few more sweet potatoes. Thought you could use them."

"Thank you for the other gifts also," she replied. "We've made good use—"

"Ain't no trouble, miss," he interrupted, confirming her suspicions. "I got plenty. This boy here," he said while stroking Sam's hair lightly, "is going to start growing like a weed soon. It'll take a lot to keep him fed. One day, he'll grow up strong and take care of you."

"I hope so, Uncle Hiram. I do worry, though."

"Ms. Sara, I know Mr. Marion wants the boy because he's got no one to—"

"He can't have him, Uncle Hiram," she stated forcefully.

"Yes, ma'am. I know you'll do your best, but he's a right mean man, miss. Not trying to make you worry, but it would help if you could get away from here."

Twilight was drifting into darkness as Sara looked down. "I'd love to leave, Uncle Hiram, but that would take money."

"Ms. Sara, if you could help me for a bit," he said as he lowered his voice, "you might make enough for you and the boy to slip away."

"Why do you need help?" she asked.

"See this hand, miss?" Uncle Hiram extended his empty hand, holding it close to her face so she could see his fingers. "Some days, I can hardly open it. Uncle Hiram's getting old."

"What would I have to do?" she asked, her voice a blend of excitement and fear.

"Ms. Sara, if you'd help me tend the still—not sell it, mind you—and make the whiskey, in a little while, you'd have enough to leave. Go to Birmingham or Nashville where there's lots of folks. Maybe one day, after this boy's grown, you'd come back with him to see ole Uncle Hiram." Sara could see the flash of his teeth as he smiled. "Be right funny, the folks around this town saying, 'What's that woman and boy coming back and seeing that old nigger for?'"

"Uncle Hiram," she asked solemnly, "I can't risk getting caught and losing Sam. How have you avoided arrest all these years?"

"Well, miss"—he chuckled—"those folks that have been trying to catch me, they think like white folk. They ain't tried to think like a nigger. About the time I'm just getting ready to work—I always work at night, miss—they're getting tired of stomping around the woods. I wait until they're gone to start.

"Every now and then, one tries to follow me at night, but it doesn't take long to wear them out. One trip across the flats always does it. That sandy bottom and moving water can sap a man quickly. Miss, if you do what I say, there's not much of a chance of getting caught. I've been making whiskey a long time, and no one has managed yet."

"All right. What do I need to do, Uncle Hiram?" she asked anxiously, her own breathless words ringing in the still night.

"Uncle Hiram will come tomorrow night. I'll bring my girl Bessie to keep the boy the first couple of times until you learn the way. Ms. Sara," he continued, "you know I could just give you the money, but if I did, you'd never take it."

"How do you know that, Uncle Hiram?"

"You have a proud look, and I know more about people than anyone else because I'm so old."

His statement prompted her to boldly ask, "Do you know who my daddy is?"

"No, miss," he answered solemnly. "Uncle Hiram doesn't. I know a lot of secrets, but not that one." Her shoulders slumped, and he tried to change the subject. "Ask Uncle Hiram something else, and maybe I can answer it."

"How'd you get your land?"

He chuckled for a moment before answering. "Many times, I've heard people say, 'How'd that nigger get that prime river land?' After the war was over, the man that owned this land found himself without any heirs. All of his sons had died in the fighting, so he left it to the one slave that didn't run off after being freed."

"That was your kin?" she asked.

"Sure was, Ms. Sara, my great-granddaddy. You want to know something else that nobody knows but me?"

"Sure. I'd love to hear something scandalous about someone besides myself."

"You know Mr. Marion's granddaddy was a Yankee carpetbagger?"

"No, I didn't know that!" In Roxboro, being descended from carpetbaggers was akin to stealing from the collection plate at church.

"Yes, ma'am. He came down here with nothing but holes in his pockets and stole everything they got. Milton Marion is always bragging about how his ancestors fought for the South. Ain't true. I told the last sheriff, and it kept the man off his back. That's why, child, he hates this nigger. I know the truth about him. Ms. Sara?"

"Yes?" she said, enjoying the singsong of his voice.

"I'd better be getting home, but before I go, there's something else you need." Uncle Hiram leaned over, trying not to wake Sam, and pulled a shotgun from the sack. "I brought this for you because of Eugene. He's a bad man, miss. If he shows up around here, trying to bother you, you shoot his sorry hide. Uncle Hiram will come and take the body away, and nobody will ever find it."

Sara took it the way Uncle Hiram intended as he passed Sam to her. As he stood to leave, she said, "We'll do that one day, Uncle Hiram." He turned to face her, not sure what she meant. "Come visit you, me and Sam."

Uncle Hiram smiled brightly. "That'd be right nice. Mean a lot to an old nigger like me."

Chapter 8

"Clinton, Papa wants you at his office at seven tonight," Ruth stated.

Clinton's appetite immediately disappeared. "What does he need?" he asked, dreading the answer.

"How do I know, Clinton?" she replied with her normal irritated voice. He fought the urge to look away from his plate and tried pushing the peas around, hoping she would leave. "You know," she started. Clinton felt as though someone had just scraped a chalkboard with fingernails. "Papa's done a lot for you."

Yeah, he thought. *And both of you remind me every day.* Clinton laid his fork down and sat back knowing they were nowhere near the end of this conversation. Looking at her, he wished she had inherited Clair's looks instead of Marion's.

The reddish-brown color of her hair reminded him of when the river flooded and washed the land away. Her skin always carried a raised red blotch or two. Tonight, a patch was inflamed between her thin upper lip and her nose. Clinton sighed, wishing her mother or someone would tell her about the long black hair protruding from her chin. He didn't dare.

"And he helped you to become sheriff."

Clinton nodded, willing himself not to take the bait. Ruth's face glowed red, and he could see she was spoiling for a fight. *Drinking whiskey with Uncle Hiram sure would be more pleasant,* he thought, wishing her away.

"What the hell are you staring at, Clinton?" she asked, her voice pitching high.

"Oh, I was just thinking about a case," he lied.

"You're going to help me put the rest of dinner away," she demanded. "Jessie left early again today for the second time this week," Ruth emphasized as if a murder was at hand. "Are you listening to me?" she asked. "I want you to fire her because there's plenty of other niggers that need work!"

Their maid, Jessie, was a scant of a woman. On windy days, Clinton worried that she might be blown into the next county if a strong gust came along. Besides being one of the best cooks around, he found her pleasant, efficient, and affable. She ironed his uniforms with perfect creases, polished his boots to a mirror shine, fried cornbread and chicken just like his mother, and worked long days under Ruth's tyrannical rule, all without complaint. He knew she worked diligently, trying to keep her own kids fed; and every week, he slipped her a little extra for all the effort.

"Clinton, are you in some other damn world?" Ruth shouted, her whole face now bloodred. "I told you, you need to fire Jessie!"

"I'll have a talk with her," he replied hastily. "I've got things to check on before I see your father."

Clinton used a long stride to get out of the kitchen and then bolted to the living room, grabbing his gun belt and hat. Ruth was soon left to argue alone. She felt the wind of his wake and hurled several curses. She knew all too well what her father wanted with Clinton.

Ruth had watched for years as Trace was spoiled, pampered, and given whatever he desired at every moment. Her jealousy grew each time her father primed Trace, saying, "And you'll take over for me one day." All the while, she stood in the background, being given no consideration that she could run the business.

Ruth picked up Clinton's plate and hurled it toward the sink, scattering peas, butterbeans, and cornbread across the floor. The sound of breaking glass gave her a few seconds of satisfaction knowing she created more work for Jessie.

"Show me that you can find a husband," Milton Marion had said when she inquired about her rightful place. "And maybe I'll give you a chance."

"What do you mean Clinton's going to college and I can't?" she had screamed after trapping Clinton into marriage. "Why can't I go too? I deserve it more than him, and it will help me take over!"

"Pregnant women don't go to college," Marion replied with a snort, once again pushing her to the side.

Ruth pitched Clinton's tea glass against the wall in a fit of anger knowing that the evening's meeting was about the child her father wanted so badly.

*****

The warm Indian summer night felt pleasing to Clinton despite the fact that he had to meet with Milton Marion. One distinct fact remained, he thought. Uncle Hiram couldn't make enough whiskey nor could Clinton drink enough to make Ruth pleasant or pretty. He didn't hate her. No, indifference best described his feelings.

Sound carried well on the still night, and voices rose and fell as his slow walk continued. The town was laid out in a disheveled fashion. Main Street ran north and south with the courthouse sitting in the middle of town. The road split there, making a Y around the building. His office and the county jail were directly across from the courthouse on the west side.

Two blocks to the south, Milton Marion's bank stood prominently, and one block farther was his general store. Peppered up and down the main square were the barbershop, Blackwell's diner, a seven-room hotel, the fire station, Roxboro's Baptist church, the doctor's office, and assorted other buildings all owned by Marion.

Clinton's slow walk came to an end as he turned into the tree-covered, vacant small lot between the bank and the general store. Milton Marion insisted on using two entrances to his office. He could utilize the grand entrance, walking through the bank and greeting customers, or use the back one, slipping in and out unnoticed. Clinton could see that the door was cracked with light spilling through the opening. The lock consisted of a simple hasp screwed into the wooden door and frame.

With a deep breath, he pushed the door open and stepped inside the room. He saw that Milton Marion was squatted on his heels in front of his personal safe. "I'll be with you in a minute," he said over his shoulder. Clinton watched as his father-in-law started moving the dial.

He knew Marion kept cash there, but how much would be pure speculation. Every peek he had gotten always revealed neat stacks of green bills. He had a knack for remembering numbers and committed what he saw to memory as Marion moved the dial. Clinton then shuddered at the dishonest implications of what he was thinking.

Milton Marion closed the safe while Clinton pretended to study the door that separated the office from the bank. "Sit," Milton commanded, pointing to the straight-back wooden chair facing his oak desk. Clinton did as instructed. Milton took his seat and peered over the desk.

Clinton spoke first, trying to move the conversation away from the subject he knew was coming. "You need a better door and lock for your outside entrance," he said. "It'll be too easy for someone to break in here."

"It's your job to see I'm not robbed. Do that and we won't have a problem, will we?" There wouldn't be any response that would satisfy the man, so Clinton remained silent. Milton rose, pushing back his chair, and walked to the front of his desk.

"Clinton, when you married my daughter, did I not send you to college?"

"Yes, sir," he answered evenly.

"And when you returned from Auburn, did I not buy y'all a house to live in?" Clinton could see Marion's face beginning to turn red and knew he was seething with anger.

"Yes, sir."

"And put you to work in my store until you were elected?"

"Yes, sir." Clinton felt the heat of his own temper rising but fought it back.

"Who put up the money for your campaign, Clinton?"

"You did."

"Did I not endorse you and go out and find votes?"

"Yes."

"How long has your daddy been dead now?"

The question carried a cruel tone. Clinton didn't know if it was the pneumonia that killed his father or if it was the hard work and constant stupid things he did to increase his debt. "A little over a year."

"And if I remember correctly, I bought his land for a right fair price so your mama could live nice."

The fair price part could be debated if Clinton thought there was any use. His mother could sell the land for what she was offered or have Marion call in the note and take it away. After the sale, she moved to Montgomery to share a small apartment with her only sibling.

The place was barely fit for humans. Between his widowed aunt's small pension and the little money his mother received from the sale of the farm, the two lived a meager existence. Clinton contributed what he could, always feeling guilty that he should do more, but the two women would never complain.

"If I added up all my help to you, there'd be quite a tidy sum owed, wouldn't there?"

"Yes, sir," Clinton answered, trying to keep his voice even and hoping for a short conversation.

"After doing all this, I expected you to do certain things. And so far, you've done nothing." Marion's tone deepened, giving it a sharper edge. "That nigger Hiram is still walking around doing whatever he pleases."

"Why do you hate Uncle Hiram so much?" Clinton instantly regretted the question as Milton Marion's face scowled and his body puffed.

"Because he is the scourge of the earth, damn it!" Marion shouted, causing spittle to fly. "He makes a laughingstock of the church and every God-fearing person of the county." Clinton understood that only something personal could cause this kind of loathing.

"I want him caught, Clinton, and I want him caught now! It's gone on long enough, so put his ass in jail! Do you understand me?"

I have no intentions of catching Uncle Hiram. He is my friend, Clinton thought. "I'll see what I can do," he replied, rising from the chair.

"Sit back down! I'm not through with you yet!" Marion shouted so loudly that Clinton wondered if his voice was carrying down the street. He eased back into his seat as Marion looked down and said in a lower, more even voice, "Billie Ewell got that girl living in that shack on the river. Both she and her boy are liable to starve to death this winter. You do what I tell you to do. Find a way to take the boy and let me and Clair raise him proper-like. Adopt him and make it all legal. I don't give a whit what happens to the girl, but get her gone."

It wasn't that Clinton didn't expect this. He knew that when Mr. Ewell took the two in, Marion would be furious. Clinton thought, *I can't live with myself if I participate in adding more misery to Sara's life.* "I respectfully decline," he answered evenly.

"That's not an option!" Milton spat. "She can't raise that child on nothing. You make this happen and I'll do right by the boy."

Clinton stood quickly, his patience worn and his face hot. He looked down, finding Marion's eyes burning with fire. The thought of hurting Sara made Clinton's temper soar. "If you wanted to do right by the boy, then you'd take both of them in and show some of that Christian love you and the preacher are always talking about. You know Trace raped her!"

"He didn't!" Milton returned sharply. "She's trash and enticed him into relations, trying to find a way to take care of her crazy mama! It's your job to do what's right and take the boy from her!"

Clinton leaned down, putting his nose one inch from Milton Marion. With pent-up venom and spittle flying, he screamed, "She's done nothing to deserve that, and I'll be damned to hell if I'll help you take the boy away from her! The only mistake that girl made was being born in the wrong town!" The urge to strangle the man rose so violently that his hands jerked toward Marion's throat. Clinton's sanity returned, and he dropped them to his side.

"You'll be damned to hell, huh?" Milton said in a mocking tone while he slipped away and retreated to his chair. He grinned slyly. "You know that nigger Tug that works for me in the cotton gin?" Clinton felt the blood drain from his face, and it wasn't lost on Milton Marion. "You know, the one that's your half brother?"

"I don't know what you're talking about," Clinton lied, trying to keep his voice even.

"Yeah, you know he's your brother," Milton replied smugly. "And I'll bet your mother doesn't know your fine, upstanding daddy fathered a nigger child, that he laid with a common field hand. Yes, your daddy, Clinton," he boasted callously. "It would be a shame to have that secret revealed over something as silly as that little tramp."

Clinton's legs suddenly felt weak. It wasn't that long ago when he had made the same discovery. There had been a stabbing, and Uncle Hiram pointed him toward the culprit. After nosing around the settlement, he found that his knife-wielding assailant had already fled. Yet as Clinton drove by Tug's little shotgun house, it dawned on him that something felt familiar, and he made another loop. After seeing the man working on his flowers, he stopped.

*****

The front of the home held rows of gladiolas, which Tug was carefully weeding. Neat lines of nandinas, bridal wreaths, camellias, and gardenias graced the landscape. Clinton then realized this was a copy of his daddy's yard. Stu Barnes toiled the land, trying to grow cotton, and worked with a vengeance each day. But returning from the fields and digging in his flowers was what he loved the most.

Tug stood, brushing his knees clean of sand, and asked in the suspicious nature all Negroes carried for the law, "Something I can do for you, Sheriff?"

Clinton responded gently. "Naw, Tug, just admiring your pretty flowers." All the while, he was studying Tug's face. Tug carried his father's ears—long with short lobes. His nose was broader, but still, he could see a family resemblance. He dropped his eyes to Tug's boots and saw that his pant legs were tucked inside them, again a trait of Stu Barnes.

"I see you're digging out a little nut grass, Tug. Daddy always said that the only way to get rid of it is to move off and leave."

Tug's face broke in a small smile, and Clinton could see the shape of his father's lips. "He's probably right," Tug replied. "If you don't dig deep and get the nut out, it'll keep coming back."

"Well, it sure is a pretty yard. Just wanted to tell you."

"Many thanks, Sheriff. You know, your daddy gave me most of this." Clinton knew the words weren't meant to sting, but they did.

*****

Clinton had buried the thought, deciding the subject would be better off left alone, but as he struggled with his very life, Stu Barnes didn't. In a moment of candor and last breath honesty, he pulled his son close and said with a raspy and painful voice, "You have a brother, Clinton." He nodded his head, letting his dying father know he was aware, and he really didn't want or need any details.

Thankfully, his father only said, "You're in a position to help him if he gets in trouble. Watch over him, son. I've made my peace with God, but spare your mama. She doesn't deserve what I've done." Those were the last words he ever spoke.

The air suddenly became stuffy, and Clinton felt a bead of sweat break out on his upper lip. "I'll see what I can do," he said weakly.

"That's not the answer I want," Milton replied sharply, still wearing a smirk. "I want results, and I want them now, and I don't care how you do it. Now that we're on the same page regarding the, shall we say, consequences…" His voice trailed off.

Clinton felt defeated. "I'll report back soon," he mumbled, turning to leave.

"She doesn't have to know, Clinton," Marion replied with a parting shot as Clinton walked toward the door. "You know how bad it will hurt her. I believe that Tug's mama was only fourteen when she had him."

*****

The air felt cooler outside as Clinton worked his handkerchief from his back pocket, removed his cowboy hat, and wiped his face. It required all his strength for the simple task. After taking a few more steps, he stopped again, unsure of what to do or where to go. Home held no appeal. He needed somewhere to think.

Minutes later, Clinton found himself standing outside the jail. He pushed the door open, entered the darkened vestibule, and fumbled for the light switch. He opened his office door, turned on the light, and hung his hat and gun belt on two wooden pegs.

Then he journeyed down the foyer in search of the night deputy, Johnson Harvey. He normally slept on a cot outside of the two cells of the jail. Most times, when Clinton worked at night, he chose to let Johnson sleep; but tonight, he needed something. He tried the heavily fortified wooden door that separated the prisoners from the offices, but it was locked from the inside.

Johnson spent seven nights a week at the jail from six to six. Clinton needed more officers, but the county couldn't or wouldn't increase his budget. He called through the small barred opening at the top of the door. "Johnson, wake up. I need to see you a minute." He waited several seconds and, hearing no response, called again louder. "Johnson, wake up!"

Several more seconds clicked by, and he called again, this time more forcefully. Only a lone chirping cricket answered. "Damn it, Johnson, wake your drunk ass up," he shouted, surprising himself with his lack of patience. Clinton heard a soft, husky voice say lowly as if scared to wake the deputy, "Mr. Johnson, the sheriff wants you."

Clinton heard a muttering, and soon Johnson's unshaven face appeared. His salt-and-pepper hair stood up on one side, adding to his unkempt look. Clinton could smell whiskey on his deputy's breath, though their faces were separated by a foot. It wasn't unusual, though. The smell was permanent.

70

The heavy metal bar squeaked as Johnson lifted it from the rack. Clinton could hear him propping it lengthwise in the corner, and soon, the door swung open. He walked two steps forward and said, "Just needed to see you for a minute."

Before the deputy could reply, the prisoner interrupted. "Sheriff," the man asked timidly, "they going to be mean to me over there at Atmore?"

From the dim light of the jail, Clinton saw pleading, childlike dark eyes beckoning and hoping for comforting words. It saddened him deeply, adding to his wonder of human nature. Joe Marsh was a hardworking man with a nice family, but he willingly killed a man over a whore.

"Joe, after you confessed to killing Charlie Ed," Clinton answered, "I called the warden. He assured me that if you kept out of trouble for a year or two, he would make you a trustee, maybe work outside the prison in the hog parlor or collect the garbage or something like that. But that's only if you stay out of trouble."

"Yes, sir, Sheriff. I'll do my best." Clinton saw a bit of relief on the man's face, but he resisted the urge to pat his hands, which were clinging tightly to the bars.

"Can I help you with something, Sheriff?" Johnson asked sheepishly.

Clinton pulled out several bills from his pants pocket and pushed them in the man's direction. "Thought you might have a bottle around here somewhere, Johnson," he asked. "Sorry to wake you, but I could use a drink tonight."

"Yes, sir," Johnson replied. "Let me see what I can find. Can't take your money, though. Wouldn't be right." Clinton resisted the urge to argue, stepping aside to let his deputy make his way down the hall. He watched as Johnson shuffled by, planting his left leg, tilting his body toward the left, and then dragging his right leg forward with an awkward motion. A shootout with two escaped prisoners years before had left the deputy crippled.

Clinton honored the previous sheriff's wishes, keeping Johnson on as a paper tiger until he qualified for his pension. He easily overlooked Johnson's drinking. The pain that permeated his face wasn't a show. One of the bullets shattered his hip, and Clinton knew the only way the deputy functioned was to dull the pain with whiskey.

Two months prior, Clinton's youngest deputy, Ronnie Meeker, thought it would be quite the joke to find Johnson's whiskey. One day, while Clinton testified in court, the young man spent a day combing the county jail, discovering all of Johnson's hiding places and removing the bottles. Fred Sprigs, the other deputy and another aging holdover from the previous administration, tipped Clinton off. He didn't like or trust the young deputy and dealt with him accordingly.

*****

"Meeker," Clinton said sternly from across the desk, "by the time Johnson arrives tonight, his medicine better be back in its proper places."

"Sheriff," Meeker replied, revealing his arrogant nature by not understanding Clinton's tone, "just playing a joke. And you know old Johnson drinks too much. I'll give it back to him in a couple of days."

The statement reeked of smugness, and Clinton wondered if somehow, Milton Marion found it necessary to play Meeker behind the scenes. "Keep an eye on him, Meeker," he could hear Milton saying. "He's not doing the job. Play your cards right and you'll be the next sheriff."

Clinton studied Meeker's narrow face and beak-like nose for a moment. His eyes carried a hint of yellow, much like pinewood after being darkened from the sun. The gun on his hip appeared too big for bones so narrow. The jaunty angle of his hat angered Clinton the most. He perched it on the back of his head, giving him a bandy rooster appearance.

Clinton stood and moved around the desk, giving Meeker a chance to see his angered face staring down at him. "Meeker, let me tell you a few things," he said. "You're just a little pissant compared to Johnson." Ronnie tried to back up a step but couldn't. Clinton had clasped his shoulder, digging fingers into bone. "Old Johnson might be just a drunk to you," he spat. "But he's a real hero to me."

Ronnie made an effort to twist his body, hoping to escape Clinton's strong grip. It only caused the fingers to dig deeper, ratcheting up the pain. "The men who shot him were escaped convicts, rapists, and murderers. They butchered a family over in the next county. Took their sixteen-year-old daughter, raped her in front of her parents, then slaughtered all of them.

"While on patrol, Johnson found those two animals walking down the road as if they were on a Sunday stroll. Both were covered in blood, and it was obvious to him they were of a criminal mind. Being a brave man, he didn't hightail it back to town, screaming for help. He took them on and managed with a bullet in his hip to kill both of those animals. So tonight, when Johnson arrives, his whiskey better be in its proper place, and I don't give a rat's ass if he stays drunk all the time! He's earned it, you little shit!"

*****

Clinton heard the clinking of glass, and soon, Johnson appeared, holding out a mason jar of whiskey. "Here you go, Sheriff," he said, happy to please his boss.

Clinton took the jar and patted Johnson softly on the shoulder. "Thanks, Johnson. Now go back to sleep. Sorry I had to disturb you."

The first sip revealed that the whiskey was Uncle Hiram's. There was just a slight burn as the clear liquid slid down Clinton's throat. After several more drinks, the heat of the liquor found its way to his head. It offered no relief, and it didn't change the problem he faced.

He knew his mother had sacrificed too many times for the sake of the family. As he grew older, he witnessed the selfish streak that ran through Stu Barnes. One thing that bothered him the most was when his father purchased a fine suit on credit after becoming a deacon in the church. His mother didn't complain, only bragged about how handsome her husband looked.

She then patched her faded, worn, and threadbare coat to make it through another winter. Her butter-and-egg money, pennies and nickels that she had saved for years, disappeared without cause. Georgia Barnes had taken it in stride, never batting an eye when his father came home leading a fine bay mare. "Gonna breed her to a jack," his father had bragged, "and get us some mules, and we'll make a fortune."

Clinton took another drink, remembering that the mare never conceived or broke to the plow. He took his last drink and rubbed his face vigorously with the palms of his hands. *A choice between two evils,* he thought. His mother might be able to stand what her husband had done, but Clinton couldn't live with himself if he was the cause of her finding out. He couldn't add another hardship or hurt to his mother's life.

He felt like a coward for not having the courage to choke the life out of Milton Marion and throw his body in the river. *Oh, Sara*—his last thought as he staggered home.

Chapter 9

Sara fed Sam while sitting in the slight shade of the last peanut stack. The harvest would be over this afternoon, and she feared the winter could be a lean one. The river provided meat, but the greens were slow to grow with the lack of rain. She wiped Sam's hands and mentally counted her savings. Sara heard a man cough and knew, without looking up, that it was Mr. Ewell.

"Ms. Sara," he said, "I've been thinking about that work for you."

Sara exhaled a great breath of relief, so afraid that he had changed his mind. "Yes, sir," she responded gratefully, but then she grew alarmed after seeing his troubled expression.

"Could you come twice a week and do a little cleaning for us? Danny and me get by all right cooking, but we're a little slack on housekeeping. I'll pay you what I can."

"Mr. Ewell, whatever you can afford will be fine with me. I'd be honored to put your home back in order." Sara saw his forehead wrinkle in thought.

"Are Monday and Thursday all right?" he asked with a slight tremor coloring his voice.

"That'll be fine," she replied knowing that something else was on his mind. He turned to leave, walked a few steps, then stopped again. "Mr. Ewell," she asked, staring at his sweat-stained back, "is there anything—"

"Yes," he said, walking back. He removed his hat. "I need to ask you something, but I'm afraid it'll come out all wrong."

Sara saw his jaw muscle twitch twice. "You've shown me great kindness." She stepped closer. "Whatever you say won't bother me." Sara kept her face open, encouraging him to speak, all the while terrified of the possibilities.

"I've noticed that Danny is quite taken with you," he said in a rush. "He doesn't know the ways of the world, and I'd be right obliged if you wouldn't encourage him."

Sara covered his stinging words with a smile, hoping he wouldn't see how badly they hurt. "Mr. Ewell, I certainly understand your point, and let me put your mind at ease. He's a fine young man, but I'd hate for him to fight battles over me that he can't win." Sara saw relief wash over his face.

"Ms. Sara," he said, "thank you. I was so afraid you'd—"

"No, sir," she replied, covering her lie. "You've already taken on Milton Marion, and I'm eternally grateful. I won't add anything else to your troubles."

*****

Sara sat on the porch, watching the last vestiges of sunlight disappear. Her nerves sang, and her heart tittered as complete darkness engulfed the woods. She never heard Uncle Hiram and his daughter Bessie arrive. Neither a footstep nor rustling broke the night air.

"Ms. Sara," Uncle Hiram called gently from the bottom step, causing Sara's already frayed nerves to jump.

"Yes, Uncle Hiram," she answered. Her heart was pounding.

"My girl Bessie is with me. Why don't you light a lamp, and let's get her and the boy acquainted."

Sara stood and opened the door to the cabin with Sam following close behind. She struck a match and got the old lantern going as Sam clutched her leg. As the light filled the room, Uncle Hiram stood with Bessie at his side. He gently squeezed the girl's shoulder.

"Ms. Sara, don't know if you know my girl or not."

"I know her by sight, Uncle Hiram, although we've never been properly introduced."

The crafty nature of the old man impressed her because Bessie could neither hear nor speak. It would be difficult for anyone to gain any information. Sara was comforted by her appearance—small in size like her father. Her face shone with the same gentle nature of Uncle Hiram, and it helped alleviate her fear of leaving Sam.

"Sam, this is Bessie," Sara said, trying to pry Sam's arms from around her leg. "She's going to stay with you tonight." At first, he tightened his grip, making her worry that she would miss out on this chance. But suddenly he let go as Bessie squatted down in front of them with her palm open. Sam grabbed one of the three red gumdrops she held and promptly stuck the candy in his mouth.

Sam grinned. "I'll be all right, Mama."

"Let's go, miss," Uncle Hiram urged. "Bessie here, she right good with children." Sara followed Uncle Hiram out the door. At the bottom of the steps, he paused, leaning in close enough that she could feel his warm breath. "Miss," he whispered, "be careful about speaking because sound carries a long way in the night air. And never walk the same way twice, because it won't be long before there's a path." Uncle Hiram paused for a question and, finding none, continued. "Just hold on to the back of my shirt. It'll take a few times, but then you'll be able to find the way alone."

A layer of thick clouds hid the moon, making the night inky black. Sara soon realized she was lost, and if they somehow became separated, she would have to wait until first light to find her way home. The lack of moonlight didn't seem to faze Uncle Hiram. She clung to his shirt, breathing sharply from the brisk pace. Several times, she stumbled over protruding roots. Soon, she didn't try to look ahead. She just watched her feet to keep her balance.

About the time she needed to ask for a break, Uncle Hiram came to a halt. "Miss, stand right here," he whispered. "Don't move a muscle, and I'll be back."

Sara released her grip and breathed deeply, trying to slow her heart. She could hear rushing water and wondered where they were in relation to the river. A soft grunt drifted to her ears, letting her know Uncle Hiram wasn't far away. Suddenly a faint light appeared from the ground not three feet in front of her. Uncle Hiram's head protruded out of a hole in the ground.

"Come on, miss," he whispered. "Walk here, sit down at the edge, and put your legs through." Sara did so and felt her feet dangling in the air. "Drop on down. It's not another foot before you touch." Sara followed his instructions and felt her feet hit a solid surface. "All right, miss, just bend on down," he said softly. Sara did as asked, finding that she had just entered an underground cavern. "Just squat right here, and Uncle Hiram will get some more light going."

Sara waited patiently as Uncle Hiram walked the cave and lit five kerosene lamps. As soon as she could see well enough, she made her way down the stepping-stones. Uncle Hiram soon returned, grinning as broadly as a young boy who had skipped school on a spring day.

"Miss, you seeing something that nobody else knows about, not even my boy Johnny."

"This is how you've gotten by all these years," Sara stated matter-of-factly.

"Sure is."

Sara looked around the lime rock cavern, taking it all in. The smoke-stained ceiling rose and dipped unevenly. The floor slanted downward, away from the river, giving the cave the illusion of a funnel opening. The air felt moist and smelled slightly of burnt wood. It suddenly occurred to her exactly where she was, and Uncle Hiram clucked softly.

"You know now, don't you?" he asked with amusement.

Sara turned to face the rock wall next to the river and pointed to her left. "The flats start about fifty yards downstream from here, don't they?" she asked. "And this is the big rock face on the edge of the river that runs for a hundred feet or so," she said, placing her hand against the wall. Uncle Hiram nodded in agreement.

"And I would guess the river comes up to about here." She held her hand about waist-high. Again, he confirmed her suspicion with an amused nod. "Also, I would assume this is where the riverbed drops off and forms the deep pool."

"You're right, miss," he answered, once again grinning as if he was a little boy caught in something naughty.

"You wouldn't be the one who started all those stories about the huge snakes that live in the deep water, would you?" Sara asked, shaking her head.

The standard lore of the county caused every child to be scared of swimming in this part of the river. The story went that if you did, a huge water moccasin of storybook proportions would rise up from the deep and swallow you whole. No child, Negro or white, would come near the place. Even her brother, whom she knew to be brave, always swam elsewhere.

"I might have told a few whoppers to keep the little ones away," Uncle Hiram replied dryly. "Not only did it scare them. Ain't many grown men come near here either. None of them would admit it, though."

"Uncle Hiram," Sara said with a snicker, "you're quite a peach."

"Come here, child," he said, stepping away and shining the lantern in front as he walked. "This is the best secret of the cave." In the rounded corner of the cavern, Uncle Hiram showed her a natural-rock well rising out of the floor, reaching almost to her chest. "You're right when you said that the river's this high," he stated, using his hand to agree with her measurement.

"This water comes from a hole 'bout two feet wide and ten feet down in the rock face. If you were outside, you'd see a big cottonwood tree directly across the river. Here, miss, you taste it," Uncle Hiram suggested, using his hand as a cup.

Sara followed suit. "It's almost sweet," she said.

"It is, miss. The water, it swirls around in this well, and all the sediment falls to the bottom. Now," he lectured with concern, "if anyone ever gets after you, you just jump in the river. When you're directly across from the cottonwood tree, swim down and come through the hole and into the cave. They'll never figure it out. Now, miss, this is the wood we use," Uncle Hiram said, pointing to a stack of driftwood cut in two-foot lengths.

"Doesn't it smoke more than dry wood?" she asked.

"It does, but it also burns cooler and makes better liquor," Uncle Hiram answered.

Sara walked around a slight right turn in the cave and saw several wooden bins. Uncle Hiram lifted the top of the first one, and Sara peered inside. It was full of whole corn.

"Most years, I grow enough myself. But if I'm short, Billie Ewell sells me some." He eased the top down and moved to the next one. "This is where I keep the corn after it's been ground," he said, opening the container. They moved a few more steps, and Uncle Hiram hefted another top. Sara saw that this one was filled with bags of sugar.

"Mr. Epstein from across the river sells me my sugar. That's how the law trips a bootlegger up. They watch and sees who's buying too much." He lowered the top gently and moved to the next one. Sara peered inside, finding an assortment of glass bottles. Uncle Hiram reached in, removed a clear Mason jar, and handed it to Sara. "Hold this," he said. He then found a glass top and lowered the lid.

"Ms. Sara, when you make some money, take it and put it in this jar and melt some wax around the top, then push the lid on tight and pull the metal clamp closed. That'll keep the water out. Bury it somewhere around the cabin, but don't forget where."

"I don't think I will, Uncle Hiram," she answered respectfully.

"I know you won't," he said, scratching his chin. "Ms. Sara, you fill up a bunch of these, and you and the boy will be able to leave. But be careful. Don't buy too much at the store. That'll get folks talking."

"I won't," Sara replied, taking the warning seriously.

Uncle Hiram opened the last bin that was full of bottled whiskey. "We're going to remove this over the next couple of nights to make room for more."

Sara noticed the once curled fingers, his very reason for needing her help, now functioned fine. Her mind formed a picture of her sitting on Uncle Hiram's porch. Sam would be standing tall and proud, looking at the two of them as they talked and laughed. No fear, hunger, or loneliness would be felt. She would reach over and hold his weathered old hand and say, "Thank you for making up that story about needing help, Uncle Hiram."

"You all right, child?" he asked.

Sara blushed slightly at being caught with her mind running away. "I'm fine. Please continue."

"Now let me show you how the still works."

Sara listened as he explained how each part of the strange-looking contraption participated in the process. Then in great detail, Uncle Hiram tutored her, so prideful of his art. At the end of the lecture, she asked only one question.

"How do you keep the cave from filling with smoke?"

"There's another opening at this end," he answered, pointing to the ceiling. "It's just like the one we came through, but it opens into a heavy cane break. That hides the smoke. When the fire gets going, the air draws from that hole," he said, pointing to where they had entered, "and leaves out the other one. Now we'll pack up some of this whiskey and carry it out tonight."

Uncle Hiram dragged out two cotton baskets from behind the crate. Sara watched over his shoulder as he removed a tan knapsack and laid it flat on the floor. He stood, grabbed two bottles of whiskey, knelt down, and slid them in the bag. He placed a handful of cotton from the basket between the bottles, then added two more.

"See what I'm doing, miss? Just do the same, but make yours lighter until we can figure how much weight you can carry." Sara worked, carefully following Uncle Hiram's instructions, until he said, "That's enough." He picked the bag up, and Sara worked her arms through the straps. When he released the weight, she felt her knees buckle slightly. She leaned forward, finding it easier to balance.

"Go to the opening, and I'll help you out. Then I'll come back and take care of the lanterns." Before they reached the entrance, Uncle Hiram stopped. "One more thing, Ms. Sara. On that bin that holds the corn, there's a shotgun hanging by its trigger guard." She looked and saw the old double-barrel on the side of the crate.

Uncle Hiram took her knapsack while she climbed out the hole. He pushed hers through, then his. Sara stood listening to the flowing water as he blew out the lanterns. Soon, darkness engulfed her, leaving only the sounds of Uncle Hiram climbing out of the cave. This time, she managed to wiggle her arms through the straps without help. He whispered, "Just stand still, and I'll close the entrance."

Sara heard a soft grunt and then the sound of Uncle Hiram pushing the sand over the wooden cover and sweeping their tracks away. "Miss," he whispered, "if you get tired on the way back, just tug on my shirt, and we'll stop and rest."

"Okay."

*****

Even with the weight of the whiskey pulling at her shoulders, the walk home didn't seem to take as long. Soon, they were standing in front of the cabin.

"Let me help you with that, child," Uncle Hiram said, easing the knapsack from her shoulders. "After a couple of nights, you'll be able to find your way. Then little Sam can come with you."

Chapter 10

A few days later, Sara awoke as the first light peeked through the windows. She yawned and stretched carefully, trying not to wake Sam. For a few precious moments, she stroked his hair. As she eased out of bed, Sam rolled over, curling into a ball. Sara rearranged the covers, compensating for his new position. The morning air felt chilly against her skin. Quickly, she slipped out of her nightclothes and pulled on her overalls. A glance found Sam still asleep, so she quietly opened the door and stepped outside.

At the river, Sara took a moment to admire the early morning smoke rising off the water as it made its slow journey to the Gulf. Mornings such as this brought on longing memories of Stuart. Sara pulled the fish basket out of the river and harvested the catch. When the fish were skinned and cleaned, she headed back to the cabin. Entering their home, she found Sam standing in the kitchen, using his fists to rub the sleep from his eyes.

"You ready to eat?" His answer came in the form of a hug. With a tight embrace, he held on to Sara's legs, burying his face in her stomach. Sara couldn't return the affection; her hands were full of catfish. After waiting a few seconds, she said, "Come on, Sam. Let Mama fix you some breakfast. We have to go to Mr. Ewell's today."

"Will I see Danny?" he asked, his voice muffled.

"Sure," she answered. "He'll be there."

"Good," he replied, letting go and looking up at her. "He's fun to play with."

Pain jolted her heart; she knew he longed to play with other children. "Let's hurry, son," she suggested as she laid the catfish in the sink, "so we can fish this afternoon." That wasn't the real reason, although Sam wanted to. She was worried about finding her way to the cave alone. She thought walking through the woods in the daylight might help her in the dark.

*****

Sara and Sam arrived just as Mr. Ewell and Danny finished breakfast. Standing in the doorway of the kitchen, Sara said, "Sorry, Mr. Ewell. Didn't mean to interrupt, but I had a few things to do this afternoon, and I wanted to get an early start."

"'Tis fine, Ms. Sara," Mr. Ewell replied as he nibbled on a piece of bacon. "I know you have plenty to do. We're finished anyway."

Danny slid his chair sideways and turned his attention to Sara as she chatted with Mr. Ewell. In her peripheral vision, Sara could see Danny staring, and Mr. Ewell's stinging words came back. Sara sharpened her focus on the elder and pretended not to notice. Sam was hiding shyly behind her legs, but she knew he would warm up soon. All of a sudden, Sam raced forward, leaping into Danny's lap. Sam's knee struck his groin, and his face turned beet red with pain.

"Sam!" Sara scolded harshly. "Be careful. You've hurt Danny."

"It's all right, Sara," Danny replied through gritted teeth. "Just doing what boys do."

"I'm sure you'd like to have children one day, though," Sara joked, and then she regretted her words, knowing she had added to his embarrassment.

"Hmm," Mr. Ewell said, stifling a laugh.

"Sara," Danny asked, sucking in his breath, trying to regain his composure, "we're going to blow some stumps out of the ground this morning. Thought Sam here," he said as he tousled the child's hair, "would like to watch."

"Can I go with them, Mama?" Sam asked excitedly.

Mr. Ewell added, "Ms. Sara, Danny lights the fuses, and I'll keep the boy a safe distance away with me."

"He won't be underfoot, Mr. Ewell?"

"Naw, he'll be fine."

"Sam, you stay out of the way," she commanded. "And do what they tell you to do."

"Yes, ma'am," Sam replied quickly as he hopped out of Danny's lap. Mr. Ewell had risen from his chair, and he didn't want to be left behind.

"Sara," Danny asked, "down in the lower forty where we're working, I've been seeing some fox squirrels. Mind if I take my .410 and let Sam hunt for a little while?"

His eyes were so soft and pleading that they reminded Sara of Stuart. "Danny, I'd be right pleased if you would," she answered. "He needs to be around men like you." Instantly, she regretted her words. His eyes shone with encouragement, and his chest swelled. She had done exactly what Mr. Ewell had asked her not to do.

"I'll take good care of him, Sara," Danny stated, smiling brightly.

"I'm sure you will," Sara replied, now unsure of the damage she had done.

*****

The first time Sara cleaned the house, it took most of the day to scrub away the layers of dirt. Today, as she stripped the sheets from the bed, she knew it wouldn't take as long. She replaced the dirty linen with ones she had washed earlier in the week. After the beds were made, she started in the front of the house, sweeping and dusting.

The whitewashed farmhouse was huge compared to what she had known in her own life. There were four bedrooms, each filled with stout beds and dressers. The ceilings were high, giving it an airy, comfortable feeling. Each room contained its own fireplace, and she noticed the wood racks were already filled.

Sara washed the sheets and hung them on the line to dry. Then she moved to the front porch, sweeping the fallen leaves into the flowerbeds. Time moved quickly, and now Sara wondered why Sam was hiding behind Mr. Ewell and Danny as they stood in the kitchen.

"Sam, what are you doing?" Sara finally asked.

Sam stuck his head from around Danny's legs as though he was a wise old cat checking out what was around the corner of the barn. "Got a surprise for you, Mama," he said proudly with wide, shining eyes.

"Well, what is it, son?" she asked. Sara could tell by Mr. Ewell's expression that he and Danny were part of this.

Sam slowly emerged, holding a large gray fox squirrel by its neck. "I killed it for you, Mama. You can fry it for our supper," he said, with obvious pride.

Sara was overwhelmed, seeing her son standing there with his shoulders back and face beaming. Tears started to cloud her eyes. "You're Mama's little man, Sam," she said, trying to keep her voice even.

"Sam, why don't you tell your mama about the squirrel?" Sara stole a quick glance at Danny, finding him looking proudly at her son.

"Mama, Danny took me and sat me on a stump at the edge of the woods. He told me to watch the trees for squirrels. It wasn't long before I seen one."

"You saw one," Sara gently corrected.

"Yes'm. I saw one."

"The boy's got a good eye, Ms. Sara," Mr. Ewell interjected. "Especially this time of year with so many leaves still on the trees."

"In a little while," Sam said, anxious to finish the story, "Danny came over and asked if I'd seen anything. I told him I had, so we walked down there."

"It took him a minute or two, Sara," Danny explained. "He had lost sight of the squirrel while we were moving, but I didn't help. He found him again on his own."

"Danny showed me how to hold the gun, and I shot him," Sam quickly interjected.

"Did you thank Danny for—"

"Yes, ma'am, I did."

"Good, Sam. I'll cook it for our supper," Sara said. "Be a nice way to end the day."

"Ms. Sara," Mr. Ewell said, "he's a fine little hunter." Sara looked from father to son, giving each a silent thank-you.

*****

As they walked home, Sara took a moment to look back and admire the farmhouse from a distance. She pictured herself sitting on the covered porch, shelling fresh green butterbeans and enjoying the summer breeze. After a minute of quiet gazing, Sara pushed the thought away. It was too dangerous to let her mind wander.

The day had warmed nicely from its cool beginning, and now Sara felt a fine bead of sweat on her forehead. Sam walked behind her, dragging his fishing pole along. Reaching the river, she felt more confident about being able to find the cave in darkness. In the distance, the sunlight gleamed and twinkled off the flats. She also spied the huge cottonwood tree Uncle Hiram mentioned. Given the makeup of the area, she now understood how the cave remained undiscovered all these years.

"Sam," Sara commanded, "sit right here on the sand, and Mama will show you how to fish." As Sam plopped down and wiggled his butt around to get comfortable, Sara unwound the line and threaded a worm on the hook. "Here you go, Sam. Watch Mama." Sara swung the line out and saw the bait hit the water. "You hold the pole still. If a fish gets on the hook, you'll feel a tug."

"What do I do then?" Sam asked, unsure of himself as he grasped the cane pole.

"Tell you what. You feel a fish pull, let me know. I'll help you catch the first one, then you can do it yourself." A slight dry gust blew, rippling the water. That added with the dapple sunlight made Sara sleepy. "Sam, Mama's going to lie back and take a little nap. Just call me if you need something."

"Yes, ma'am," he replied, intent on holding the pole as his mother had shown him.

*****

"Mama!"

Sara awoke, pushed herself into a seated position, and looked at her son. She knew his urgent voice wasn't from being scared, just wary. She followed his eyes and saw Eugene leaning against a pine tree, staring at them from the other side of the river.

She could see that his face was twisted in an angry sneer. Sara matched his look, determined to show him she wasn't afraid. Then she realized something wasn't right with his face. It dawned on her that his right cheekbone was sunken where the sheriff had hit him.

Sara broke her stare and pushed Sam to his feet. "Get your pole, son. No, I'll get it. It's time to go home." Thinking quickly, she felt confident that they would be in reach of the shotgun before Eugene could swim the river or walk to the flats and cross.

Instead of following the winding river, Sara cut directly through the woods, quickly reaching the safety of the cabin. She double-checked the shotgun, making sure it was loaded. Then taking a piece of cloth, she fashioned a sling. *From now on, it moves with us*, she thought.

Chapter 11

Uncle Hiram's natural intuition came to life as he moved through the woods by the dim light of a freshening moon. He stopped for a moment under an oak tree, squatted on his heels, and let out a low, quiet breath. The familiar night sounds no longer existed, not the chattering of a squirrel or the call of an owl. He cocked his strongest ear, and seconds later, the snap of a dry branch confirmed his fears. He then walked toward the flats, making enough noise to give his position away.

Clinton peeked around the trunk of a tree as Uncle Hiram nonchalantly strolled into the shallow water. He gave the old man enough time to make it across the river, then followed, hoping to pick up his trail on the other side. Clinton's breath sharpened as cold water filled his boots. It seemed to him that Uncle Hiram didn't walk as much as he glided. But for Clinton, it was much more difficult to navigate the uneven bottom.

Several times, he almost lost his balance after stepping into deeper holes. His chest grew tight, and his breathing became labored by the time he reached the other shore. He found Uncle Hiram's footprints and rested for a moment, trying to catch his breath.

He diligently followed the trail but soon lost it in the leaves of the deeper woods. As he turned to leave, Uncle Hiram watched from his perch high in a mossy tree, his face puzzled by the sheriff's actions. Clinton opened the door of the patrol car and sat down with a tired thud. He removed his wet boots and socks, tossing both into the back seat. After sitting for a moment and thinking, he knew that the logical thing to do was follow Sara, but he just didn't have the heart. At that moment, he decided there might be another way.

*****

Sara watched the first few drops of whiskey drip from the copper tubing. She removed the metal cup, tossing the liquid away, as Uncle Hiram had instructed. After replacing the cup with a green glass jar, she checked on Sam. He was sleeping soundly on a makeshift pallet of quilts. She reached for the bucket to mix some more mash and jumped slightly when she saw Uncle Hiram standing close by.

"Didn't mean to slip up on you, child," he said.

"Lord, Uncle Hiram," she said, breathless, holding her hand to her chest. "You scared me to death."

"Well, miss, sorry about that," he replied, his face still puzzled over the sheriff.

"Is something wrong?" she asked. "I was beginning to wonder if you were going to make it."

"Yes. Not meaning to scare you, but the sheriff tried to follow me tonight."

The shocking statement numbed her body. "Why would he do that?" Her voice was fearful.

"Don't rightly know," Uncle Hiram replied, scratching his head thoughtfully. "I thought we had the same agreement with the old sheriff. He might have gotten bored." Uncle Hiram shrugged his shoulders. "He'll get tired and leave me alone. They always do."

"I can't lose my boy," she stated with tears welling in her eyes. "Is he still out there looking?" She had grown comfortable with the cave in the last couple of weeks, but now she looked at the entrance fearfully.

"No, ma'am," Uncle Hiram said with an easy smile. "I wore him out crossing the flats and leading him away from here. He's at home now, cussing this old nigger and so tired he won't be good for days."

90

"I can't help but worry, Uncle Hiram," she said, nervously looking toward the entrance again.

"Ease your mind, child. Uncle Hiram has been doing this a long time, and there's a lot of them that have tried to catch me. Let's finish this batch up and lay off a couple of days. You check around your cabin each morning for footprints to see if he's watching you too."

"Why would he do that?" she asked, her voice fearful.

"Don't you fret," he said reassuringly. "I've always had someone trying to catch me, and I want you to think the same way. That's so you'll always be careful. He'll get tired of stomping around the woods, miss. You'll see. If you're going to get away from here, we got to take a little chance."

Suddenly, as if some revelation came forth that caused her desire to leave to override her fear, she said, "I know, Uncle Hiram, and we'll—"

"Oh, miss, I almost forgot. Time for you to be paid."

Sara's hand shook as she reached for the green bills that he pulled from his pocket. "Thank you, Uncle Hiram," she said while hugging the old man. "Thank you so much. I don't deserve this."

"Yes, you do," he said quickly, slapping a tear away from the corner of his eye. "You've helped me a lot. All that whiskey we carried out filled a big order. Now let's get this finished and go home."

*****

Clinton pushed the light switch of the patrol car and killed the engine, coasting to the back of his office. After several unsuccessful attempts to pull on his wet boots, he gave up and decided to walk barefoot. Using the shadows of the night, he slipped quietly to Marion's office.

The moonlight provided enough illumination for him to see the hasp and lock. He pulled a screwdriver from his back pocket and removed the four wood screws. After checking his surroundings carefully, he pushed the door open and stepped into the office. He crossed the room and sat down in front of the safe. Clicking on his flashlight, he saw that the dial rested on the number 22. After committing that to memory, he went to work.

The first attempt failed. Clinton felt sure of the numbers, but the turns of the combination were left up to chance. He tried again with no luck. After several more tries, desperation set in knowing that Sara's life hung in the balance. There had been another ugly confrontation that morning with Milton Marion about his delays. "Your mother will know soon, Clinton" was still ringing in his ears.

The temptation to try the combination again felt strong, but he knew he had already stayed in the office too long. Even if he opened it, he hadn't developed a plan yet.

*****

Sara undressed Sam as the first light of morning peeked over the horizon. She tucked him into bed and then walked to the kitchen. Opening the front pocket of her overalls, she reached in and removed the money. Slowly and surely, she counted forty-two dollars, the largest amount of cash she had ever seen.

Chapter 12

Two days later, Uncle Hiram appeared at the cabin late in the evening. "Have you seen anything, miss?" he asked.

"No," Sara replied. "I and Sam walked semicircles between here and the river each day and didn't find any footprints."

"It's like I said. He's gotten tired and given up. Most white people like that."

"You sure, Uncle Hiram?" she asked.

"Yes, ma'am," he answered. "Let's start again tomorrow night. I'll meet you there."

*****

A strong wind gusted out of the south and pelted Sara and Sam with falling leaves and acorns as they walked through the darkened night. Occasionally, the moon peeked out between the layers of moving clouds, giving her just enough light to reassure her path.

Sam clung tightly, making the walk that much more difficult. Grateful to reach the cave, she dropped to her knees and dug the deep sand away. A heavy rumble of thunder rolled, causing Sam to squeal in fright.

"Mama!" he cried.

"Shhh, baby," Sara whispered close to his ear, always mindful of Uncle Hiram's orders on making noise. "Let Mama help you into the cave. Nothing can hurt us there."

Sara lowered Sam through the entrance and then followed. He settled down after the lanterns were glowing, but he still wore a troubled expression. Sara quickly started the fire, then mixed the mash. As the smoke gathered at the top of the cave, she realized the other entrance was still closed. She climbed the stepping-stones and pushed the wooden cover away. The smoke began to evacuate, but the heavy south wind created an eerie moaning sound as the trapped air escaped.

"Mama, I'm scared," Sam said loudly, his words echoing.

"Shhh, son," Sara urged. "It's just some wind. There's nothing to be afraid of."

*****

Uncle Hiram moved quickly through the woods, angling toward the river. He had wanted to make it to Sara's cabin before she left, but one of his customers, Mr. Benton, showed up just before dark. He insisted that it wouldn't do for Uncle Hiram to sell him the whiskey right there. It had to be brought into town and left in his car shed. Several times, he felt his front pocket, making sure the money was there. He knew she would smile and then protest when he placed the three hundred dollars in her hand.

He had awakened last night and came to the conclusion that he could no longer jeopardize her and the boy. Early that morning, he had ridden his mule across the river and made a deal with Mr. Epstein to help the two disappear. That took most of the day, and then Mr. Benton took the rest. Uncle Hiram picked up his pace knowing that the coming weather would hide many sounds.

*****

Clinton sat in the soft sand of the riverbank. Tired of trying to follow the old man, an impossible task, he reasoned bootleggers needed water, and the river had to be the source. So for the last couple of nights, he had staked out a place in hopes that Uncle Hiram would come to him.

As the weather grew closer, he let out a sigh; the constant threats were taking their toll. As the wind gusted and lightning moved closer, Clinton took stock of his life and the consequences of letting his mother find out the truth. Each and every time he tried to apply reason to the problem, he knew his father's indiscretion should remain secret. His mother loved Stu Barnes, and he couldn't be the one to sully her memory. It was the only thing she had left.

The heaviness of his heart and what he had become created a sick feeling in his stomach. To think of something else, Clinton ran the combinations he had tried through his mind. A patient process of elimination would sooner or later produce results, but he would much prefer blind luck.

The first heavy drops of rain pelted him as lightning flashed. Suddenly his heart jumped. Not twenty yards ahead, Uncle Hiram walked briskly, headed upriver. Clinton eased along the bank and began to follow.

*****

Eugene pulled a pint of whiskey from his back pocket, removed the cork, and took a long drink. His intention for the night was to fish, but now it seemed getting drunk was a better idea. He rubbed his disfigured cheekbone gingerly, his mood dark. He hated the fact that the girl treated him like trash, and the sheriff did also. And today, Mr. Marion had done the same when he had asked for a raise.

"If I give you more money, I'll have to give everyone a raise," Milton Marion had shot.

"I'm worth it because I do more work," he had hotly argued back.

"Well, if you are, then find another job that'll pay you what you want," Marion had challenged.

Eugene took another drink, then pushed the bottle back into his pocket. The first fat raindrop hit the top of his head, so he decided to leave. As he rose, the sound of a child squealing caught his attention. He scrambled to the top of the bank and peered over, seeing nothing but blackness. He waited for the flash that would come after the thunder. As the sky crackled with fingers of electricity, there stood Sara and her boy. He held his position, waiting for the right time to even the score.

*****

As Sara worked, she glanced at Sam on his pallet, assuming he had fallen asleep. She then turned toward the entrance, expecting Uncle Hiram. But instead of her friend, she saw Eugene standing there, scowling.

"So this is the old nigger's hiding place," he said drunkenly, gazing around the cavern. Sara feinted to the right and, when he moved to block her, cut left, reaching for the shotgun. He caught her by one strap of her overalls, dragging her back.

With a quick right, she smacked him on the side of the head with her closed fist, then lurched again. The effort was wasted. He was much too strong. Eugene used his other hand and grabbed her crotch and, with little effort, picked her up and slammed her into the lime rock floor. He sat on her stomach and used his knees to pin her arms.

"Mama!" Sam cried, now awake. Black eyes stared at her as thin lips twisted into a sneer.

"Seems to me, Sara, you're in a hell of a mess," Eugene spat wickedly.

"What do you want, Eugene?" Sara shot back, trying to hide her fear and disgust. The smell of his unwashed body filled her nose, causing nausea to rise from her stomach.

"You know what I want, Sara," he said. "And you're going to give it to me anytime I want. If you don't, I'll tell the sheriff what you and that old nigger are doing here."

"Not in front of my boy, Eugene. Don't do this in front of him," Sara said, trying to hide her desperation.

"I want it right now!" His dirty, stringy hair fell into her face as he reached to unsnap the hooks of her overalls.

Sara fell to pleading. "Not in front of my boy!"

"In front of your boy!" Eugene shouted, the harsh sound bouncing around the cave. "You didn't mind beating me in front of your…"

Sara saw the weathered dark hand catch the front of Eugene's hair and jerk him backward. Wet, sticky blood sprayed her face as Uncle Hiram savagely slit Eugene's throat. As the weight lifted, Sara scrambled away, crawling to Sam. Behind her, she heard the gurgling sound of a dying man. She wrapped her arms around her child and began to sob.

Uncle Hiram stood over the body until the last jerky moments of death were finished. Calmly, he walked to the end of the cave, washed the blood off his knife, and snapped it closed. Sara's crying deepened into mournful sobs racked with pain as she clung to her child.

Squatting down, Uncle Hiram placed his hand on her back. "It's all right, Ms. Sara. That white trash can't hurt you now. Sam, he did real good. Saw me coming and didn't say a word."

"Oh, Lord, my God! What am I going to do with this?" Uncle Hiram stood and faced the sheriff. Clinton was amazed at his benign expression as if he had slaughtered a hog instead of a person.

"That man tried to rape this girl, Sheriff. Right in front of her boy too," he said in a tone that relayed, "Why should you care?"

Sara slowly realized that Uncle Hiram wasn't talking to her and looked up to find the sheriff looking around the cave. Her heart sank; blood drained from her face as she fainted. Uncle Hiram quickly dropped to his knees, grabbing her before her head could hit the floor. "It's all right, miss," he said, holding her tightly. "The sheriff is a good man."

The words stung Clinton as they sank in. Uncle Hiram was assuming that he and the girl would walk away from this. Not knowing what to do at the moment, he opened a bottle of whiskey and wet his handkerchief. "You need to clean her face," he said, handing it to Uncle Hiram.

He gently began wiping Sara's face while whispering, "Ms. Sara, it's going to be all right." Clinton couldn't look at her anymore, afraid that he would be the cause of her death.

"Mama!" Sam called.

The tenderness with which Uncle Hiram ministered to her was that much more disturbing to Clinton. He took a large drink of the whiskey, hoping that in reality, it was poison. With the soft urging of Uncle Hiram, Sara's eyes opened, and she looked at Clinton pleadingly.

"I've got to figure out what to do," Clinton said, avoiding her ashen face.

"Sheriff, ain't no problem," Uncle Hiram piped up. "We get rid of that man, and you let us go home."

The sheer simplicity of his statement made the hair on Clinton's neck stand up. "Uncle Hiram," he said sternly, "I've got a dead body lying here, and I'm just supposed to walk away from this?"

"He was trying to rape this girl, Sheriff!"

"You've killed a white man, and no juror in this county would believe you or her! You'll get the death penalty, damn it!" Clinton hung his head, wishing for the courage to run away and disappear forever. "I've got to figure this out," he said, shaking his head.

"Sheriff, you arrest her and she'll lose her boy. Just take me!"

Sara spoke, her voice trembling. "Uncle Hiram, I can't let you—"

"Yes, you can," Uncle Hiram objected, much as a parent would correct a youngster. "Besides, Sheriff, I thought we had an agreement just like the one I had with the old—"

"I've never said that, Uncle Hiram." Clinton saw the old man's face harden.

"Yes, you have—not with words, but every time you came to me, I gave you what you needed."

"Damn it!" Clinton shouted in frustration. "I've got a dead man, and the two of you have obviously been making whiskey. What in the hell do you want me to—"

"Let the girl go!" Uncle Hiram shouted back. "She ain't been helping long, only till she could get enough money to get away."

Uncle Hiram eased around Clinton, but he did nothing to block the old man's movement.

As Uncle Hiram pointed the shotgun at Clinton, Sara screamed, "No, Uncle Hiram!"

Somewhere inside Clinton's heart, he didn't give a damn whether Uncle Hiram pulled the trigger or not. Faced with the horrible feeling of destroying three lives for the necessities of his father-in-law or getting it over with in an instant left him indifferent.

"Sheriff, I'll kill you if I have to."

"Uncle Hiram, don't," Sara pleaded. "I can't live with it."

"Just let her and the boy go, Sheriff," Uncle Hiram said, his tone less threatening. "I got the money in my pocket for her to leave now."

Clinton didn't turn or move a muscle. "You and I will hide the body, and I'll only charge the two of you with bootlegging. It's the best I can do. You—"

"Go to hell, Sheriff," Uncle Hiram said, raising the gun an inch.

"Uncle Hiram, please put the gun down," Sara asked, tears streaming down her face. "He doesn't deserve to lose his life. He treated me kindly when Mama died."

"She'll still lose her boy, Sheriff," Uncle Hiram said with almost more sadness than Clinton could bear.

"It's the best I can do. Either pull the trigger or do what I ask."

"Let's move the body, Sheriff," Uncle Hiram said, defeated. He had grown too fond of the sheriff to carry it through.

*****

The air outside the cave felt cooler and contained a hint of briskness as the two wrestled the dead body to the shoreline. "Sit still, Sheriff," Uncle Hiram whispered. "I'll take care of it from here." Clinton shuddered as Uncle Hiram pulled his knife and went to work on the body. He started to turn his head, not wanting to watch. Nevertheless, he found himself fascinated with the process. Uncle Hiram returned to the cave, bringing back the blankets that comprised Sam's makeshift bed and a long length of rope. He quickly created a shroud, then weighted the body with large rocks.

After tying the quilted coffin, Uncle Hiram said, "Come on, Sheriff. Take one end, and I'll get the other." With great exertion, the two threw the body into the river. "The river's deepest right there and has a rock bottom. Ain't a chance in hell he'll float."

"You sure?"

"Yes," Uncle Hiram stated as he spat into the water, indicating either disrespect or good riddance. Clinton couldn't guess which. "He's meeting the devil right now, and that's the best thing for him. Ain't nobody going to miss him," Uncle Hiram stated as he cleaned up at the edge of the river. "Mama and Daddy both dead."

"Let her go and just take me, Sheriff," Uncle Hiram pleaded as he dried his hands on his pants leg.

"Why do you care so much for her?" Clinton asked sadly knowing he couldn't let them go.

"'Cause she ain't never had nobody. I'm better than nothing even if I'm just an old nigger."

*****

Clinton parked at the back of the jail, hoping it was early enough in the morning that no one would notice his prisoners. Johnson neatened his bed and tucked his blanket under the cot's mattress, then limped around to the other side and did the same. Both cells were empty, so the normally barred door remained open. Clinton acknowledged Johnson with a nod as he led the three into the cellblock. Johnson watched silently as the sheriff unlocked Uncle Hiram's handcuffs and closed the jail door behind him.

The deputy continued to observe as the sheriff took the boy into his arms, then locked the woman in her cell. The child cried softly at first but then began to wail. "Mama! Mama!" Johnson didn't know or ask what was happening. As the sheriff walked away, the girl's eyes followed, and then her voice sailed a mournful quiver. "Mama loves you, Sam. It'll be all right." As they disappeared from her sight, she sat on the jail bed and began to cry.

*****

He walked the short distance to Milton Marion's house, feeling the enormous gravity of the situation he created. Sam began to hiccup between sobs as Clinton's boots thumped on the wooden porch. Not bothering to knock, Clinton opened the door and walked in. Willie May, Marion's maid, looked up from her ironing.

"Take care of Sam if you will, Willie May," he said, gently handing the crying child over. Without waiting for a response, he did an about-face and walked out of the house. The last thing he wanted to see was the smug look on Marion's face as he finally laid claim to his grandson.

Chapter 13

Clinton jotted down a few notes at his desk, then decided to check on Sara and Uncle Hiram. As he stepped into the cellblock, low threatening words from Ronnie Meeker drifted through the air. "You'll have to talk to me sooner or later, Sara."

Uncle Hiram lazily opened one eye as the sheriff caught Ronnie by the scruff of the neck and slammed his forehead into the bars, shaking the adjoined cells. "You will treat her with respect, Ronnie!" he snapped through a clenched jaw. "If you don't, I'll stomp your skinny little ass into the dirt! Do you understand me?"

"Yes, sir, Sheriff. Wasn't meaning no harm," Ronnie quickly pleaded.

Uncle Hiram smiled and opened his other eye. *Bang!* The deputy's forehead slapped against the bars again, causing his cowboy hat to fly. "Respect, Ronnie. Remember that!" Clinton growled. "Where the hell is Fred?"

"Fred's running a little late, Sheriff," Ronnie replied as he rubbed his forehead. "I told Johnson to just go ahead and leave, and I'd tend to everything till he got here."

Clinton glared at Meeker but resisted the temptation to do more damage. Following the sound of the voices, Fred stepped into the cellblock, and Clinton glared at the man angrily. "We'll talk about you being late some other time," Clinton said hotly. "You and Ronnie, come to my office." Fred stepped aside as the sheriff stomped by.

Ronnie scrambled, retrieving his now bent hat, and double-stepped along with Fred, trying to catch up with their boss.

Clinton sat down hard and wrote one more note on the paper, then provided a short and significantly edited overview of the arrest. "Meeker," he commanded, "you stay here at the jail for another hour or so, and then we'll go clean out the cave. We straight on how we treat our prisoners?"

"Yes, sir, Sheriff," Meeker answered while rubbing the red whelp on his forehead.

"Good. Now this applies to both of you. I don't want anyone coming into the jail to gawk, visit, or try to get a peek so they can gossip. I don't give a damn," he semishouted, "if it's your mother, wife, or the damn preacher in here trying to save their souls. The only person who can freely come and go is their lawyer.

"Fred, get them something to eat soon, and tell Blackstone I don't want the usual slop he pawns off on my prisoners." Blackstone Shelton ran the local diner and had the county contract to feed the prisoners. They all knew that the meals amounted to three-day-old leftovers he couldn't sell.

*****

Clinton walked across the street at a fast clip, carrying the anger of the events with him. Not bothering to knock, he plowed into the young prosecutor's office and found him in the usual feet-propped-on-desk position. Their relationship bordered on open hostility, so Victor looked up and said with a stiff smile, "Morning, Sheriff."

Victor was dressed as usual—pressed white shirt, expensive dark pants the color of charcoal, bright-red suspenders, and matching tie. His hair was parted down the middle and slicked back with hair oil. What Clinton resented the most was Victor's complaints to Milton Marion that he played too soft with the Negroes.

"What brings you over so early?" Victor asked. Clinton remained standing as he recited the synopsis of the previous night. The DA whistled softly. "You finally got that old nigger, didn't you?"

"Yeah, and another one to boot."

103

"Well, good. It's about time some of this white trash got cleaned up."

Clinton refused to take the bait knowing that Victor thought anyone who didn't have his breeding was trash. "I'll go back to the scene, gather the evidence, and give you a report in the morning."

"Fine," Victor agreed as his highly polished shoes hit the floor. "But I think I'll just ride out there and see it for myself."

"No need, Victor. It's down in a cave on the river, so it'll be pretty dirty work bringing the evidence up from underground." Clinton knew the thought of getting his clothes dirty would change his mind.

"Make sure you get everything," Victor said. "We need to make the charges stick to that old nigger. Hell, half the county will sober up with him in jail," he said, laughing.

"You might be right," Clinton agreed in an effort to keep the meeting short.

"What about the boy? Have you taken him to Martha Reid?"

The thought of poor Sam in her hands sickened Clinton. She had no love for the children she supposedly served. He knew the wheels of fate would turn quickly for the child, and Milton Marion would soon have custody. He had just expedited the process, cutting Martha out of the equation.

"No. He's at Marion's house," Clinton answered, his mouth dry.

Victor frowned deeply. "You sure that's what he wanted?"

"Didn't ask," Clinton answered, his tone darkening.

"I'll see Martha today," Victor said, now wearing a slight smirk, "and tell her where the boy is. I'll talk to Conway Moon also. He'll be the one to get the case."

"Fine, Victor. One less thing I have to do."

*****

Clinton understood his own nagging need to check on Sara, but after what he had done, trying to protect her seemed ridiculous. He peered through the iron bars and saw her sitting with her back against the stone wall, knees drawn tightly to her chest, crying softly.

He walked to the opposite corner of Uncle Hiram's cell and beckoned him with his hand.

"Keep an eye on her," he whispered in the old man's ear. "If she tries to hurt herself, holler for Fred."

"I'll do that, Sheriff," Uncle Hiram softly answered. "Can you help me get a telegram to my boy Johnny?"

"Let me take care of a few other things, Uncle Hiram, and I'll do it this afternoon or tonight. Is that soon enough?"

"That'd be good."

"All right, then. Remind me if I forget," Clinton said before walking away.

Uncle Hiram stuck his hands through the bars, gently urging Sara. "Miss, come here and talk to Uncle Hiram." Sara opened her eyes and wiped the tears away with her sleeve. She met his warm, outstretched hands through the bars, and his dark dancing eyes locked onto hers. "Don't you worry none, child," he said softly. "Uncle Hiram got plenty of money buried around his land. There'll be someone to take some of it and help us get out of this."

Her solemn look added to the misery cast in her eyes. "Why would anyone help us?" she asked, defeated.

An easy smile waxed across his face. "Sometimes, help comes from somewhere you don't expect. Don't you worry. Let me work a little magic. My boy Johnny will be here soon, and he'll help."

Sara smiled briefly until she thought of Sam. She returned to her cot, and soon the mournful sobbing began again.

Chapter 14

Danny sat on the front steps, sharpening a hoe, as the sheriff's car crunched the gravel of their drive. Mr. Ewell walked out the door, stood behind his son, and waited. Meeker began to get out of the car, but a muffled command drifted through the air, and the deputy sat back down.

Clinton adjusted his hat as he walked to the stoop. "Morning, Mr. Ewell, Danny," he said.

"Sheriff," they both returned in unison.

The meeting was twofold. Clinton thought that Mr. Ewell should be told in person what had happened, and he also needed him to help with the contents of the cave. "Mr. Ewell, there's no easy way to say this but to be blunt. I caught Sara and Uncle Hiram making whiskey last night, and they're both in jail."

Danny's face turned ashen as his father grunted in surprise. "After all these years, you finally caught—"

"'Fraid so, Mr. Ewell."

"And he had the girl helping him?"

Clinton saw Danny swallow hard. "Yes, sir."

Mr. Ewell's shoulders slumped slightly. "Sure wish Hiram hadn't done—"

"Me too, Mr. Ewell," Clinton replied wistfully.

"What about Sam, Sheriff? Where's he?" Danny looked as if his stomach hurt.

"He's at Milton Marion's house," Clinton replied, having to force the painful words out.

"He just got what he always wanted, Sheriff," Mr. Ewell stated.

"He did, Mr. Ewell, he did." Silence fell on the three for a moment. "Mr. Ewell, I'm going to need your help."

"How's that, Sheriff?"

Clinton saw Danny staring at him, looking so hopeful. It dawned on him that the young man was taken with Sara and understood more than he cared to admit. "If you will, I need you to drive your wagon to the site and haul the evidence to the county warehouse. You can snake your way in there, but it's too tight to try it with a truck." He saw Danny's face fall.

"Where is it, Sheriff?" Mr. Ewell asked, suddenly intrigued.

"You'll be surprised. It's almost on your property line. It'll be easier to understand once you see it."

*****

After helping load the wagon, Clinton removed his hat and, using his handkerchief, wiped the sweat from his face. "Ride in with Mr. Ewell and Danny," he ordered Meeker. "When you get everything unloaded, lock the warehouse tight and go home from there."

"All right, Sheriff," Meeker replied. "See you tomorrow."

After watching the three pull away, Clinton entered the cave and took one last look around. He opened one of the two bottles of whiskey that he had managed to hide and took a long, deep swallow. He knew Ronnie would probably steal several bottles as well. Tomorrow or the next day, he would check the warehouse and take a count just to be sure. It might be something he could use against the deputy later.

*****

Clinton returned to the jail and found Johnson sitting in a cane-bottomed chair, playing checkers through the bars with Uncle

Hiram. "Johnson, would you leave us alone for a minute?" he asked quietly.

"Sure, Sheriff," Johnson answered. "Just come get me when you're done."

Uncle Hiram whispered through the bars, "Sheriff, she ain't eaten anything today. I tried to get her to, but she just lies there and cries."

Clinton opened Sara's cell door, and the squeaking of the hinges caused her to sit upright. He felt the weight of her green eyes penetrating him. "Sara," he said gently, "you can't go all day without eating."

"Why'd you do this?" Sara asked, her face swollen and tender with pain. "I was just trying to find a way to leave. Can't you understand that?"

"Sara, my job is to enforce the law," he answered. "It could be a lot worse," he whispered. "There's a dead body, and I—"

"I know, Sheriff, but you don't understand what it's like. Where's Sam?" she asked, shaking her head. "I know he's scared. He's never been away from me."

"He's at Milton Marion's," Clinton answered, wishing he had the courage to lie. He cursed himself as her face twisted in pain.

"Will you tell him that I love him?" she begged.

"I'll do that," he promised.

"Can I see him?"

"I don't know," he answered, "but I'll see what I can do."

"Would you, Sheriff?" she pleaded, dropping her chin to her chest and starting to cry again.

"I'll do my best, Sara," he said, resisting the temptation to push her hair out of her face. "I'm going to tell Johnson to let you out of the cell so you can bathe. Would you promise me you won't run away?" She answered with a nod. "Good," he said gently, wanting to hold her so badly. "I'll see if I can bring you some more clothes tomorrow, okay?"

"Okay."

"Sheriff, I was to remind you about getting in touch with my boy," Uncle Hiram said as Clinton locked Sara's cell.

"Yeah, Uncle Hiram. I'll walk over to the freight station right now." Clinton walked out of the cellblock and located Johnson. "Give me a moment," he said to his deputy. "I'll be right back." A minute later, he returned and handed Johnson a bottle of Uncle Hiram's whiskey. "They're in your care," he said. "See what you can do to make them comfortable."

"Much obliged, Sheriff," Johnson replied, smiling. "I'll do just that."

*****

Clinton opened the door not expecting a warm greeting but hoping the homecoming would be civil. Instead, Ruth was wrestling with a screaming Sam. Between wails, tears streamed down the child's filthy face and turned brown as they dropped off his chin.

"Did it occur to you, Clinton," Ruth hollered, attempting to be heard over Sam, "to carry this boy to Martha instead of dumping him on Willie May? Mother and Daddy are in Montgomery and won't be back for three or four more days."

"I thought it would have been what your father—"

"You thought, Clinton? You didn't think! She brought him here, and I didn't even know what was going on until Jessie told me. I'll be damned to know how these niggers get their information so fast!"

"I just thought it was the best thing to do—"

"No, damn it! You should have taken him to Martha. After Jessie left today," she shrilly bitched, "he's been running away. I've chased him all over the streets with the whole town watching."

Clinton resisted the urge to say "Who cares?" Instead, he asked, "Has he had anything to eat?"

"No, Clinton. I was waiting for you to get home!" She half-tossed, half-thrust the squirming, screaming child toward Clinton and stomped out of the room. He didn't know why it happened, but as he gathered Sam in his arms, the crying stopped.

*****

Danny looked across the dinner table. "Daddy, we have to help her."

"Not much we can do," Billie Ewell replied flatly. "What money we have is already committed to next year's crops and taxes."

"We can't do anything, Daddy?" Mr. Ewell shook his head. "I want to marry her," Danny boldly stated. "Wait," he said as his father started to protest. "Maybe if I talk to the sheriff, tell him how desperate she was. Hell, Daddy," he cried out, "I'll go talk to Mr. Marion, and maybe he'll understand and—"

"Son," Billie Ewell replied harshly, "Milton Marion will eat you alive. He got what he wanted, and you're no match—"

"I can try to do something," Danny said, his frustration filling the room.

"Leave it alone. There's nothing you can—"

"I can marry her! There's nothing wrong with that!"

"Danny, I know best! There ain't—"

"Why are you being so stubborn?" Danny shouted, his temper rising.

"I'm trying to keep you from making a mistake! She's going to prison!" Billie Ewell responded, matching his son's volume.

"Why can't we borrow some money against the land and try to get her a better lawyer?"

"The die is already cast no matter who the lawyer. I've worked hard all these years to hold on to this land, and I won't allow you to throw it—"

"I can't sit back and do nothing. I love her!"

"I know you do," Billie argued hotly. "I'm not blind, but she might not agree to marry you anyway."

"She will. I can feel it," Danny cried. "She needs me!" Suddenly Mr. Ewell shivered as Danny pushed back from the table and stood. "Tomorrow, I'm going to the jail and ask her with or without your blessing!"

"You can't!" Billie shouted as if he would physically stop his son if he tried.

"Why, damn it? Why are you being so stubborn? I would think you would want to help her!"

"I know best! Leave this alone!"

"Why the hell should I?" Danny screamed as spittle flew from his mouth.

"Because she's your sister!"

The room instantly felt devoid of air. Danny sat down slowly and looked across the table at his father in astonishment. "She's my sister?" he whispered. "And her brother?"

"Mine too," his father replied faintly, the fire in his voice suddenly gone. "I'm sorry."

"You fathered those two and left them in their misery? You let the whole county talk about them and their mother all these years!"

"Yes."

"How could you? After preaching right and wrong to me day after day, how could—"

"It's a long story, Danny."

"I deserve to know, damn you, you sorry son of a bitch!"

"Yes, you do," Billie faintly agreed. "And she does too."

Danny sat astonished and wounded as Mr. Ewell began to reveal the horrible tale of injustice created by his own desires.

Chapter 15

Clinton awoke early with Sam curled into a tight small ball at his chest. He had only intended to lie down on the couch with the boy just long enough for him to drift off. In the faint twilight of the room, he stroked Sam's hair a few times, overcome with regret.

Carefully, he untangled himself from the child, hoping he would sleep until Jessie arrived. The floor felt cool to his bare feet as he walked to the bathroom to dress. A few minutes later, he quietly eased out of the house, hoping that neither Ruth nor Sam would hear his departure.

*****

It took an hour to finish the required papers for the DA. He thought about taking a sip of Uncle Hiram's whiskey, but he rejected the notion. As he walked across the street to Blackstone's, it occurred to him that it looked as though several drunken farmers decided they were master carpenters and pounded the building together.

As Clinton pulled the door open, he was struck by the odd feeling of everything being out of square. A wooden counter divided the first one-third of the diner. Behind that, Blackstone plied his trade, serving coffee, tea, and food to his customers, who sat on high-perched wooden stools. Behind him, double swinging doors reaching from the upper chest to the knees of an average man separated the kitchen area. Six tables capable of seating four people each filled the rest of the area. Generally, they were only full during trials at the courthouse or on Election Day.

Clinton spoke the obligatory "Good morning" to the regulars, men who drew paychecks from the county courthouse, as he walked to the last stool.

"Say, Sheriff," one asked, "what's going on with that old bootlegger?"

"It's an ongoing investigation, and I'm not at liberty to discuss it," Clinton answered in a tone that discouraged any follow-up questions.

Blackstone poured the last bit of coffee out of a pot and into a stone urn. "What do you need, Sheriff?"

"Cup of coffee, couple of fried eggs, bacon, and biscuits."

Blackstone took a cup, lifted the spigot on the urn, and filled it three-quarters full. He placed the coffee on the counter in front of Clinton and called the order to Pearly, his cook. "Sheriff just sent the food over for your prisoners," Blackstone said. "Checked it myself."

"I'm watching," Clinton responded bluntly, not trusting the man's word. Blackstone glared, but Clinton didn't care. He wasn't afraid of the man, but he also knew his type. Blackstone wasn't tall, but Clinton knew his low center of gravity could aid the man in a fight. His sleeves were rolled up, revealing thick, powerful forearms. Strong wide shoulders filled out the rest of his shirt. A hard line rested on his square jaw, and a broad, flattened nose marked his face. His dark eyes carried a familiar menacing look that he had seen too many times in evil men.

Most wondered why Milton Marion had plucked him off a farm and made him a business partner in the diner, but Clinton understood the reasoning. They both belonged to the same pod. He also knew that Marion wanted to make sure every nickel that flowed from the county coffers first passed through his own hands. Marion used his influence to ensure that Blackstone won the bid for the jail and county prison farm, and that created another problem with Clinton trying to fight Blackstone and Milton Marion over the quality and the lack of food for his prisoners.

Blackstone set the plate down hard in front of Clinton, causing the eggs to slide to the edge of the dish. Ignoring the obvious taunt, Clinton took his fork and began cutting the eggs into small pieces.

*****

The door opened as Clinton finished breakfast and pushed the plate away. Victor made his usual entrance, greeting everyone brightly, as any politician would.

"That the arrest reports and the inventory of the evidence?" Victor asked as he swept his tie over his shoulder, making sure it wouldn't get spotted with food. Picking up the papers and opening them, he asked loudly, "How much whiskey did you find?"

"Victor, do you want the whole county to know our case, or would you rather I come by your office and discuss this later?" Clinton asked sharply.

"Yeah, that'll be fine, Sheriff. Just come by in an hour or so," Victor replied, ignoring Clinton's displeasure.

"Fine, Victor," Clinton answered, pushing off the stool. "Be there in an hour."

*****

Roger Ellis was sweeping the last vestiges of dirt off the wooden sidewalk of Milton Marion's store as Clinton walked up. The whole county knew that Mr. Ellis was paid to marry Milton's spinster cousin, but he didn't blame the man for taking the money or the job. Someone his age wouldn't last very long doing heavy, backbreaking work.

Before making his request, Clinton checked the street to make sure no one was within earshot. "Mr. Ellis, I need to get a few things for a prisoner's son."

"Sara's boy?"

"Yes, sir. He's staying with us a few days until Milton and Clair return." Clinton felt no need to explain further.

WHERE THE COTTON ONCE GREW

"Come on in, and I'll fix him up. I know his size. Sara bought him something not long ago."

Clinton leaned against the counter, pretending to study the latest catalog, as Mr. Ellis scurried about the store. The pants, shirts, and other necessary items were piled up on the counter. He flipped another page in the book as Mr. Ellis wrapped everything in brown paper and tied the bundle with white cotton string.

"Be back directly, Clinton," he said, walking to the back of the store. It was a few more minutes before Mr. Ellis returned and placed another brown bundle on top of the first one. "Clinton," he said, checking the door for unwanted ears, "our inventory came up a little over. This is for Sara," he pointed and then pulled a pencil from his pocket and made a mark on the paper. "Some nice dresses for the trial and underthings and such, and it'll be our secret, okay?"

"You're safe with me, Mr. Ellis," Clinton replied, trying to hide his emotion.

"You know," Roger Ellis said softly, "nobody except Mr. Ewell tried to help that girl, and I feel right ashamed of myself. So young and pretty. And that boy, he's just as sweet as he can be. They'd come in here, and he'd never ask his mama for…" The sad look in Clinton's eyes spurred Roger Ellis to add, "I know you were just doing your job. He always gets what he wants."

"That doesn't make it any easier, Mr. Ellis."

Long, delicate fingers tapped the brown packages, drumming a tune. Mr. Ellis's gray eyes blinked slowly, giving contrast to his white skin. "Maybe a good man will be placed on the jury, Clinton, one who will stand up and do what's right."

The subtle offer surprised Clinton, and he wondered if his feelings were so transparent. He also understood the abuse someone who opposed Milton's obvious will would take in the jury room, and it would be more than most men could bear. Not wanting to hurt Mr. Ellis's feelings, he said with a wink and a nod, "Might happen, Mr. Ellis. You never know."

*****

Long strides made the trip back to the office short. He dropped the package for Sara on his desk, then left again to carry Sam's home. With a slower gait, he pondered the statement made by Roger Ellis. Amusement crept into his mind, thinking about the possibility of an acquittal.

Uncle Hiram probably had enough money that he could bribe half the county, but Clinton also knew the best anyone could do was hang the jury. Victor would just find twelve more men and retry the case until the proper result was achieved. He smiled at the possibility, though, and decided to pass Mr. Ellis's comment along to Conway Moon.

Clinton opened the front door and dropped the brown package on the floor. Jessie stood, holding Sam, while the child rubbed the sleep from his eyes. *Funny,* Clinton thought, *how the lives of the Negroes and the people they work for are so tightly wrapped. Many white people in Roxboro wouldn't trust their own relatives to care for their young, yet Negro nannies are given the ultimate respect.*

The whites and Negroes didn't share their tables, schools, or churches, but many a wedding found a proud nanny sitting on the front row of the church, dressed brightly in her Sunday best, beaming as the child she nursed through each illness and diapered, fed, and corrected got married. Funerals were much the same. Respect crossed the color line as natural as summer turned to fall, except when it came to the court system and justice.

"Never seen you home this time of day," Ruth said with a biting edge as she walked into the room.

"Just dropping off a few things for Sam to—"

"I thought I told you to wash his clothes, Jessie!" Ruth challenged.

Jessie tried to shrink her already thin body, making a smaller target for Ruth. "I did, missus," she replied quickly. "They ain't dry yet."

"My breakfast?"

"On the table, Ms. Ruth," she replied. Ruth shot a hard look at Clinton as if he had created all this for her displeasure.

116

After the swinging door to the kitchen closed, Clinton leaned in and whispered, "See if you can keep Sam out of her way, Jessie."

"Do my best, Sheriff," she whispered back.

*****

Clinton crossed and uncrossed his legs while Victor read the reports.

"Where'd you store the still and the whiskey?" Victor asked.

"In the county warehouse," Clinton answered, shifting his weight in the hard wooden chair.

"Got it locked up and secure?"

"Yeah. Ronnie took care of that."

This brought a frown to Victor's face; everyone in town felt the deputy wasn't that bright. "You check it yourself?"

"Haven't had time, Victor. Too many—"

"Don't you think you should?"

The question started Clinton's temper rising. "I made the arrest and gathered the evidence, and if you're so damned concerned about how I do my job, go check on it yourself," he shot.

"No need to get in a huff, Sheriff. I was just asking," Victor replied, propping his feet on the desk. Clinton resisted slapping him into an upright position as he reviewed the papers once again. He finally looked up and brought his feet to the floor.

"The grand jury will convene next Monday," Victor said. "Won't take much to get the indictment, because everybody in the county knows the old nigger has been selling whiskey for years. The girl will be no problem either because no man I know will approve of her taking up with a nigger."

Clinton's face grew warm over the provocative statement, but he let it pass. "What are the charges, Victor?" he asked in a tired fashion.

"Well, being the sheriff, you should know."

"Victor," Clinton responded hotly, "I'm not a damn lawyer. It's my job to catch them, and it's your job," Clinton emphasized, "to convict them, so just give me the overall picture."

"You sure are testy today," Victor replied with a smirk.

117

"Listen, Victor, I've got other things to do, and I'll come back later if this is going to take much longer."

"There are several charges," Victor lectured as if talking to a waif. "The making of illegal whiskey to sell, possessing excessive quantities of liquor in a dry county, and the illegal revenue."

The last statement made Clinton frown because the last charge could bring in federal agents from Atlanta if the DA chose. "You going to call the—"

"Naw," Victor replied, smiling smugly. "We'll handle this ourselves. Haven't got much use for those boys."

Clinton hid his relief. "What kind of time are they looking at?"

"Ten years," Victor replied smartly. "I plan to get the max, and that'll send a message to the next wannabe bootlegger."

"You're the DA, and you know best," Clinton said, shrugging his shoulders. "Have any idea of the time frame before we go to trial?"

"We should be able to get it done before Christmas. I checked the calendar yesterday, and it's not too full, just some petty stuff that will move quickly. Talked to Judge Beech, and he seemed anxious to move forward."

Clinton controlled his face, not letting his disgust for the Honorable Winston Dillon Beech show. Judge Beech, as most people referred to him, was a motley old man. The governor appointed him to the second district more than twenty years earlier, and no one had dared run against him since.

Being from one of the old money families in Montgomery got him the appointment. Milton Marion's influence held him in place. Judge Beech always sided with the DA in his rulings. Such a judge should be a delight to any sheriff, but for some reason, it bothered Clinton. Maybe it was because of the callous way in which the judge conducted his trials.

"You talked to Conway Moon yet?" Clinton asked.

"No. He's been away the last couple of days. I left a note on his door, though, informing him of his new clients."

The emphasis on the word *clients* showed the amount of disdain that Victor had for Conway Moon and the indigent people he fought for. Clinton had come to admire the lawyer even though they were generally on opposite sides. He had come from a well-to-do family in Richmond and came south to gain courtroom experience under the most difficult conditions. He was a loud, boisterous lover of food and spirits and wore the tag of nigger lover proudly.

Clinton realized his mind had wandered and quickly turned his attention to Victor. "When's the bail hearing?"

"Today at two o'clock, and I left that on the note for Conway. If he doesn't make it, the judge said he'd postpone it until tomorrow."

*****

Clinton saw that his office door was already open with Mr. Ewell leaning against one wall and Conway against the other. A younger version of Uncle Hiram stood beside Conway, and he wondered how Johnny had gotten here so quickly. Martha Reid, the county social worker, sat stiffly in a chair facing his desk.

"Let me first get the good morning out of the way," Clinton said after reaching his desk. Mr. Ewell murmured his reply, but Conway and Martha both asked questions, overriding each other and causing neither to be understood.

"Look, y'all, I know everyone needs to see me." Holding up his hand, Clinton stopped Martha and Conway, as both pursed their lips. "I'll see Ms. Reid first out of deference to her being a lady." At that point, Conway snorted, causing Martha to glare. "Conway, then I'll see you, and, Mr. Ewell, you'll be next. If you don't mind, Johnny—"

"He's with me, Sheriff," Conway interrupted, then boomed, "I just need to see my clients." Clinton knew the lawyer spoke louder than usual just to irritate Martha. "If you'll let me visit them in their cells, that'll be all I need for now."

"No, Conway. I'd like to talk to you first. Then I'll let you use my office."

"Sheriff," Mr. Ewell interjected, "I'll ease across the street for coffee and be back in a while."

"Thank you, Mr. Ewell," Clinton answered with grace as the man slipped from the room.

"Sheriff, me and Johnny will wait outside while you talk to Martha." Using her first name signaled disrespect, and Martha's face darkened in anger. "Try not to be long-winded, Martha," Conway shot as Johnny followed him out the door.

"Sheriff," Martha asked tersely as the door closed, "have you ever heard of proper procedure?"

"Yes, ma'am, but—"

"The child was supposed to be brought to me because I'm charged through the state with his welfare," she said in a raised voice.

"Yes, but—"

"The proper channel is me first, and then I make the determination on placing the child." Her scowl deepened, and Clinton could easily understand how she had become a spinster. Every day, she looked and dressed as though always ready for a funeral. He guessed that even Milton's money couldn't buy her a husband. "Milton won't be pleased with how you've handled this, Sheriff!"

"You're probably right, Ms. Reid," he replied through clenched teeth. "But I made the decision, and I'll stand by it. Now if you'll excuse me," he said, rising from his chair and opening the door, "I have other people to see."

Conway Moon and Johnny were standing at the entrance to the vestibule. The lawyer bowed at the waist as Ms. Reid walked by, and her walk accelerated into quick, angry steps.

"Sheriff, you must have really pissed her off," Conway remarked, jowls shaking.

"Doesn't take much," Clinton replied lightly. "I'll be back in a minute with your clients."

Chapter 16

Clinton entered the cellblock as Uncle Hiram nibbled the last half of a biscuit. "Breakfast any good?" he asked while peering through the bars.

"Stale as last week's preaching," Uncle Hiram replied, dropping the uneaten portion on the tray. Clinton glanced at Sara's cell and saw that her food was untouched. Uncle Hiram followed his gaze. "She ain't ate a thing since we got here, Sheriff," he whispered. "Can't do anything but lie there and cry."

"Fred," Clinton said, "why don't you take a walk around town and check things out? Conway Moon needs to talk to these two, and I'll take care of the jail."

"Okay, Sheriff," Fred replied, dropping the leaned back chair down with a thud.

Clinton opened Sara's cell, stepped in, and squatted beside her cot. Her eyes were dull, lifeless, and covered with red spider veins. "Sara, I know this is hard, but starving yourself won't help."

"I need to see my boy, Sheriff," she replied softly as new tears sprang to life. "Please, I'm begging you."

Her pleading eyes disturbed Clinton so much that his heart hurt. "I can't promise," he answered. "But if there is any way possible, I'll bring him tonight."

"Would you?" she asked, suddenly looking hopeful. "I know he's scared and doesn't understand what's happening."

"I'll do my best," he answered. "Now stand up so I can walk you and Uncle Hiram to my office. Your lawyer is waiting."

Sara stood, pushed the hair out of her face, and tried to smooth her dirty overalls. Clinton wondered how he and life itself could treat this kind and gentle creature so badly. A surge of pleasure ran through Clinton as Johnny and Uncle Hiram hugged tightly. The introductions were short. Only Sara was unfamiliar with the lawyer.

"Before you get started, Conway," Clinton asked, "could I see you in private for a moment?" The lawyer followed him out the door and pulled it closed. "There's a brown package on my desk that's for Sara. If you'll see she gets it after your visit, I'd be appreciative."

"Sure, Sheriff," Conway agreed.

Almost to himself, Clinton said, "Roger Ellis might be a good man on the jury. I'd pick him if I was their lawyer."

*****

Conway looked from Sara to Uncle Hiram. "I've done a review of the charges and the evidence. It doesn't look good, especially with Milton Marion having a vested interest." Then drawing his face into a scowl, he asked, "Uncle Hiram, they've been after you for years. Why would you involve this young mother in your operation?"

Uncle Hiram's face grew dark, but before he could respond, Sara spoke. "Mr. Moon, Uncle Hiram was trying to help me, and I was of my own free will." Her tone relayed deep affection for the old man.

"Still—"

"I'll have none of that," Sara said forcefully. "Uncle Hiram treated me with great respect and warned me of the risks."

Conway shot a look at Uncle Hiram and saw that he was smiling. "Take no offense," he said lightly. "These are questions I have to ask. The DA will insist the two of you be tried together and use that, Sara, to inflame the jury."

"Mr. Moon," Uncle Hiram injected, "I got a few ideas—"

"Don't tell me," Conway responded, rolling his eyes. "I can't know about anything illegal."

"Well..." Uncle Hiram said, catching the lawyer's drift.

Leaning forward, Conway asked Sara, "If you want, I can go in and fight and maybe get you a separate trial. The odds are stacked against us, but I'm willing to try."

Sara shot Uncle Hiram a look, asking for an answer. He answered back with an expression that said, "Whatever I do will help you also."

"No, sir, Mr. Moon," Sara answered.

"Okay, Sara. I have no doubt the court will declare you indigent, so the county will pay me for defending you. Uncle Hiram," he said, "it's different with you."

"How much you need, Mr. Moon?" Uncle Hiram asked.

"A hundred dollars for now." Johnny pulled a roll from his pocket and counted out the cash. "Good," Conway said, taking the bills. "Now this afternoon, you two have to enter a plea in court. Do you want me to talk to the DA about a guilty plea to a lesser charge?"

"Mr. Moon, we'll see if we can get acquitted," Uncle Hiram answered for both.

"You know that your chances are slim," Conway said honestly.

"I know, Mr. Moon. We'll try, though."

"All right, then. After we enter your plea, I'll request bail, but I can say with certainty that it won't be allowed."

*****

"Sara," Clinton said as the three walked out of the office, "Mr. Ewell would like to see you for a few minutes."

"You need me to sit in?" Conway asked Sara.

"No, sir."

"I'm done, Sheriff, but there'll be many more times I'll need to see my clients," Conway stated.

"Just let me know when," Clinton replied.

A few minutes later, as Conway and Johnny walked toward his office, the lawyer stopped as if contemplating something important. "I bet that Roger Ellis would be a good man if he's selected for the jury," Conway said.

"Sir?" Johnny asked, looking somewhat confused.

"You didn't hear me say a damn thing," Conway groused, already on the move again. Johnny thought for a second, then smiled as the big man strolled away.

Chapter 17

"Mr. Ewell," Sara started as he closed the door, "I'm so sorry that I've embarrassed you."

"Ain't nothing, Ms. Sara, 'cause it's me who is sorry."

"Why would that be, Mr. Ewell?" she asked.

"I need to tell you—"

"I wish I could change what I've done," she interrupted, distraught over the situation. "But I—"

"Ms. Sara, please hear me out before you say anything else," he said nervously, clutching his hat tightly.

"Mr. Ewell," she asked, her eyebrows arched, "what's wrong?" She couldn't understand the strong man looking so weakened and strange.

Mr. Ewell lifted his chin from his chest and said, "Most of my life, I've only pretended to do what's right. I'm no better than a Pharisee."

"What are you talking about?" she asked in a flat tone.

"Ms. Sara," he mumbled, "I'm nothing but a hypocrite, just like Jesus talked about in the gospels."

Suddenly her suspicions rose. "What are you trying to tell me?"

His syllables came out slow and painful as the climax of a boil. "I'm your father."

The room began to spin, and Sara leaned against the wall, grateful for its support. Her chest tightened, and her breathing grew shallow. Slowly, years of anger, the countless days of hunger, desperate poverty, and cruel whispers surfaced all at once. That combined with the memories of Stuart's and her mother's deaths robbed Sara of the words she wanted to scream.

"Ms.—"

"Don't say anything," Sara whispered fiercely, surprised that she had managed to speak. Carefully, she reached for the chair and sat down. Her temper boiled dry, flushing her face with more heat than she'd ever known. "May you burn in hell!" she hissed like a viper.

"Ms. Sara, that's what's going to happen and what I deserve."

Sara willed herself to stay seated and not rise and strike him. She crossed her arms on the desk and laid her head down, hoping he would leave. But minutes later, he was still standing there, holding what remained of his twisted and broken hat. Somehow, her rage cooled, and she spoke.

"Does Danny know?" she asked with her heart in her hand. "He doesn't deserve this."

"I told him last night, and he took it real hard. He was quite sweet on you, and he said this morning that it's your right to inherit half the land, so I'm going in the next day or two and have Mr. Moon—"

"Little good it will do me in prison," she said.

"I can't make up for what I've done to you. It's the best I have to offer."

"No, there's something you can do, Mr. Ewell," she pronounced strongly. "You're Sam's grandfather too, and you have as much legal right to him as Mr. Marion."

"I do, but what can—"

"No! Damn it, I dictate the terms, and you listen," she demanded. "If you want to make up for the wrongs you caused me and my family, this is what you'll do. We'll keep this new information to ourselves." Sara walked over and stood directly in front of Mr. Ewell and began to lay out her terms.

"When the proper time comes, you will go to court and fight for my boy. I don't want him being raised by Mr. Marion. The very thought makes me ill. While I'm sitting in prison, at least spare me that nightmare, because he wants him for the wrong reasons.

"Let Sam know that he's loved by you and Danny while I'm rotting away. It's not what I ask, Mr. Ewell. It's what I demand you do," she finished emphatically.

Mr. Ewell didn't or couldn't match her eyes. "I will, and for what it's worth, I give you my word."

"It's all I ask. Just protect and love my boy."

"I've used up enough time," he stated as if asking for permission to leave.

"Not yet, Mr. Ewell," she ordered. "Tell me about my mother. There's so little I know. You do owe me that much."

His feet shuffled a few times as if he was going to turn and run, but he didn't. He started slowly then, after a few words, found some rhythm and strength. "Lilly and I were distant cousins. Third or fourth, I think. My father always kept in correspondence with our extended family, and one summer, we were invited to visit. That's when I first met your mother. Her beauty could captivate any young man, and you remind me so much of her.

"They were different from us in many ways, very cultured. They enjoyed drinks before dinner and then had wine with their meals and didn't try to hide it even if company visited. They didn't work in the fields. The old man, your grandfather, Mr. Cunningham, his holdings were very large, two thousand acres or so. And the house was huge. Four white columns and more rooms than you could count. Lilly's older brothers, two of them, were wild as March hares but mannered. Wouldn't no more curse in front of a lady than a preacher would. I think both spent some time in boarding school up in Atlanta."

"Where are they?" Sara asked, hoping it wasn't the obvious answer.

"One fell off a riverboat that served as a gambling house and drowned. The other brother got drunk one afternoon and bet a friend he could swim the Chattahoochee River. That muddy water claimed both Lilly's brothers."

"How did Mama end up here?"

"This part ain't going to be pleasant."

"My mother and brother are dead, Mr. Ewell, and I'm headed to prison. I don't expect pleasant!"

He took a deep breath and plunged on. "About a year before my own father died and left me the farm, he received a letter that your grandfather wanted to sell a matching pair of mules. Papa thought that was strange because all farmers took pride in identical stock. Papa wrote him back and agreed to the purchase. He sent me over to retrieve the animals.

"After arriving and shaking off three days of dirt, who comes flittering out of the house but Lilly. I figured, by that time, she'd long since married. Not so, because her daddy didn't think much of the local suitors and wouldn't hesitate to run them off. Sometimes, a well-placed shotgun blast did the trick.

"Lord, her beauty overcame me. We sat at the table and had dinner, and then later, we sipped wine and talked on the porch. But that night, lying there on that feather mattress, it dawned on me that she needed someone better, not a plain dirt farmer but a man who could take her places and buy lots of fancy clothes and such. I slipped out early that morning before she woke.

"Not long after that, I inherited the land. And about a year later, I married Danny's mama. It wasn't long before she started getting sick and staying weak all the time, and the local doctor couldn't find what or why. He said to take her to Montgomery, so I did. The doctor there did some tests and told us to come back in a month.

"The news wasn't good. He said she had some type of leukemia and that she might live four or five years at the most. Nothing could be done to stave off her impending death. He tried a new treatment and gave her doses of arsenic, but even he was surprised at how long she lived.

"It wasn't four or five days after I got the diagnosis that a pitiful tearstained letter arrived from Lilly. Your grandfather, it seemed, had been losing money for years and was heavily mortgaged. Your grandmother had long since died, so the only ones left were Lilly and her daddy.

"He'd already borrowed from all his friends, and they'd grown tired and written him off. The old man grew more erratic as the bankers closed in." Sara's belly clenched, afraid of yet knowing what his next words would be. "Your mother heard the blast and found your granddaddy lying dead on the porch. He'd stuck an old cap and ball pistol in his mouth and pulled the trigger.

"She didn't have anywhere to go, Ms. Sara. I made up a reason to travel there and brought her here under the cover of night. She rented that place from Milton Marion with the money I'd given her."

"And she just readily agreed to live as your mistress?"

"Not at first. I only intended to help her because of family ties, but later, it changed after thinking about my wife's impending death. And, Ms. Sara, anything I say from here on will sound like an excuse," he said nervously.

"Mr. Ewell, my brother and I grew up without you, and if it's punishment to keep talking, then so be it." Her words cut through him, but he started again.

"I promised Lilly I'd marry her when Mary died. I wouldn't leave Mary, though. Wouldn't be right."

His mistake made Sara's face grow red, and she angrily shot back, "You have a funny way of looking at right and wrong."

"You're right," he agreed weakly. "I might as well be blunt and get it over with. I didn't think Mary would live that long after Danny was born, and I spent more time wondering and worrying about what he would think of his father and what people would say. I put your mother off all those years, and each time, she believed that next month or next year, I would do right by her."

"Mr. Ewell," Sara asked, dropping some of her venom, "how in the world did you get her not to talk?"

"I don't know. Either I'm the best liar in the world, or Lilly thought that if she did, I'd deny the fact and stop supporting her. I wish she'd dragged me out to the courthouse square and shouted it to the whole county."

Sara admitted the truth sadly, not wanting to hear anything else. "My mother carried an inherent weakness of the mind, and she believed what she wanted to. As much as I'd like to curse you, she has to share the blame. This is our secret, and we'll use it at the proper time if it will help."

"Ms. Sara, I'm so sorry."

She shared his hesitation as he placed his hand on her shoulder and, for the first time, felt his fatherly touch.

Chapter 18

Johnny and Danny were sitting on the redbrick stoop as Mr. Ewell drove the wagon into the yard. He went directly to the barn and took his time unhitching the mule. They stopped their conversation in midsentence as he approached. Danny's face was painted with sheer contempt, and he made no effort to hide it. His father ignored the rightful anger for now because bigger things needed to be accomplished.

"Johnny," Mr. Ewell said, taking a seat on the stoop, "it's nice to see you."

"Yes, sir, Mr. Ewell. It's good to be home, but I wish the reason for the visit was more pleasant."

"I know, son." Mr. Ewell reached over and squeezed his knee. "I'm glad you're here, though. I need you to help me and Danny tonight."

"To do what?" Danny asked.

"Well," Mr. Ewell explained, his face passive, "the sheriff is coming for a visit—I'd say tomorrow afternoon—to question Johnny about his whereabouts tonight."

"Why's that, Mr. Ewell?" Johnny asked, puzzled. "I have—"

"'Cause the county warehouse is going to burn and destroy the evidence against Ms. Sara and Uncle Hiram. He'll come looking, thinking Johnny did it."

"And just who is going to set this fire?" Danny asked, looking at his father incredulously.

Mr. Ewell answered both of them by tapping his chest. "It's the least I can do," he said dryly. "Now you boys hitch the wagon late this afternoon and load the johnboat. Run a trotline, and I'll catch up with you before daylight so we can all claim we were together. And we'd better catch a tubful of fish, boys. The man ain't dumb."

"How do you know he'll believe us?" Danny asked with narrowed eyes.

"Leave the lying to me, boys," Mr. Ewell said. "I'm older and have had more practice."

*****

Clinton's spirits were already low as he walked home, but seeing Milton Marion's car parked in front of his house caused them to drop even further. Before he reached the first step, he heard Sam's wailing. Alarmed, he pushed the door open to find Milton Marion and Ruth struggling to quiet the child.

Sam, spying Clinton, wiggled free and leaped into his arms. Instantly, the crying stopped. As Sam hugged him tightly around the neck, Ruth glared, and Milton Marion's face flushed. Clair looked bemused as if pleased with the child's reaction. She winked quickly at Clinton, causing his uneasiness to grow.

"Clair," Milton said, "why don't you and Ruth take the boy and let me and Clinton talk?"

"He won't come with me, Daddy," Ruth sniped. "He only likes Clinton and Jessie."

"Very well, then," Milton said, not wanting to fuss with his daughter. "We'll talk in the kitchen, and the boy can stay with us." The kitchen door had no more swung closed before accusatory words flew from his mouth. "Pray tell, Clinton," he said, his blue eyes glowing, "why didn't you take the child to Martha Reid instead of bringing him to our house?"

Clinton returned fire in a low growl, determined to never again be his father-in-law's whipping boy. "I did your bidding, and there are two people sitting in jail who don't deserve to be there all because of what you wanted, so don't give me any damn lectures on how I've embarrassed the family."

Marion backed up one step, pretended to straighten his tie, and then locked his eyes on Clinton, showing he wasn't afraid. "Very well," he said. "Now that you've created this situation, it's up to me to make it look better. I'll talk to Martha tomorrow and get her to issue temporary custody to you and Ruth till after the trial. Then I and Clair will pursue legally adopting him."

Clinton didn't respond as Milton Marion spun on his heels and barged through the kitchen door. The one thing that he felt the most grateful for was that Sam would stay with him. He had become attached to the little boy.

*****

Although late enough for the night air to cool, Mr. Ewell had sweat gathering along his hatband by the time he walked to the river. The camp was empty, but he could see the light of the lantern as the boys worked the trotline. The washtub was half full, and it pleased him. He sat on a log and rested as the two paddled the boat ashore.

"Did it burn?" Danny asked while pouring this run's catch in the larger tub.

"Like sagebrush on a windy day," Mr. Ewell proudly announced.

"Anybody see you?" Johnny asked cautiously.

"Nope," Mr. Ewell replied. "We'll go home about noon tomorrow. The sheriff will probably be tied up with the warehouse in the morning. Then, Johnny, he'll come looking for you."

*****

After listening for a minute at the door, Clinton felt sure Ruth had fallen asleep. He and Sam eased out of the house and quietly walked down the steps. He leaned down and whispered into the child's ear, "I'm going to carry you somewhere, and you've got to promise that you won't tell anyone."

"You mean like when Mama and me were going to the cave?" Sam whispered back, his breath soft against Clinton's face.

"Just like that, Sam," Clinton answered, amused. "Don't tell Ruth or Jessie, okay? It will be our secret."

"I promise," Sam answered easily.

Clinton walked into the cellblock, carrying Sam in his arms. Uncle Hiram and Johnson were engrossed in their checkers game. Looking through Uncle Hiram's cell, he could see Sara lying on her cot, facing the opposite wall. *This is no place for a child*, he thought. *But there's no other way.*

Clinton saw that her cell door was open, just as he had instructed. Johnson spied the sheriff and started to speak but stopped when Clinton put his finger to his lips. He moved slowly, careful not to thump his boots across the stone floor.

Sam's eyes wandered, taking in the new sights and smells until he saw his mother. "Mama!" he called excitedly, his legs already pumping as Clinton set him on the floor. She sprang from her cot as though lightning had struck and engulfed her boy. Clinton turned away, so moved by the scene that he felt hotness growing behind his eyes. Trying to give Sara and Sam privacy, he motioned for Uncle Hiram and Johnson to follow.

After they all sat in Clinton's office, he rummaged around in his desk, then tossed a pack of playing cards to Uncle Hiram. "Why don't y'all play cards in here and let the two have a little time alone?"

"Fine by me," Uncle Hiram said, grinning. "Johnson ain't much of a checker player. I hope he's better at cards."

"Maybe Sam will go to sleep in a while," Clinton said hopefully, "and make it a little easier on Sara when we leave."

"Sheriff, I've checked the food like you asked," Johnson said, changing the subject. "It ain't no good. Just what Blackstone can't sell."

"He's right, Sheriff," Uncle Hiram agreed, wrinkling his face. "Ms. Sara, though, she did eat some today."

Clinton pushed his hat back. "I'll see Blackstone tomorrow and convince him to do better. Oh, and by the way, Johnson, I checked, and you're one month from your official retirement date."

"You reckon the trial will be over by then?" Johnson asked.

"No—"

"Let me stay till it's over, Sheriff," Johnson interrupted. "Don't want to leave them in someone else's care."

Clinton was relieved and touched by the request. "Just let me know when," he replied. "And I'll sign the paperwork and send it in. I'll be back in a while."

*****

Clinton took a careful look around before removing the wood screws and breaking into Marion's office again. He took long strides across the room and sat cross-legged in front of the safe. On the sixth try, it opened, and he saw five neat large stacks of cash. Resisting the urge to take the money and run, he pushed the door closed and spun the dial.

Holding his breath and willing his pulse to slow, he ran the numbers again. When the door opened the second time, he couldn't tell if the feeling that flushed his face was euphoria or plain old relief. *I've got it,* he whispered in the empty office. *Now what do I do?*

Chapter 19

Victor Turlock viewed the smoky remains of the county warehouse as the misty morning started to warm. He watched as the sheriff and his deputy poked through the ruins, looking for the remains of the still.

"I found it, Sheriff," Ronnie announced. The deputy hooked the edge of a molten piece of metal with a hoe and flipped it over. He repeated the process several times until the still landed on clean ground.

Victor looked at the flattened mess. "Sheriff, what are you going to do about this?"

"What do you mean, Victor?" Clinton responded.

"You know what I mean!" Victor said angrily. "You know that nigger's boy set the fire!"

Victor's irritation amused Clinton, but he also knew that Johnny was the most likely suspect. "Yeah, I'll go question him today and see where he was last night."

"You know," Victor said, his displeasure showing, "I think I'd have put a guard on the warehouse as soon as that young nigger returned."

The back of Clinton's neck grew red from the catty remark. "Just who do you think could be here both day and night? I've only got a few deputies," he replied testily. "Two of them are old as hell—"

"You have Ronnie," Victor curtly interrupted. Now Meeker became uneasy. He had lied to his wife last night, saying he was chasing another bootlegger. The true cause of his absence was another woman.

"Victor," Clinton stated flatly, "Ronnie has enough to do, and he's the only one young enough—"

"Then you should have used him properly," Victor snapped, missing all the signs of a growing temper.

Clinton stepped close to the DA, determined, once and for all, to shut the little bastard's mockingbird mouth. "Victor, I am the duly elected sheriff of this county, and since taking office, you have insulted me, pushed me around, and generally been a pompous little jackass! Between you and my father-in-law, you'd wonder who wore the badge!"

Victor tried to respond, but Clinton's large hand was clutching his tie just below the knot. He pulled upward, dragging the DA's face close to his own. "And if you say one more thing about how I run my department or whine again to Milton about how I do my job, I'll stomp your sorry little ass in the ground!"

Victor was gasping for air, but he managed to squeak out, "I understand."

Clinton released him with a hard shove. He then turned toward Ronnie, eyeing him warily, as the DA scuttled away. "Meeker, you wouldn't have kept a few bottles for yourself, would you?"

Ronnie pondered a second before answering. "Naw, Sheriff," he lied. "I put every bottle in the warehouse."

"Good. I wouldn't want you getting in trouble over a few bottles of illegal whiskey."

*****

Mr. Ewell hung the blue catfish on the third step of the windmill and quickly skinned and gutted the fish. Johnny thoroughly washed the body cavity before handing it off to Danny. He rolled it in a mixture of flour, cornmeal, and salt and pepper and then tossed it in the black pot of boiling cooking oil. As each fish floated to the top, Danny removed it, adding to the growing stack. Each man heard the sound of the car but pretended not to.

Clinton cursed under his breath as he opened the door. He didn't want to pursue Johnny and secretly hoped he had a good alibi. Intuition brought him to Mr. Ewell's after checking Uncle Hiram's house. A wonderful aroma drifted in the air, causing his empty stomach to rumble.

"Looks like I got here at the right time," Clinton said, eyeing the food.

Mr. Ewell diverted his attention. "Hello, Sheriff. You did. Get a plate and help yourself."

"I think I will."

"Come on over to the fire, Sheriff," Danny suggested, "and get some hush puppies."

"Go ahead and start eating," Billie Ewell urged. "We'll catch up with you in a minute."

"Naw, I'll wait," Clinton answered politely. He noticed that none of the three seemed surprised to see him.

Within a few minutes, the last of the fish was cooked. Johnny poured each a glass of sweet tea and then sat down after Mr. Ewell quickly prayed. Soon, all were silent, peeling off the flaky white meat and stuffing it in their mouths.

After he had consumed more food than a stomach should hold, Clinton pushed his plate away. He scratched his head. "Mr. Ewell, you hear about the warehouse burning last night?"

"Naw, Sheriff, hadn't heard. How'd it catch fire?" Mr. Ewell asked, his eyebrows arched in surprise.

"Best I can figure, someone set it," Clinton replied calmly, glancing at Johnny to gauge his reaction. The young man didn't flinch and only seemed intent on finishing another fish. "That's the reason I'm here, Mr. Ewell."

"Why's that?"

"Johnny would be the most likely suspect," Clinton said plainly.

"Yeah," Mr. Ewell replied. "I'd guess so with Hiram being in jail."

"Where were you last night, Johnny?" Clinton saw that his reaction was completely calm as he answered.

"We were fishing on the river all night."

Clinton assumed "we" meant just Johnny and Danny. "That's very well," Clinton said. "But you could have easily left the river and set the fire, and no one would have known but Danny."

Danny's eyes narrowed, but before he could speak, Mr. Ewell chimed in. "Sheriff," he explained, "I decided to go with them. Haven't had that much fun in years."

"So the three of you were all together last night?" Clinton asked, seeking complete clarification.

"We were," Billie Ewell answered. "I'll vouch for both the boys."

"Okay," Clinton replied. "You're known as a man of your word, so that's all the questions I have for now. Thank you for the meal," he added, rubbing his stomach. "It was mighty good."

Clinton walked slowly to his patrol car, enjoying the warm sun. It was not until he drove a good distance away that a deep rumble of laughter escaped. *Mr. Ewell was lying through his teeth*, he thought. *The table was set for four, and they were expecting me.*

*****

Clinton stood from his desk and jammed his hat on. After strapping on his gun belt and checking to make sure his sap and handcuffs were in place, he let out an audible sigh. He hoped Blackstone's place would be empty this late in the day. He marched across the street, clearly agitated. Opening the diner door, he saw Blackstone leaning against the counter, reading a newspaper. Clinton didn't speak, nod, or acknowledge his existence but walked to the back table.

"Cup of coffee please," Clinton said loudly.

"That's all you need, Sheriff?" Blackstone asked lazily.

"Yep."

Clinton removed the lead sap from his belt as Blackstone turned to pour the coffee. Keeping his hands hidden, he secured the leather strap around his wrist. Blackstone's boots dragged across the floor as he eyed the sheriff carefully. Keeping his body outside of striking distance, he extended his arm to place the coffee cup on the table.

Clinton struck with the sap, hitting the top of Blackstone's hand dead center. A terrific grunt of pain filled the air as his hand jerked back in reaction. Quickly, Clinton rolled from the chair and swung the sap viciously, striking Blackstone's right temple. His eyes rolled and his body crumpled, unconscious, to the floor.

Clinton turned Blackstone over on his stomach, dropped one knee hard into the center of his back, and secured both hands with the cuffs. Pearly stuck her bandanna-covered head out the kitchen door but quickly retreated when their eyes met. Clinton heard her snicker before going back to work.

Clinton squatted on his heels and waited patiently for Blackstone's mind to reenter the world. When the dark eyes began to focus, Clinton grabbed a handful of curly hair. He looked deep into Blackstone's cold eyes, finding nothing but a bully, charlatan, and thief. He banged Blackstone's head on the floor twice.

"This is your last warning," Clinton commanded through clenched teeth. "I don't like you or your kind. You feed my prisoners inedible slop again, and damn you, I promise you'll never see it coming." Clinton banged his head against the floor once more, then rolled him over and removed the handcuffs. Blackstone lay motionless until he heard the sound of the door closing.

*****

Johnny took a deep breath as he entered the store. Mr. Ellis bustled from one customer to another as he walked over and began patiently rifling through a stack of work pants. Finally, Mr. Ellis approached and asked, "Can I help you?"

"No, sir," Johnny answered, looking up. "Just found what I needed."

"Good," Roger replied. "Come on, and let's get this paid for."

Johnny took a careful survey of the other customers, measuring their distance, as Mr. Ellis wrapped the pants. Almost without moving his lips, he whispered, "Need to see you tonight, Mr. Ellis."

Roger Ellis paused for a second. "Back of the store?"

Johnny quickly shook his head, because hanging around in the alley could get him shot. "Old cottonwood tree," he said quietly.

Mr. Ellis nodded his head. "Good. Right after dark."

*****

The huge cottonwood marked the beginning of the town, although one had to travel another quarter mile to reach the first house. Johnny sat beneath it, looking up through the limbs, and saw a few clouds hiding a quarter moon. His discomfort grew with each passing minute.

In an effort to calm his nerves, he rehearsed over and over again what he would say if Mr. Ellis came with the sheriff. Tired from lack of sleep, Johnny nodded off, his chin dipping to his chest. He didn't know if the nap lasted an hour or a minute but awoke to the sound of footsteps.

"Johnny," he heard Mr. Ellis calling softly.

"I'm here, Mr. Ellis," Johnny replied. "You alone?" he asked, not yet able to see the man.

"Yes, I'm alone." Mr. Ellis chuckled nervously. "I can understand why you're worried, though."

"Yes, sir." The two met at the edge of the shadow cast from the tree. "Daddy wanted me to talk to you."

"Figured that might be the case," Roger replied.

Johnny dug in his pocket and pulled out a roll of money. "He asked me to give you this, Mr. Ellis." Roger Ellis took the money. It felt soft and warm in his hand. "You think you'll be on the jury?" Johnny asked.

"Can't say for sure. I've been on a lot of them, though."

"If you are, can you help us?"

Roger wanted to strike a blow for all who had been mistreated by Milton Marion, but his gentle nature made lying difficult. "Johnny, I'll do my best, but there'll be a lot of pressure on me," he said, his voice tiny and childlike.

"That's all we ask, Mr. Ellis. Daddy said you were the only one that we could trust."

"My dear boy," Mr. Ellis replied gently as he stood a little straighter, "I hope I don't let you down."

141

Chapter 20

Early the next morning, as Conway walked to his office, Deputy Johnson limped by. "Morning, Mr. Moon," he said, looking a little more chipper than normal.

"Morning," Conway replied, returning the greeting.

Normally, that ended their conversation, but Johnson added, "Mr. Moon did the warehouse burning help your case any?"

"What do you mean, Johnson?"

"The warehouse. I mean, doesn't it help that it burned and took all the evidence—"

"I'm sorry, Johnson," Conway said. "I was away the last two days."

"Oh, Mr. Moon, thought you knew already. The warehouse, it burned slap down to the ground. Not a thing left 'xcept the old still, and it's flat as a pancake," Johnson added cheerfully.

"Any idea how it burned?" Conway asked with a touch of dread in his voice.

"Naw," Johnson replied. "The sheriff talked to Uncle Hiram's boy, but he had a good alibi. I'd guess the DA be pissing and moaning now."

"Johnson, that's his natural state," Conway replied dryly.

"Mr. Moon, you reckon you can win now?"

Conway's curiosity rose. "Why does it matter to you, Johnson? You've got no dog in this fight."

"You remember when I got shot by those convicts and almost died?"

"Yes," Conway lied; he wasn't in Roxboro at that time.

"Before I could get back on my feet, my daughter Missy got the scarlet fever and died." With tears welling up in his eyes, he continued. "And the county cut my wages when I couldn't work. I barely had enough to feed my wife and my other two girls. You know who helped me and paid to have my Missy buried, Mr. Moon?"

"No," Conway said, shaking his head.

"Uncle Hiram. Came to my house, gave me the money, and said there was no need to pay it back. There were a lot of people who turned their back on me, Mr. Moon, but Uncle Hiram didn't."

*****

Later that day, while Sara seemed to be napping, Uncle Hiram whispered in Johnny's ear, "You know OT's son Tribune, the one that ain't quite right?" Johnny nodded in agreement. The boy's mind never fully developed, and everyone still thought of him as a child. "Go find him," Uncle Hiram insisted. "And give him two dollars to go with you to Judge Beech's house tonight."

"Why?" Johnny asked.

"I was making a delivery one night and saw the judge letting Tribune in his back door. He was looking this way and that way, so I eased over there and peeked in the window."

"What did you see, Daddy?" Johnny asked, dreading the answer.

"Ain't going to say. I just banged on the window and then ran back and hid in the shadows. Not a minute later, Tribune was pushed out the door. I told OT the next day to keep a watch on his boy."

"I'm old enough to know," Johnny insisted.

"No, you're not. You just take Tribune with you and hand the judge this note."

Johnny took the piece of paper and put it in his pocket. Later, sitting at the kitchen table, he read his father's words.

It was me at the window that night, and I saw what you were doing to the boy. If you don't help us, I'll talk. You'll be surprised how many people will believe me.

Uncle Hiram

*****

As Clinton opened the morning mail, someone rapped lightly on his office door. "Come in," he said, looking up, expecting Fred but finding Victor instead.

"We need to talk about the case, Sheriff," Victor said.

Clinton was mildly surprised that Victor stood so apprehensively, waiting to be asked in. *Maybe I got to him,* he thought, but he quickly dismissed the notion. Victor would be his arrogant old self once the jury was seated.

"The trial," Victor said after sitting down, "is two weeks from today. Evidence-wise, we don't have anything except the still. You or Meeker wouldn't have kept a bottle or two for personal use, would you?"

The question tilted toward the pleading side, signifying that Victor's confidence level wasn't as high as he liked. "No," Clinton answered, enjoying the lie. "It never occurred to me to keep any. Asked Ronnie too. He said no, so for physical evidence, the still is all we have."

"Well, it would help if we could positively say to the jury that the bottles contained whiskey. But everyone in this county has probably bought a bottle or two from that old nigger at one time or another."

"Yeah, probably so," Clinton agreed in order to move things along.

"I'll use the testimony of you, Meeker, Mr. Ewell, and his son as to what y'all brought out of the cave. Between that and the common knowledge, that should be enough." Clinton remained silent, finding no reason to agree. "Strange, though," Victor added. "I talked to Mr.

Ewell this morning to advise him that he and Danny would have to testify for the state, and it wasn't a warm conversation."

"Their land joins, and the two boys grew up together," Clinton explained. For most, that explanation would have been enough, but Clinton read Victor's quizzical look. "You grew up in the city, didn't you?"

"Yeah, Birmingham, why?"

"It's different in the country," Clinton said, but he quickly gave up. Being a city boy, Victor would never understand. "How do you think Conway is going to defend them?" Clinton asked.

Again, the DA's face sparked with concern. "He'll come after you, Sheriff," he replied, "and say that you trumped up the charges to help Mr. Marion. I'd advise you to keep your head and give me time to object." Clinton shrugged his shoulders, indicating his indifference. "I can't imagine that Judge Beech will allow Conway to go down that road," the DA said, now smiling. "He is for law and order, isn't he, Sheriff?" The mere mention of the judge caused Clinton's stomach to roll. "Can you think of anything I've missed?"

"No," Clinton replied. "That's pretty much it. Surely, Conway has something else in mind to defend his clients." The word *client* bothered him slightly less than *prisoner* when thinking of Sara, and to be honest, he was finding every excuse to visit her jail cell. He had even quit wrestling with the vivid dreams about her.

"Yeah," Victor said, fishing in his shirt pocket and pulling out a piece of paper. "He gave me his witness list last night. He's going to put that nigger on the stand and the girl plus several others that are unfamiliar to me. Alva Siler?" Victor asked, looking up from the list.

"A widow," Clinton answered. "She lives in a ramshackle farmhouse on the east side of the county. Milton bought the farm after her husband died, but she still lives in the house."

"She colored?"

"Naw, white woman."

"Why do you think Conway would want her to testify?" Victor asked.

"I have no idea," Clinton replied, puzzled.

"Delphi Hobart?"

"Another widow. Milton bought their land after her husband died. Don't know her very well. She rarely comes to church and kinda keeps to herself."

"She white too?"

"Yeah."

"Hmm," Victor murmured. "Well, Sheriff, I appreciate your time."

Clinton watched him turn and then broke into a smile. *Funny,* he thought, shaking his head, *you choke someone just a little bit and their tune will change.* Victor opened the door and ran into Milton Marion, bearing the brunt of the collision. Milton glared at the DA as though he had done something terribly wrong. As Victor scuttled away, Clinton braced himself for the coming onslaught.

"Clinton," Marion began, "my foreman at the mill said he hasn't seen Eugene for a while. He hasn't shown up for work or anything."

"Eugene who?" Clinton bluffed, pretending not to know the man.

"Eugene Bryan! You know who he is, that scrappy fellow who works for me," Milton said.

"Oh yeah, the one with the long, greasy hair. You say he's missing?"

"That's what I said, Clinton!" Milton snapped, his face tingeing a darker red. "What do you intend to do about it?"

"I'll fill out the paperwork and get Meeker to start asking around, but you know how these young guys are. He might have just taken off or could have gotten drunk and fell into the river and drowned."

"Find him, damn it! He owes me money, and I want it back!"

"I'll see what I can do," Clinton replied.

"You and Turlock got this trial nailed down?" Milton asked, changing tact and narrowing his eyes.

"We're working on it."

"You better," Marion threatened, then spun and left as abruptly as he entered.

*****

146

Each night, the same routine occurred as Clinton returned home. Sam would leap into his arms, desperate to escape Ruth's hatred. "I'll be glad when this trial is over," Ruth spat while Sam hugged Clinton's neck tightly. "And Daddy and Mama can take possession of this brat!" Clinton didn't offer an argument, because nothing he could say would change her feelings.

Clinton and Sam shared a cold dinner of fried chicken and potato salad while waiting for Ruth to settle for the night. He would wait until midnight if necessary just to spend a few more minutes in Sara's presence.

"Are you my daddy?" Sam asked later as they strolled to the jail.

Clinton was taken back, then realized it was an innocent inquiry that any little boy in his position might ask. "No," he replied gently. "I'm not your daddy. I'm just taking care of you for a while."

"If you're not, who is?"

Clinton's throat grew tight. "Why don't we wait a few years before I answer that question?" he stalled, not knowing what else to do.

"Can my mama tell me?"

The sheer innocence of the child was overwhelming, and the last thing Clinton wanted was to burden Sara. "How old are you, Sam?" Five little fingers were held up. "Five, huh? Tell you what, if you'll wait till you're seven," Clinton said, holding up seven of his own fingers, "I'll tell you then."

"That's a long time."

"It seems so, but it's really not."

"Why can't Mama tell me?" Sam asked while rubbing his left eye.

"She can, son, but right now, your mama has a lot on her mind. That's why we need to wait, okay?"

"Okay," Sam agreed, seemingly satisfied for the moment.

As they started walking again, Clinton asked, "Who's been teaching you your numbers?"

"Jessie."

The two entered the jail and found a familiar scene—Uncle Hiram and Johnson locked in battle over the checkerboard while

Sara sat reading a book. Normally, Clinton left to find something to do in his office; but tonight, he decided to watch the checker game, hoping to eavesdrop on Sam and Sara's conversation. He prayed the child wouldn't ask about his father. After a few minutes, Clinton relaxed. Sam seemed to be content to sit in his mother's lap and be held.

Clinton stole a glance and saw Sara kissing her son on the forehead. "Sheriff," Sara called gently from her cell. He exhaled a low breath, relieved that she hadn't caught him watching her. "You think you can get Sam's hair cut? It's getting mighty long."

"I'll get Jessie to carry him tomorrow, Sara," Clinton answered. "Sorry. I should have already taken care of it."

Sara stood and walked out of the cell, carrying Sam on her small hip. Uncle Hiram stretched out his arms. "Come here, boy, and sit with Uncle Hiram. See if you can help me whip old Johnson." Sam crawled into Uncle Hiram's lap as the deputy reset the game.

Clinton fidgeted nervously, wondering if he should stay or go. Finally, he found the courage to turn toward Sara and steal another glance. He felt his adrenaline drop. She caught him looking, and her green eyes locked onto his.

"Thank you, Sheriff, for getting us better food," she said.

"Yeah, Sheriff," Johnson said, diverting his attention. "Pearly has spread it all over the county how you beat the hell out of Blackstone. Sorry, Ms. Sara," he quickly apologized.

"It's all right, Johnson," she replied lightly. "Sheriff, you did that for us?"

The question put Clinton on the spot because she was the true motivation. "Sara," he stammered nervously, "he's been shorting the county for years. Just sending him a message."

"You better watch him, Sheriff," Uncle Hiram piped. "He's a mean one, and he'd as soon cut you as to look at you."

"Yeah, Sheriff," Johnson added. "Next time, shoot him, and maybe he'll die before reproducing and bringing more meanness into this world."

Clinton then realized that being here with this beautiful woman and her child, a drunken deputy and medicine man, and bootlegger and murderer was the closest thing to happiness he had experienced in a long while. He stole one more glance at Sara and found her staring at Sam with moist eyes and a trembling lip. Not being able to stand the havoc he created, he said, "Uncle Hiram, need to talk to you after you finish this game."

"I'll be through in a minute, Sheriff. Won't take long to beat old Johnson."

It might have relieved a tiny part of Clinton's guilt if he had only known Sara's thoughts. She had given up on any hope of Mr. Ewell being able to wrestle control of Sam away from Milton Marion, but in its place, she prayed with a new hope. The sheriff seemed to care so much for her child, and she was trying to find the courage to ask him for the greatest favor.

Chapter 21

Clinton yawned deeply. He was exhausted from his late return from Montgomery the previous night. *It was worth it,* he thought as several wagons rolled by the courthouse. Two days prior, he had observed the process of jury selection. Some satisfaction came from having Roger Ellis seated, but the other eleven men were farmers, which meant they were all beholden to Milton Marion.

Clinton watched as Ronnie crossed the street, returning from the courthouse. "It's already full, Sheriff," he announced. "Even the nigger balcony."

"With whites?" Clinton asked, yawning again.

"Yeah, Sheriff, except Uncle Hiram's boy, Johnny. The rest of them stayed away for some reason."

"They already know how it's going to turn out," Clinton guessed. "There's a lot of respect for Uncle Hiram in the settlement but some envy too."

"There are a lot of whites that feel the same way," Ronnie said in a surprising moment of clarity. "They're jealous of him owning land while they have to sharecrop with your daddy-in-law."

Clinton nodded in agreement. He fished his pocket watch out. "It's time. Go get Uncle Hiram and the girl." Meeker returned a few minutes later with Uncle Hiram and Sara bound. "Take those handcuffs off," Clinton sharply commanded.

"Just following procedures, Sheriff," Ronnie replied, trying to excuse his actions. He quickly tried to unlock Sara's handcuffs, but he dropped the key twice in the process.

"Let me have it," Clinton demanded, wanting to wring the deputy's neck. His hand touched Sara's as he unlocked the cuffs, causing a jolt to run through his body.

"Thanks, Sheriff," Sara murmured while rubbing her wrists.

Clinton was lost for a second when he saw how her red hair clashed against the blue sky. Her cotton dress was white and simple, fitting snugly against her thin body. He couldn't help but admire how proud she held her shoulders and knew that in another place, she would be the belle of any church social.

Uncle Hiram grinned as Clinton removed his cuffs and took a moment to straighten the old man's gray tie. "Let's go," he said, leading the two across the street.

*****

Conway Moon waited at the defense table as Clinton ushered Sara and Uncle Hiram up the aisle of the packed courtroom. All three felt the stares as Conway boomed, "Sara!" and then hugged her tightly. Clinton felt a twinge of jealousy over the embrace. Conway released her and then shook Uncle Hiram's hand. He leaned in close and whispered to Clinton, "Don't take it personally. You know I have to come after you."

"I understand."

Clinton slowly checked the courtroom and noticed that Milton Marion was missing. *He's pretending not to care,* he thought. But then he spotted Granby Galesburg, one of Milton's bank clerks, wearing overalls as if his pale-white face wouldn't stand out among the weather-beaten crowd. *He might as well be naked,* he thought, taking his usual seat, a lone wooden chair directly parallel to the prosecutor's table.

The clock on the wall ticked, showing one minute to nine. The judge's chamber opened, and Fred, with the judge following, walked into the courtroom. "All rise for the Honorable Winston Dillon

Beech," bellowed Fred. Clinton gave Fred credit. His strong voice demanded compliance. Chairs squeaked, shoes hit the floor, and many cleared their throats as they stood.

"You may be seated," said Judge Beech. "Read the charges, Fred."

"The state of Alabama…"

Clinton's mind drifted from Fred's words to the judge. He could see several new age spots on his face. The black robe hung loose, and he looked older and more disheveled this morning. His brown eyes were fatigued, and several strands of his thinning hair were out of place and hanging over his forehead.

Judge Beech banged his gavel as Fred finished the charges. "Victor, your opening statement," he ordered without looking at the DA.

Victor rose from his chair and walked slowly to the jury box. "Gentlemen of the jury," he started.

Clinton drifted away from Victor's words and looked at Sara. Her hair hung loosely over her shoulders, and she sat stiffly as if recording the DA's words.

"You'll see that the state's case is overwhelming," Victor delivered in his usual monotone. "And as you hear the testimony, it will be clear that the two defendants are guilty." Victor then leaned on the fact that Uncle Hiram was a Negro and that Sara, being white, saw no better than to be in business with him.

Several times, Clinton thought Victor was winding down, only to hear his tone change and reiterate several points he already covered. Clinton glanced at the judge and saw his old face sink into a scowl until the DA finished. Judge Beech took two fingers and adjusted his glasses. "Conway, you want to make an opening statement?"

The lawyer stood as if he was unaware of the proceedings and boomed loudly enough to wake all sleeping babies. "No, Your Honor." Victor turned to Conway in surprise, but the lawyer paid no attention to the DA.

"Victor," Judge Beech said, "call your first witness."

Victor stood. "The state calls Sheriff Clinton Barnes." Clinton walked to the stand and said, "I do," after Fred administered the oath. He sat down and looked at Victor. "Sheriff, how long have you been in office?" Clinton answered. "What made you think the defendant, Hiram Macarthur," Victor asked, pointing at Uncle Hiram, "was making illegal whiskey and selling it?"

"Several reasons," Clinton lied. "There were rumors, and sometimes, that's all we have. But a tip from Seth Walker, an agent from the State Revenue Department, was the main reason I started following him."

"Why did the investigation fall into your hands instead of Mr. Walker's?" Victor asked, playing to the jury.

"Whenever Seth or any of the agents arrive, it doesn't take long for people to get the word out. He thought I'd stand a better chance of catching Hiram than he would." Clinton looked at Uncle Hiram, and his wise old face didn't seem the least bit bothered.

"Now, Sheriff, lead us through the investigation and how you caught the defendants." Clinton took several notes from his shirt pocket and carried the courtroom through the process. "And where did you store the evidence?" Victor asked.

"We, meaning me and Ronnie Meeker with the help of Mr. Ewell and his son, Danny, moved everything out of the cave and into the county warehouse."

"Tell us the exact contents, Sheriff," Victor said. Clinton gave an account of how many glass bottles there were, never saying they were full of whiskey. That caused Victor to frown. Then he told of the still, wood, mash, sugar, and the rest. "And what happened to the evidence, Sheriff?"

It was obvious to Clinton that Victor was trying to convince the jury early on that they didn't need physical evidence to convict. "It was destroyed in a fire."

"It burned, you say? Who do you think set the warehouse fire?"

The inflammatory question sailed across the courtroom. Judge Beech and Clinton both expected an objection, but Conway just leaned back in his chair. "I don't know," Clinton answered evenly. "It's still an ongoing investigation."

"Was anything left after the fire, Sheriff?" Victor asked, irritated. He and most of the courtroom expected the sheriff to openly name Johnny.

"The still."

"I would like to show the still to the jury, Your Honor," Victor stated.

"Bring it in, Fred," Judge Beech mumbled. Awkwardly, Fred and Meeker paraded the flattened piece of metal in front of the jury. One of them, Saginaw Austin, snickered out loud, and the rest gave it a short look.

"Thank you, Fred, Ronnie. That's all I needed," Victor said. Clinton arched his back and caught sight of Sara's eyes, finding them fearful. He swallowed a hard knot of remorse. "That's all I have for this witness, Your Honor," Victor said.

"Conway," Judge Beech called.

Clinton's adrenaline rose as Conway pushed back from the table. As he walked slowly to the witness chair, he raked his huge fingers through his long hair. "Sheriff, this won't take too long." The friendly tone of the statement didn't put Clinton at ease. "Sheriff, you testified that you removed forty-two bottles from the cave."

"That's correct."

Conway laid his large paws on the waist-high banister that separated the lawyer from the witness. "And out of the forty-two bottles, how many did you send for testing?" His voice carried no fire and was so low that several jurors leaned forward in an effort to hear.

"None."

"So you removed forty-two bottles of clear liquid, assuming they were full of whiskey, but you didn't send a single one to be tested?" Conway asked, raising his voice an octave.

"Correct."

"Why not?"

"Didn't see any need," Clinton remarked evenly.

"Did you taste any to try and make a determination on what the bottles contained?"

Clinton knew no lawyer worth his salt would ask a question he didn't already know the answer to. He smiled slightly because Conway had asked him a few days earlier. "No, sir," he lied.

"Did you instruct your deputy to determine what was in the bottles?" Conway asked, locking eyes with Clinton.

"No, sir." Clinton felt his face burning. *Must be from Victor's blistering look,* he thought.

"So you removed the bottles," Conway boomed, releasing the railing and turning to the jury, "and just assumed it was whiskey?" The word *assumed* echoed around the courthouse.

"The cave held a still with a fire burning under it, so it was an easy assumption," Clinton answered.

"But you didn't test it?" Conway asked again loudly, facing the jury.

"Objection, Your Honor!" Victor sang. "The sheriff has answered the question three times and—"

"Withdrawn," Conway replied, unruffled. "Sheriff," he said, turning back to Clinton, "let's suppose you came to my house and I had forty-two bottles of clear liquid sitting on my kitchen table. Would you arrest me for bootlegging?"

"If you had a still going in your living room, I would."

The answer brought a round of laughter from the gallery. Judge Beech raised his gavel, but he stopped in midair as the spectators settled. Conway turned back to Clinton, his face like stone but his eyes amused. Clinton knew there was something coming. He could smell it.

"But would you check the contents of the still, Sheriff, to make sure it was whiskey I was making?"

"Objection," Victor called, jumping to his feet. "I don't see where Conway is going with this."

"Both of you approach the bench," Judge Beech commanded. As he leaned forward, the worn old glasses slipped down his nose.

"Your Honor," Victor said, "I object to this line of questioning, and the counselor knows better than this. Any fool in his right mind, if presented with a still and a burning fire, would naturally know that whiskey is being made."

"And any idiot knows that you should test evidence," Conway tersely replied. "Your damn problem, Victor, is you've had too many easy juries."

"But—"

Victor was interrupted not by Conway but by Judge Beech. "Overruled, Victor," he said, stunning the DA.

Having never won an argument in front of the judge before, Conway's adrenaline surged. He walked to the witness chair and, once again, gripped the railing. "Sheriff, let's talk about the still that you stored in the warehouse. Did you mark it in any way?" Conway asked.

"What do you mean?" Clinton asked. He stole a glance at the clock. He had been on the stand for an hour.

"To be clear, did you put any identifying mark on the still?"

"No," Clinton answered. *It was something I should have done, but I'm glad I didn't.*

"Then how do you know that piece of metal, which the DA so proudly paraded before the jury, is actually a still? And if it is, how do you know it's the one you brought out of the cave?"

"I don't," Clinton admitted. A slight murmur rumbled as Victor fixed Clinton with an angry glare. Conway eased away and faced the jury before asking his next question. "Sheriff, you were raised on a farm, weren't you?" he asked, letting his bass voice carry the distance. The unusual question caught Clinton by surprise.

"Yes, sir, I was," Clinton answered, wondering what he was up to.

"Ever raise any hogs, Sheriff?"

Victor's eyebrows furled, and he leaped to his feet. "Objection, Your Honor. This question has no relevance!"

"Overruled," Judge Beech said. The DA looked at the old man in disbelief. "You heard me, Victor. Overruled," Judge Beech repeated, shooting Victor a hard glare. Clinton looked at Conway, who remained expressionless. "Answer the question, Sheriff," Judge Beech directed.

"Yes, I've raised hogs."

"Does Hiram have hogs, Sheriff?"

"Yes, sir," Clinton answered, now knowing where the lawyer was headed. The whole idea was ludicrous because no one would carry feed that far to cook it down.

"So, Sheriff, is it possible that they were making hog feed that night?" Victor never made it out of a crouch before Judge Beech fixed him with a steely look.

"Not likely," Clinton answered, letting a smile slip. "But it could be possible. I've found, as sheriff, that not all people think or act alike."

"Have you ever seen Hiram's hogs?" Conway asked.

"Yes," Clinton said, careful not to let another smile slip.

"And what is their condition?" Conway asked.

"They are the fattest I've ever seen." Uncle Hiram could fatten a hog to the point that the flesh overlapped its eyes and blinded the animal, and the whole county knew it; most were envious.

As quickly as winter passes in the South, Conway changed tact and hurled the next question across the courtroom. "Sheriff, how long have you been married?"

"Objection, Your Honor! The sheriff's marital status has no bearing!"

Conway looked at Judge Beech. "If you'll allow me a little longer, Judge, I think you'll see the importance."

"You're overruled, Victor," Judge Beech said. Another murmur trickled from the crowd. The DA looked as though someone had slapped him and the handprint was still fresh on his cheek. "Answer the question, Sheriff," Judge Beech commanded. Clinton answered.

"And who is your father-in-law?" Conway boomed.

"Milton Marion."

"Sheriff, I want you to answer this next question to the best of your knowledge." Victor seethed while Clinton braced for the worst. "Who is the father of Sam, my defendant's child?"

"Objection!" Victor screamed in anguish. "Your Honor, the paternity of the child has nothing—"

"Overruled, Victor."

"Your Honor, this is all immaterial and has no bearing on the case!" Victor pushed.

"Both of you approach the bench," the judge ordered impatiently.

Victor reached and clasped the edge of Judge Beech's bench and pleaded as if his life depended on winning the point. "Judge, the father of the defendant's child has no relevance!"

"You're overruled, Victor," said Judge Beech.

"Judge—"

Fierceness sprang from Judge Beech. "Victor, when you sit on this bench, you can make the decisions," he spat through tight, thin lips. "But until then, this is my courtroom!"

"Judge…" Victor groveled as Milton's Marion's words rang in his ears: "You little jackass, don't you dare allow what happened between my boy and that tramp to be dragged into this," he had grunted between clenched teeth. "I'll see to it that you never have a chance in hell of replacing Beech when he retires."

"One more word, Counselor," the judge said, pointing a bony finger, "and you'll be spending the night over at the jail. You understand me?"

Clinton couldn't hear everything, but he caught enough snatches of the tense conversation to know Victor's family jewels were firmly in the judge's hand. He shot a quick look at Uncle Hiram, whose face remained mute. Conway walked to the railing.

"Sheriff, who is the father of my defendant's child?"

Clinton looked at the judge. "Answer the question, Sheriff," he said.

"I can only give you my guess," Clinton said, wondering how Sara would take what he had to say.

"Tell me, Sheriff."

"Her brother was convicted for beating Trace Marion to death, and I can surmise that he was the father."

Judge Beech banged his gavel many times before he brought the courtroom to order. Everyone in the county already knew, but to hear it in open court titillated the crowd as if the preacher had just run off with the piano player.

"Sheriff," Conway asked, rattling the windows, "isn't it true that you set up my two clients at the bidding of Milton Marion so that he could take his grandson?"

"No," Clinton lied, focusing on thoughts of his mother and feeling like the worst kind of coward.

"Hasn't he wanted custody of his grandson for years?"

"I can't answer that. You'll have to ask him," Clinton said defensively.

"If not, why did you take the child to Milton Marion's home instead of following the proper course of turning him over to Martha Reid?"

"I thought he'd be better cared for there," Clinton replied stiffly.

With that fact established for the jury, Conway changed direction. "So just in a normal day of duty, you suddenly decided to start following Hiram?"

"Yes," Clinton answered.

"After all these years, it just struck you to pursue him?"

"Yes."

"I find that hard to believe, Sheriff," Conway said, his voice full of contempt and disgust. "I'm through with this witness, Your Honor."

Clinton stood, but before he could step down, Victor said, "Judge, I have a few more questions." He eased back down in the chair and looked at Victor. His eyes glowed with anger, and both of his fists were knuckles first on the desk. Bulging veins caused stripes of red and blue to crease his forehead, making Clinton wonder if they were going to burst. "Sheriff," he asked sharply, "are you charged with upholding the laws of the state of Alabama?"

"Yes."

"And, Sheriff," he said shrilly, "do the statutes include pursuing and catching bootleggers?"

"Yes."

"That will be all, Your Honor," Victor said. As Clinton stepped down, Victor asked, "May I approach the bench?"

"Conway," Judge Beech said, waving both lawyers forward.

"Judge," Victor asked, "I need at least a twenty-four-hour recess to analyze the new revelations of this case."

"Why so?" Judge Beech asked indifferently.

Victor was exasperated. "The state is not prepared for the direction the trial has taken. I could not have imagined the paternity of a child would—"

"I'm prepared, Judge," Conway interrupted and offered cheerfully.

Judge Beech shot Victor a killing look. "I've already ruled on that issue, Victor," he answered. After glancing at the clock, he said, "It's a quarter to twelve. Who do you have next?"

"Meeker," Victor said, frowning tightly.

"Can you get it done quickly?" Judge Beech asked, his stomach rumbling loudly.

"Yes."

"Then put him on, and then we'll break for lunch," he said.

Victor turned away from the bench and said loudly, "Your Honor, I call Deputy Ronnie Meeker." Clinton sighed openly as Meeker walked confidently to the stand, wearing a cocksure smile. Victor started his questions, assuming that the jury needed to hear the same testimony on the evidence again. Several of the men shifted in their seats, becoming worn from the repetition.

"Deputy Meeker, was all of the evidence destroyed in the fire?" Victor asked, smirking.

"No, sir," Ronnie Meeker answered. Seeing Conway on the rise, he quickly added, "I was afraid something like the fire would happen, so I—"

"Objection, Your Honor!" Conway shouted, loud enough for half the county to hear. Clinton shot a killing look at Meeker and cursed under his breath. "I wasn't told of this in discovery!" Conway hollered.

"Your Honor, I only found out myself this morning," Victor said, putting on his most innocent face.

"That's a lie, and you know it," Conway shot.

"Judge—"

"Both of you, approach the bench," Judge Beech ordered, his face veiled in thin patience. He glared down at Victor. "I won't allow this to go any further. You know what the law requires!"

"But, Judge," Victor pleaded, "I just found out this—"

"Bullshit!" Conway boomed, making no attempt to keep the conversation private.

The judge pointed his bony finger at the lawyer. "Watch your language, Counselor! There are ladies in this courtroom, and if you curse one more time where they can hear you, I'll hold you in contempt!" Now glaring at Victor, he sternly said, "It's disallowed. Move on to something else."

"Your Honor, I—"

"One more word, Victor," Judge Beech shot angrily, "and you'll find yourself taking dinner with the defendants."

Clinton looked at Uncle Hiram, wondering how the old man had gotten to the judge. Uncle Hiram met his gaze and winked unabashedly.

Victor looked at his witness and shrugged. "I'm through with this witness, Your Honor."

"Conway, your witness," Judge Beech said.

"No questions."

Judge Beech wasted no time banging his gavel. "The court will adjourn until one o'clock."

"All rise," bellowed Fred.

*****

Clinton led Uncle Hiram and Sara across the street with Ronnie following sheepishly. "Meeker!" Clinton called over his shoulder, never breaking stride. "Go to Blackstone's and get food for Uncle Hiram and Sara. Get something for me, you, and Fred also, and put it on the county's tab."

When he returned, Meeker found Clinton sitting outside the cells with Uncle Hiram and Sara. Quickly and quietly, he set the stacked trays of food down, removed his and Fred's, and then scuttled outside. Fred sat on the steps of the jail, smoking and watching the spectators on the courthouse lawn unpacking baskets of food.

"Here's your lunch, Fred," Meeker said, setting the tray beside his coworker. He plopped down on the wooden stoop and began to eat.

161

Fred flipped the cigarette away and scornfully said, "Meeker, you are about as dumb a man as I've ever known."

"Why you say that, Fred?" Meeker asked, his mouth full of cornbread.

"'Cause," Fred answered, "you don't do that to a man you work for. You made the sheriff look foolish by saying you thought something might happen and sitting up on that stand all full of yourself."

"I was just trying to help," Ronnie mumbled defensively.

"Yeah," Fred said. "The other day, when your wife stopped the sheriff and said, 'I wish Ronnie didn't have to work so many nights,' the sheriff didn't blink an eye. He just replied, 'I'm sorry, Mrs. Meeker, but I sure appreciate how hard Ronnie works.' All the while, you're tiptoeing around with that other gal. He could have thrown your sorry ass out in the cold, but he didn't."

"How'd he find out? You are the only one supposed to know so you could cover—"

"He ain't dumb, Meeker! If your wife is telling him you ain't home, then he knows that you are up to something."

"Damn," Ronnie muttered, thinking about that possibility.

"Yeah, I know," Fred said with disgust. "Mr. Marion done whispered in your ear, making promises. He's using you, and when he's through, you'll be out in the cold." Silence fell as Fred picked up his tray and began to eat. Ronnie pushed his away, his appetite gone.

*****

Clinton glanced at his watch, intending to do some paperwork before heading back to the courthouse. "Roxboro Sheriff's Department," he said after the phone interrupted his plans.

"I know what's going on," Milton Marion's enraged voice shouted in his ear. "You're trying to help her get acquitted and—"

"I did what you wanted," Clinton interrupted through gritted teeth. "You should be satisfied!"

"Damn you—"

Clinton slammed the receiver back into the cradle and muttered a vile curse.

*****

"Victor, call your next witness," Judge Beech said.

"Yes, Your Honor," Victor replied.

As Victor called Mr. Ewell to the stand, Clinton counted the remaining witnesses and determined it wasn't possible to finish the trial today. He gained Ronnie's attention and waved him over. As the deputy leaned down so Clinton could whisper in his ear, he had to resist the urge to choke him.

"Go to the hotel and get six rooms for the jury. There's no way we'll finish today."

"Six rooms?"

"Yeah. They'll have to share." Ronnie spun on his heels, suddenly wanting to please his boss.

Mr. Ewell sat stiffly in the wooden chair, casting a menacing look toward the DA. Victor covered the same ground again with him, causing several jurors to yawn deeply. Clinton knew that in most counties, this case wouldn't have come to trial after the evidence was destroyed. He had done a poor job and was grateful for doing so. After stealing a look at Sara, who was strangely focused on Mr. Ewell, he swallowed hard.

"Your witness, Conway," Judge Beech said.

Conway stood, removed his coat, and hung it on the back of his chair. "Mr. Ewell," he asked, "did you know about the cave before the night of the arrest?"

"Yes, sir, Mr. Moon," Mr. Ewell lied convincingly. "Hiram has been mixing hog feed down there for years." Victor's body recoiled, and the audience murmured loudly.

"That's all I needed, Mr. Ewell. I'm through, Your Honor," Conway said as Billie Ewell stood.

"Judge Beech," Victor said, jumping to his feet, "I have a few more questions for this witness." The judge motioned for Victor to continue, and Mr. Ewell sat back down. The DA eyed the man warily.

163

He was on such strange ground, having a prosecution witness turning to the defense. He sucked in a deep breath and bore down in full attack mode, but little good it did him. Mr. Ewell stuck to his story, not letting the DA shake him. Victor questioned him from several different angles, trying desperately to prove that the farmer was lying.

"Yes, sir, Mr. Turlock, I knew about the cave," Billie Ewell proclaimed. "Uncle Hiram has been mixing hog feed down there ever since I can remember. And no, Mr. Turlock, I don't think it's strange that Sara and Uncle Hiram were there at night."

Clinton, the jury, and the entire courtroom knew that Mr. Ewell's story was thin, but the side effect made Victor sound defensive.

"I'm finished with the witness, Your Honor," Victor said tersely.

"Conway," the judge asked, "any more questions from you?"

"Yes, Your Honor," Conway said, delivering a winning smile. "Just a few, though. I think this witness is pretty well questioned out." A slight chuckle rose from the courtroom. Judge Beech frowned but waited for it to pass. "Mr. Ewell, why were you asked to leave Roxboro Baptist Church?"

"Objection, Your Honor!" Victor screamed. "Irrelevant!"

"Judge," Conway stated calmly, "let me ask one follow-up question, and you'll see the validity."

"Overruled, Victor. You may proceed, Conway." Victor rolled his eyes and cursed under his breath.

"Why were you asked to leave the church, Mr. Ewell?"

"'Cause I took Sara and her boy in after her mother died," Mr. Ewell answered.

"And who asked you to leave?" Conway asked loudly, expecting an objection.

Mr. Ewell hesitated briefly, expecting the same, but Victor didn't rise. "Milton Marion," he said.

"That's all, Your Honor."

"Victor?" the judge asked.

"No more questions, Your Honor."

Clinton guessed by the look on the DA's face that he was thinking about calling Danny to the stand. He also knew that Victor would assume the two had practiced their stories and that nothing could be gained.

"The state rests, Your Honor," Victor added after a few more seconds.

"Conway," the judge called.

"Your Honor, I call Hiram Macarthur." A slight murmur rose as Uncle Hiram eased from his seat and made his way to the witness stand. "Hiram," Conway asked while rising and pushing back his chair, "tell me why you and Sara were in the cave that night."

Uncle Hiram calmly rubbed his hand across the top of his head. "We were making up a little hog feed, Mr. Moon."

"If you will, tell the court how you make this feed."

"Well, Mr. Moon, I like to cook my corn down into mash. Then I stir in food scraps and let it sit for a while before hauling it out and feeding it to my hogs."

"Why go to so much trouble? Wouldn't it be easier to do this beside your hogpen?"

"No, sir. Some might think that, but I'm an old man. Sometimes, I think walking so much has kept me alive all these years. Also, the feed is protected from the weather and animals in the cave."

"Why was Sara helping you? I mean, why would you need help?"

Uncle Hiram shifted his weight and suddenly looked uncomfortable. "Mr. Moon, I just wanted to be nice to her."

"What do you mean, Hiram?"

"Well, sir, she had the boy to take care of, and she didn't have much work. Mr. Ewell could only use her a little in the winter. I just felt the need to make her life a little better."

It suddenly dawned on Clinton why the two other women were on the witness list. In Roxboro's society, Sara's sin of associating and being friends with a colored man was charge enough. Conway would try to mitigate that and show the jury that Sara wasn't the only one.

"Now, Hiram, you don't have to be afraid of the truth, so tell the court why you went to so much trouble to help Sara."

Calm came over Uncle Hiram as he began to speak. "Mr. Moon, if she couldn't feed the boy, then he'd be taken away. She loves her child, Mr. Moon, just like I love all mine."

Conway nodded appreciatively, and the gallery seemed to agree. "Why did y'all work at night?" he asked, leading Uncle Hiram down the script.

"Mr. Moon, I always kept the cave a secret from most folks."

"Why's that, Hiram?"

"Well, sir, if children knew about it, they would play there and wouldn't know to read the signs if the water was to rise. They could get trapped and drown."

"How's that?" Conway asked as Victor furiously scribbled notes.

"If it rains real hard upstream, the water flows down, and the river rises really fast. Children wouldn't understand how quickly water could fill the cave."

"Why work at night, then?" Conway asked. "Couldn't you get trapped?"

"No, sir," Uncle Hiram said easily. "The old rock pool, when it spills over the top, it's time to start leaving."

The day after jury selection, Judge Beech had allowed Victor to take the jury to see the cave so they could visualize the upcoming testimony.

"But why did you ask Sara to work at night, Hiram?" Conway prompted.

"So these folks," Uncle Hiram said, "wouldn't see her working with an old nigger. With all her troubles, I didn't want to cause her more."

Conway turned to the jury. "What was in the bottles, Hiram?"

"It's a special concoction. Wish they'd taken a little taste," Uncle Hiram said, giving the jury a mischievous grin. "Can't tell you, Mr. Moon, what all the ingredients are, because then I might not have the fattest hogs."

"Well, how about a simple overview?" Conway asked.

"It's got a little mineral oil in it, along with some wheat germ and a few other things. Now, Mr. Moon, I'd be lying if I claimed it didn't have a spot of mash in it because it does. But if you took a taste, it'd give you a case of the green apple quickstep that you wouldn't forget." Judge Beech reached for his gavel but allowed the crowd to laugh a moment before he banged it against the bench.

"Thank you, Hiram," Conway said. "Judge Beech, I'm finished with this witness."

"Victor?" Judge Beech said.

Victor walked close to the witness stand and said, "Now, Hiram, you stated several things that I'd like to address. You want this court to believe that to fatten your hogs, you haul corn all the way to the river and then mix the feed up in a cave? If that is so, why does it take sugar? That was part of the inventory."

"I said, Mr. Turlock, there's a bit of sour mash mixed in my feed."

"So you admit you were down there making whiskey?" Victor asked with a raised voice.

"No, sir, Mr. Turlock. I said we were making hog feed."

"And, Hiram, you've kept this cave a secret all these years just out of your concern for the children? That's mighty noble of you," Victor said sarcastically.

"Yes, sir, Mr. Turlock. My boy Johnny is named after my little brother who drowned in that cave."

A small murmur made its way across the courtroom. Victor had already been embarrassed too many times today, and his cheeks flushed, and his anger boiled. "So," he said, gripping the wooden banister, "you want the jury to believe that with all the ingredients to make whiskey, the two of you were just making feed?"

"Yes, sir," Uncle Hiram answered, unmoved and unshaken.

"And out of the goodness of your heart, you gave Sara work?"

Clinton sat up straighter knowing this was the only significant thing Victor could use: the division of the races. Most of the county would agree with Victor. In their eyes, Sara should lose her child before associating with a Negro man. *Still,* Clinton thought, *Victor has got to know what the two other witnesses are waiting to do. Surely, he's that smart.*

"Wasn't there something else, Hiram, for a nigger like you to show such kindness to a young white woman?" Victor asked, seething.

Son of a bitch! Clinton wanted to scream. Even he hadn't considered that Turlock would stoop this low.

"No, sir," Uncle Hiram responded before Conway could object. "I know what you're trying to say. I'm too old, Mr. Turlock," he shouted for all to hear. "My thing ain't worked in years!" The laughter started and then took on a life of its own. Even the judge took a moment to chuckle before trying to bring order. And in the midst of all the noise, Uncle Hiram shouted, "You wait and see, Mr. Turlock. One day, the sap won't rise for you!" Laughing and slapping his old knee, he finished, "Be like pushing a chain!"

"Order!" Judge Beech said, banging the wooden gavel. "Order in this court!" Slowly, the laughter died down.

Quite a quandary, eh, Victor? If you stop now, you'll lose face, and the crowd at Blackstone's will wear you out, Clinton thought. Uncle Hiram remained perched, smiling brightly, ready for battle again.

"I need just a moment, Your Honor," Victor said. Judge Beech granted the request, then sat back in his chair. The DA conferred with Troy Prince, his assistant, for a few moments before turning back to the judge. "That'll be all for this witness, Your Honor."

You were counting on that dark suggestion working, you little bastard, Clinton thought. *You don't have anywhere else to go.*

Judge Beech took it in stride. "Conway, any redirect?"

"No, Your Honor."

"Call your next witness, then," Judge Beech said.

Several people stood so Alva Siler could make her way to the witness stand. Her old, worn, printed dress looked as though it was more suited for dusting than wearing. Everyone rightly assumed it was the best she owned. She sat nervously on the edge of the seat, clutching a worn cloth purse. One long braid trailed down her back, keeping her gray hair neatly in place. The sight would be more pitiful if the county didn't hold so many who looked the same.

"Mrs. Siler," Conway asked with a gentle tone, "where do you live?"

"At the end of County Road 21," she answered timidly.

"And how did you come to reside there?" he asked.

"The eighty acres were passed on to my husband from his family," she answered.

"How long have you lived there?"

"Thirty-one years," Alva answered with a spot of pride.

"Are you married?" Conway gently probed.

"No, sir. I'm a widow," she replied wistfully. "My husband, Lewis, passed six years ago."

"How did he die, Mrs. Siler?" Conway asked gently.

"An unbroken horse kicked him in the head."

"Any children?"

This question made her sit up a little straighter in the chair. "Yes, sir," she announced proudly, "two boys. Dilley, he's eighteen, and Wheeler, twenty."

"Do they work the farm, Mrs. Siler?"

"No, sir. The oldest one, he's down in South Florida and works the watermelon fields in season. The other one, Dilley, is in New Orleans and unloads barges and ships when he can. They're good boys, Mr. Moon," she volunteered. "Send me what they can."

"I'm sure they are, Mrs. Siler, but why don't they farm your land?"

"When my husband died"—she choked on emotion momentarily—"we had to sell the land since we couldn't pay the mortgage."

"Who owns it now?" Conway probed.

"Objection, Your Honor!" Victor said, rising. "That has no bearing on this case."

"Your Honor, the prosecutor knows Mrs. Siler is just a character witness for Hiram Macarthur. I'm only helping the jury to understand her situation."

"Overruled, Victor," Judge Beech said. "Continue," he ordered.

"Mrs. Siler?" Conway asked. "Who owns the land now?"

"Mr. Marion," she answered as though it frightened her.

"But he allows you to live in the home?"

A touch of anger crept into her pale-blue eyes before answering. "Yes, sir," she said bitterly. "He said at first I could live in the house for free till I died, seeing how he'd gotten the land. Then the next year, he told me I needed to pay a little rent."

"How much?"

"Just three dollars a month. I took in enough washing, ironing, and sewing, and between that and selling my eggs in town, I could get by." There, she stopped and wrung the top of her bag again.

"What happened the next year?" Conway asked, leading her.

"Mr. Marion doubled the rent, saying that it would set a bad example for the rest he rented to if he didn't."

"And the next year?"

"He added another three dollars a month," she answered bitterly. "He said the house was falling apart because of me and that I was living off his charity."

"What did you say in return?" Conway asked.

"I said, 'Mr. Marion, I can't pay that,'" she answered pathetically. Tears cut trails down her face, wetting the front of her worn dress. "Mr. Moon, he claimed I was no better than a squatter, and if I couldn't pay, I'd have to leave. I didn't have anywhere to go."

Clinton stifled his own emotions and looked at Sara, wondering how many times she had gone through the same thing. He then turned to the jury and saw Roger Ellis wiping his eyes with a handkerchief while several others wore scornful looks.

"What happened, Mrs. Siler?" Conway asked. "You're still living in the house."

She broke into wrenching sobs. "Uncle Hiram just showed up one night. Said he heard I was in trouble and gave me the money. And every month since then, he's helped me."

Conway hesitated a few moments, giving her time to regain a semblance of composure. Judge Beech looked away, giving the indication that she could take the time needed.

"I'm sorry, Mr. Moon," she sniffed, dabbing at her running nose.

"That's okay. Just one more question. What will you do if Hiram goes to prison?"

"I don't know, Mr. Moon, but I do know this." She turned and shouted at the jury, "There ain't a damn one of you fit to wear Uncle Hiram's boots if you convict him!"

Conway let the direct challenge echo around the courtroom. "I'm through with the witness, Judge."

"Victor?" Judge Beech asked.

"No questions, Your Honor."

Clinton resisted his need to chuckle. There was no way Victor would walk into that quicksand. Lost in her testimony, Clinton didn't realize that it was completely dark outside. He heard Judge Beech calling his name and turned toward the bench. Victor and Conway were already approaching as he stood.

"Who's left, Conway?" Judge Beech asked with tired eyes.

"Two, Judge," he answered, "Delphi Hobart and my client Sara. If you can keep Victor from being so long-winded on his closing remarks…"

Victor cast Conway a catty look. "I'm sorry your vocabulary is so limited that you can't—"

"It's a shame you weren't born a woman," Conway snapped.

"Enough," Judge Beech warned. "Clinton, it's after seven. We really need a break to let everyone eat, but that would put us after eight starting back. See if you can get rooms for the jury, and we'll hold them overnight."

The peculiar way Judge Beech addressed Clinton, using his first name, caught him by surprise. It was always Sheriff or Sheriff Barnes, and his tone was never friendly or familiar.

"Already have, Your Honor."

"Good," he said, obviously relieved. "Fred," Judge Beech said loudly.

*****

Clinton had grown weary battling Ruth about Sam and was grateful she had already settled in. He wondered if he should wake the child and take him to the jail, but as Sam's green eyes opened, all doubt was removed.

*****

171

Sam raced past the checkers game and skidded on the stone floor before making the turn into his mother's cell. She hugged him tightly, then kissed both cheeks.

Uncle Hiram looked up from his game and caught Clinton watching. "Sheriff," he said, "we had a pretty good day."

"Yeah," Clinton agreed, buoyed by Uncle Hiram's infectious smile. "I imagine Victor doesn't want to cross-examine you again."

Johnson cackled. "The DA probably feels like he's wearing women's bloomers right now."

"I hope tomorrow night to be sitting at my table," Uncle Hiram planned. "If you'll give Johnson the night off and you come too, we'll take a little sip."

"We'll do that, Uncle Hiram," Clinton replied, wondering how the old man could show such affection after what he was putting him through. "But please, let's—never mind." *What could it possibly hurt,* he thought, *for them to already think the case is won?*

Sara emerged from her cell and touched Clinton's forearm, gaining his attention. "I'm sorry Mr. Moon was so hard on you. It wasn't deserved." Before he could respond, she looked down at Uncle Hiram. "Would you let Sam play checkers with you again?"

"Sure, child," Uncle Hiram agreed, reaching for the boy. "Come here, Sam. Help old Uncle Hiram beat Johnson."

As Sam climbed on Uncle Hiram's bony knee, Sara asked, "Could we talk for a minute, Sheriff?" Clinton nodded and followed. She sat demurely on the edge of the old cot, and when he hesitated, she insisted that he sit next to her. "Sheriff, what do you think will happen?"

"Honestly, I don't know. Things went well today, but I can't lie to you. It's still a long road to acquittal." *I've done enough lying already, and for the life of me, I can't fathom not seeing you again*, he thought.

"I know this is a lot to ask," she said, swallowing her fear, "but can you try to get permanent custody of Sam if they find us guilty?"

"Sara!"

"He loves you, Sheriff," she pleaded. "I see how gentle you are with him, and he needs someone like you."

"I dunno," Clinton resisted, stunned by her request. *And to be honest, I'm perfectly flattered,* he thought.

"Sheriff," she said, clutching his arm tightly, "you're in the family. Maybe that'll satisfy Mr. Marion."

"I'll try, Sara," he promised, willing his heart to stop banging against his chest. "I'll do my best."

"Thank you, Sheriff," she said, so thankful he had agreed.

Every fiber in Clinton's body screamed for her touch, but in the end, he just stood and walked away.

Chapter 22

"Roxboro Sheriff's Department," Clinton barked into the office phone early the next morning.

"Don't you hang up on me again, you bastard," Milton Marion demanded.

"I've done my part," Clinton replied, trying to hold his anger.

"No, Clinton," Milton screamed. "You and that damn worthless Turlock will get this done. I just took a chunk out of his ass, and if that whore walks free, I'll be in Montgomery by nightfall, you son of a bitch!"

*****

Judge Beech banged his gavel, and the court came to order. "Conway," he said. Clinton wondered if the old judge went home last night or just slept in his office. *The man looks barely above the grass line,* he thought.

"Judge Beech, I call Mrs. Delphi Hobart."

Everyone watched as the blue-haired woman waddled to the stand wearing a pair of faded overalls, brown work shirt, and scuffed old boots. Clinton sank back in his chair as she took the oath. Something told him that this woman was not to be taken lightly.

"Mrs. Hobart," Conway asked after standing, "would you tell us why you agreed to testify?"

"Yes, sir. I sure will," she answered firmly. "I can tell you this right off that after my husband died, old Marion came slinking around, wanting to buy my land. I sold it, but I made him cut the house out of the deal. But Marion, he's slick. Lord, that man can steal the shortenin' out of a biscuit."

The crowd chuckled as Victor leaped to his feet. "Objection, Your Honor!"

"Sit down, you little jackass!" Delphi shouted at the DA. "You ain't no smarter than a green mule! And if you was mine, I'd take a hickory limb—"

"Judge!"

"And whop you between the ears—"

"Your Honor," Victor begged.

"To give you some manners."

Judge Beech rapped his gavel and shouted at Conway, "Counselor, control your witness!"

"Mrs. Hobart," Conway boomed, trying to get her attention.

"You, mister, ain't worth no more—"

"Ma'am," Conway hollered in an effort to drown out her voice.

"Than fish manure—"

"Mrs. Hobart," Conway screamed, now patting her fat arm.

"In the bottom of the river." Finally spent, she looked up at Conway. Even with his imposing frame, everyone waited for her to let loose on him.

"Mrs. Hobart," Conway calmly advised, "when Judge Beech speaks, you stop talking and look at me, please."

"I thought you said for me to tell the court why I was here?" Mrs. Hobart huffed.

"Yes, ma'am, but there are rules to follow. So anytime you're not sure, just look at me. Okay?"

"I don't like that feller there," she said, pointing at Victor. The crowd chuckled.

"Now, Mrs. Hobart," Conway coached, "I want you to look at the judge, and he's going to give you a few instructions."

"Ma'am," Judge Beech said, "another outburst and I'll hold you in contempt."

"What's that mean?" she asked. "I don't have that much schooling."

"It means the sheriff sitting right over there," Judge Beech explained while pointing his gavel, "will carry you to jail if you start hollering again. Understand?"

"Sure," she said, suddenly seeing the light. "If that fellow right there"—she pointed at Victor—"jumps up and interrupts me again, I'm to look at Mr. Moon for what to do."

"That's right, ma'am."

"Your Honor," Victor asked quietly, not wanting to be the object of her wrath again.

"Overruled, Victor," Judge Beech said quickly. "Mrs. Hobart, continue."

"Like I was saying, old Marion bought my land, but I kept the house. Counting my money, I figured that it'd last me another ten years, and that would hold me till I was seventy-five. But there was something I didn't know."

"What was that?" Conway asked.

"I got this letter saying I needed to pay taxes on the house. My husband had always taken care of those things, so I didn't know what to do. The next day, I went to the courthouse and talked to that fellow sitting right over there," she said, pointing at Mason Linden, the tax assessor. "He looked in this big book and said my taxes were already paid. 'Who paid them?' I asked, and he said, 'Mr. Marion did.'

"Well, Mr. Moon, I was mighty grateful and thought maybe Marion done read the passage where Jesus commands taking care of the widows and the orphans. I forgot all about it until the next year. That same fellow said Marion had paid my taxes again except this time, Uncle Hiram was standing behind me in line.

"He followed me outside and said, 'Mrs. Hobart, if Mr. Marion keeps paying your taxes every year, your house will soon be his.' I said, 'You mean he's trying to steal my house?' 'Yes'm,' he said. 'That's what he's doing.' Lord, Mr. Moon, I liked to have fainted."

"What happened next, Mrs. Hobart?"

A faint smile crossed her face, and she looked fondly at Uncle Hiram. "I asked Uncle Hiram what to do, and he said I'd better pay that man for both years. I said, 'I only got enough to pay one year with me.' Mr. Moon, he pulled the money out of his pocket and handed it to me just to help this old woman out."

"Mrs. Hobart," Conway said, "thank you so much for sharing your story."

"Glad to, Mr. Moon. Uncle Hiram, he a good man," she announced loudly.

"Ma'am," Conway said, "this other gentleman might have a few questions for you."

With an agitated look, she locked in on Victor, forgetting the judge's order. "You say me and Uncle Hiram keeping house, I'll jump off here and box your ears, you little squirt," she shouted.

Victor quickly replied, "No questions, Your Honor!" Mrs. Hobart stomped to her seat.

"Judge Beech, I call Ms. Sara Cunningham," Conway said. The crowd immediately hushed. Clinton sucked in a sharp breath as Sara walked to the witness stand. Conway started slowly with gentle questions. "How old are you? How old is your son, and what is his name?" She answered quietly and demurely.

"Sara," Conway asked, "what were you doing in the cave with Hiram that night?"

"Helping him mix hog feed," she lied.

"Not make whiskey?"

"No, sir."

"Most importantly, why did you help Hiram?" Conway asked.

"To get away from here," she said breathlessly.

"Why was it necessary to leave?"

She drew a deep breath, swelling her chest. "I didn't want my child to grow up being called a bastard like I was."

"Where did you plan to go?"

"I don't know, Mr. Moon, just someplace where people wouldn't say, 'There he is. That boy ain't got no daddy.'"

"Sara," Conway said, "I know this isn't easy, but I have to ask." She nodded her head, agreeing, as Victor pushed to the edge of his chair, ready to spring. Conway arched his heavy eyebrows. "Who is the father of your child?"

"Objection, Your Honor!" Victor said, exasperated.

"Overruled, Victor," Judge Beech replied. "The objection is duly recorded in the record."

Sara looked from Victor back to Conway. "Again, Sara, who is the father of your child?"

"Trace Marion." Judge Beech banged his gavel, but the tittering crowd dried up quickly, wanting to hear the next question.

"Were you and Trace young lovers?" Conway asked.

"No, sir," she answered.

"How, Sara," Conway asked pointedly, "did the conception take place?"

"Trace Marion raped me," she answered evenly. Victor started to rise, but Judge Beech looked him down.

"How old were you?" Conway continued, knowing some in the jury had young daughters.

"Fifteen."

"Why do you think your brother beat Trace Marion to death, Sara? For revenge?"

The mention of her brother misted Sara's eyes. "No, sir," she answered calmly even though her hands were starting to shake. "He knew that Trace would do it again if he didn't stop him."

"Did you tell your brother that Trace raped you?"

"No, sir. He found out on his own. Trace talked, not me, Mr. Moon."

"Did Mr. Marion ever come to you and say he was sorry for what his son had done?"

"No, sir."

"Not even before your brother killed Trace?"

"No, sir."

"Has he ever offered you any help?"

"No," she answered flatly.

"What contact have you had with Mr. Marion?"

"My mother rented a house from him, and he'd come to collect the rent." Clinton could see that she had impressed the jury.

He hoped that their sympathy was strong enough to overcome their financial indebtedness to Milton Marion.

"Did he treat you fairly when he came to collect?"

"No, sir. He raised the rent every year." Judge Beech let the murmur roll across the courtroom.

"Every year?" Conway repeated, wanting the jury to tie Delphi Hobart, Alva Siler, and Sara together.

"Yes, sir."

"Thank you, Sara. Judge Beech, that's all I have."

"Victor, your witness," Judge Beech said.

Victor stood, straightened his tie, and walked directly to the left of the witness box, making sure the jury could see her. "Ms. Cunningham," he started sharply, "how long did you help Hiram Macarthur in his business?"

"What business?" she replied, sidestepping the trap.

"The business in the cave."

"That wasn't a business, Mr. Turlock," she stated.

"Then how long did you help him in the cave?"

Sara weighed the question a moment, then answered, "A little over a month."

"What were you doing in there, Ms. Cunningham?" he asked.

"I'd grind the corn for him," she stated.

"That's all? He paid you to grind corn?" he asked, tilting his voice upward, indicating to the jury that she was lying.

"Yes, sir."

"Didn't you think it was strange working at night in a cave that no one else knew about?"

"Uncle Hiram is not like most people. He thinks a little differently," she answered, smiling slightly for the jury.

"So night after night, you went to a cave in the dark and ground corn?"

"That's correct."

"And all that time, you didn't think it was strange—"

"Objection," Conway boomed as he rose. "My client already answered—"

"Move on, Victor," Judge Beech quickly commanded.

179

"With all those jugs and jars in the cave, with a still sitting there, you never once thought Hiram was making whiskey?"

"I didn't see a still, Mr. Turlock," Sara lied, dodging another trap.

"You didn't see a still?" he asked incredulously. "The sheriff stated that he removed one—"

"No, sir," she interrupted. "We had a big old black pot that Uncle Hiram used to cook the corn down, but I never saw a still, and I certainly didn't see that flat piece of metal you showed to the jury."

With disgust playing across his face, he asked, "Then what did you assume was in the glass bottles? I suppose you didn't see them either?"

"I asked Uncle Hiram one time," she said easily. "And he warned me not to drink from the bottles, that it would make me sick."

Victor changed direction and shot the question across the courtroom. "How many other boys were you having relationships with when you became pregnant?"

"None," Sara answered defiantly.

"Surely, Ms. Cunningham, there were others."

"No, sir," she answered, her green eyes glowing. "In fact," she added defiantly, "there hasn't been anyone since I was raped!" Clinton felt sure she wanted to end the sentence with *jackass* or something stronger.

"Well, Ms. Cunningham," Victor said, pushing away from the stand, "if you were raped, as you claim, why is there no record of Trace Marion's arrest? There wasn't a rape, was there? Now why don't you admit that and clear your conscience?"

"Trace Marion raped me, Mr. Turlock!" Sara quickly shot. "I know damn well he did. It was my body that was being violated while his sweat dripped in my face."

Victor seemed unperturbed by her comeback. "Then why didn't you report it to the sheriff?"

"My brother said it wouldn't do any good," she retorted, determined not to show any fear.

"Your brother?" he asked, tilting his voice again. "Your brother advised you?"

"Yes."

"Not your mother?"

"She wouldn't have understood, Mr. Turlock."

"Well, while we are here," he said, strolling away, "let's talk about your mother. She raised you and your brother alone, didn't she?"

"Yes, sir."

"How did she make a living? I mean, what did she do to put food on the table?"

"I don't know."

Victor turned to the jury and cocked his head sideways. "You don't know? Surely, you have some idea. Someone had to earn money to pay the rent."

"I don't know," Sara replied defensively.

"So your mother fed and clothed you all those years without any income?" Clinton glanced at Conway, wondering why he wasn't objecting.

"No, sir," Sara said, trying to remain calm.

Clinton knew Victor was trying to taint Sara with the implication that her mother was a whore and that she was too. He shot another look at Conway, hoping he would stand and come to her aid.

"I find that hard to believe," Victor said, giving Sara a scornful look. "Tell the truth," he seethed as he bore in. "You're just like your mother, going in business with an old nigger bootlegger so you can—"

"You little bastard!" Mr. Ewell roared from the gallery. "I supported her mother all those years!" Clinton quickly moved from his chair as Mr. Ewell bowled over people, rushing toward Victor. "I'm already going to hell, and killing you ain't gonna send me no deeper!" he shouted.

Victor began to shrink while his eyes darted left and right, too scared to stay or run. Clinton met Mr. Ewell at the low swinging gate that separated the witnesses and lawyers from the crowd. Judge Beech's gavel hung suspended in midair with his mouth gaped open in surprise.

"You son of a bitch! She's my daughter!"

Clinton crashed into Mr. Ewell as he barged through the gate. "Mr. Ewell!" he shouted, wrapping the man in a bear hug.

"I'll cut you from your ass to your lips, you little bug!"

"Daddy!" Danny hollered, joining Clinton in the fray. Finally, Fred leaped in; and with him pinning one arm, Danny the other, and Clinton tightly holding Mr. Ewell, they stopped his forward progress.

Judge Beech slammed the gavel several times while shouting, "Billie Ewell, you will leave this courtroom now! And if I see your face again, I'll have the sheriff lock you up! You understand me?"

A surprising calm came over Mr. Ewell, and he looked at the judge. "I'm sorry, Judge. Ms. Sara's my daughter, and I couldn't tolerate her being talked to that way."

"I mean it, Billie," Judge Beech warned. "You go home, and don't you come back."

All eyes of the courtroom turned to Sara, and then all heads went together to process the news. Sara looked at Conway, and he smiled knowingly. Judge Beech banged his gavel, and the buzzing around the courtroom slowly died. "Victor," he said. Clinton couldn't say for sure that the DA had wet his pants, but he looked so pale that it was a possibility.

"No more questions, Your Honor," Victor submitted, now shaken and drawn.

You are nothing but a coward, Victor, Clinton thought.

Judge Beech glanced at the clock. "We will start again at one fifteen. This court is now in recess."

Chapter 23

"You may sit," the judge said while pulling his chair forward. "This court is now in session. Victor, address the jury."

"Yes, Your Honor," Victor replied while walking to the jury box. "Gentleman, this has been quite a trial," he stated. "There have been many mistruths, but you're smart men, and you understand things clearly. The defense has managed to put Milton Marion on trial instead of the defendants."

Clinton listened with one ear as Victor started his assault, leaning heavily on the fact that the jury was obligated to convict because Uncle Hiram was a Negro. Sara was also guilty by association, a white woman who should have known better.

And then the long, tedious details started, and Clinton's mind wandered. He noticed that Sara was watching the DA while Uncle Hiram concentrated on a fly buzzing around the defense table. He tuned in again and heard Victor insisting that Milton Marion's name should never have been mentioned in the trial. Clinton knew Milton was seething by now. He had watched Granby Galesburg scuttling across the street during the recess to report.

The sun disappeared as Victor droned to a close. Conway stood to begin the rebuttal, his once-booming voice now low and ringing with sincerity. "Gentlemen of the jury," he said, making eye contact with each, "the facts of this case are simple. The state has proven nothing, and there's not a shred of evidence to convict my clients. I could bore you with the details that the prosecutor repeated over and over and dispel each one, but I trust you to know better.

"If we look at this as reasonable men, it comes down to Milton Marion wanting his grandson without admitting his son brutally raped Sara. I also know that it's likely you are indebted to Milton Marion. It is easy to understand how that can affect a man. Times are difficult, money is scarce, and there's little work to be found. But I want you to think about one thing before you judge my clients.

"One day," he said, pointing to Uncle Hiram and Sara, "you could be sitting in their chairs with your life hanging on the honesty of men like yourself. What would you want from those judging you? I implore you, gentlemen. Do what's right. Send a message to Milton Marion that you are men of conscience. Let this young mother go back to her child, and let Uncle Hiram just be Uncle Hiram."

Clinton studied their expressions as Conway closed. Mr. Ellis seemed struck and was trying to hide heavy eyes. Several wore slight scowls, because their manhood had been challenged, and some stared angrily at Clinton. He hoped they would hate him enough to acquit. Most of their faces darkened as Victor rose to speak again. An hour later, he finished in dramatic fashion, demanding that they convict.

Judge Beech gave the jury their instructions and sent them off to deliberate. Later that evening, he ordered Fred to check on their progress. He soon returned and whispered to the judge that they were still working. "Get them dinner," he said. "And tell the sheriff I need to see him."

Clinton entered Judge Beech's chambers a few minutes later, finding him looking tired and tatty. "You wanted to see me?" he asked.

The old man nervously clicked his long fingernails. "Yes," he replied, leaning back in his chair. "Take the prisoners back to jail and leave them there. I'll send Fred over when the jury comes in."

*****

Clinton leaned against the brick wall of the courthouse next to Conway Moon. He dug around in his pocket for cigarettes, offered one to the lawyer, then took one for himself. Conway lit his cigarette and then spoke in a low, somber tone.

"Clinton, I've never had a case affect me this way."

"How so?" Clinton asked. "I'm sure there were other times that you were swimming upstream against Marion."

"This one is different," Conway answered wistfully. "And you should know why."

"Because of Sam?" Clinton asked, trying to avoid talking of Sara.

"Partly, but mostly because of her."

"How—"

"She's a gentle creature and beautiful in more ways than her looks."

"She's certainly a pretty girl," Clinton agreed, wishing Conway would change the subject.

"Clinton, don't try to bullshit me," he replied sternly. "You know it's more than that."

"Conway, I've never known you to be indirect. What's on your mind?"

He turned, leaning his shoulder against the wall so he could face his friend. "She deserves better than this. Even with her harsh existence from birth, she was born a lady. Most women in this town can put on the proper airs, set their table in the right order, but none can ever claim to have what she has."

"What's that?" Clinton asked.

"Class," he answered soberly.

"You sound as if you have regrets," Clinton said evenly.

"No, that's not it, my friend. I'm spoken for."

"Really? You've never mentioned that."

"In my world, Clinton, Richmond is a closed society. She's waiting for me to finish this purgatory. We don't marry for love. We marry for matching family funds. We're so damn interbred that's it's a wonder we don't have more idiots than we do."

"Who says you have to do that?" Clinton replied, feeling slightly lightheaded.

"Me," Conway admitted. "Oh, don't be so surprised," he said, seeing Clinton's expression. "If you looked at me really close, I'm much more like Marion than you realize."

"I doubt that," Clinton scoffed.

"Sheriff," Fred called from the front steps of the courthouse, interrupting the conversation.

"Yeah, Fred?" Clinton answered, walking toward the light.

"Judge Beech needs to see you."

"Okay. Be there directly." Clinton turned back to Conway. "Did you know about Mr. Ewell being Sara's father?"

"Another time," Conway replied as he ground out the cigarette.

*****

"Clinton, the jury hasn't come to a verdict yet," Judge Beech said. "Get 'em rooms again, and we'll start over at nine in the morning."

"Yes, sir," Clinton replied.

*****

It took longer than expected to get the jury settled for the night. They were tired of the process and grumbling about being away from their own work. Standing in the small living room of the hotel, Clinton glanced at his watch. "Damn," he muttered. It was one in the morning. He walked to the jail and saw that Uncle Hiram was lying on his cot, asleep, while Johnson snored lightly from his bed. Only Sara remained awake.

"Sorry, Sara," Clinton said, sitting on the edge of the cot. "By the time I got through with the jury, it was too late to bring Sam."

"It's all right," Sara replied, making Clinton feel that much guiltier. "Maybe tomorrow night, we'll be home on the river."

"Maybe so," he replied, wishing he could be optimistic. "If not, though, I'll bring him tomorrow night."

Emerald eyes found his. "Sheriff," she said sincerely, "I meant what I said. I don't blame you."

"Thank you, Sara," he replied, rising to leave before losing control. "You're being kinder than you should."

Chapter 24

The tension rose as the first hour passed with no word from the jury. The courtroom remained full, and Clinton wondered if some slept in the wooden chairs, afraid of losing their seat. Uncle Hiram slumped casually, seemingly amused by doodling, as the third hour slipped by. Sara sat rigid, elbows on the table, staring straight ahead with just an occasional nervous glance toward the jury room.

The crowd murmured as Fred walked swiftly across the courtroom and entered Judge Beech's chambers. A minute later, he bellowed, "All rise for the Honorable Winston Dillon Beech." Chairs scraped, feet shuffled, and one baby cried out as his mother lunged to her feet.

"Be seated," Judge Beech said as he banged his gavel. Clinton sucked in his breath as the jury entered the courtroom. "Would the defendants please rise," said the judge. Conway helped Sara to her feet as Uncle Hiram stood ramrod straight. "Mr. Foreman, have you reached a verdict?" asked Judge Beech.

"We have, Your Honor," Purse Williams replied. Clinton knew the man well, and it wasn't a month ago when they had shared a noontime meal. He muttered a prayer as Purse opened his mouth. "We find the defendants guilty, Your Honor."

Clinton stifled a retch as Sara's knees sagged. Conway quickly grabbed one elbow while Uncle Hiram held the other. Her face showed no emotion but a small trickle of tears. Uncle Hiram grunted and then rubbed his chin. Clinton felt sick to his stomach, and Victor added to his pain by giving him a thumbs-up.

Judge Beech banged his gavel, hushing the growing noise in the courtroom. When the spectators settled, he thanked the jury and then said to the lawyers, "Sentencing will be two weeks from today. Sheriff, you can take the prisoners back to jail."

*****

That night, Clinton huddled over his desk, finishing the paperwork for his faithful deputy to draw his pension. After stuffing the papers in an envelope, he sealed it carefully. He walked to the post office and dropped the envelope through the slot with a satisfied breath.

*****

Low clouds brought on an early night as his boots thumped across the porch. Even before opening the door, Clinton heard the sounds of Ruth struggling with Sam. "I swear, Clinton," she said scornfully, "maybe Papa should have gotten you a job at the state prison, much as you like hanging around a jail."

Clinton refused to take part in the discussion. "Has Sam eaten?"

"No," she said sharply as if she wouldn't even bother with that detail. "I waited for you to get home, and now he's all yours."

*****

After feeding and bathing Sam, Clinton dressed him in long pants, a warm shirt, and a jacket. He watched the clock and listened for Ruth to settle. At nine thirty, he and Sam quietly eased out the door and started toward the jail.

As they walked along, Clinton surveyed the street and found it empty. A hint of fog drifted in, reducing the visibility. After a side-step into the shadows, Clinton picked Sam up so their heads would be at the same level. He whispered in the child's ear.

189

"Sam, can you be really quiet for me tonight?"

"Yes, sir," Sam whispered back.

"Good. Don't make a sound." Sam nodded, agreeing that he wouldn't.

With Clinton carrying Sam, the two crept soundlessly to Milton Marion's office. Clinton set the child down and removed the screws from the hasp. He glanced around before pushing the door open. After squatting down in front of the safe, he held his breath, dialed the combination, and turned the handle. A satisfied sigh escaped as the door swung open.

Pulling a cloth sack from his beltline, he removed the large stacks of cash, closed the safe, and spun the dial, returning it to the original number. Minutes later, the two stood by the patrol car. Clinton squatted down and whispered, "Sam, can you sit in the car all by yourself and be quiet for a few more minutes?"

"I can," Sam whispered delightfully as if they were playing a wonderful game. "Are we gonna see Mama tonight?"

Clinton nodded his head and opened the door of the car. He put the sack of money on the right floorboard as Sam crawled in and sat down. After checking the area carefully, Clinton entered the jail. With long, hurried strides, he walked into the cellblock, praying that the familiar stench would never permeate his senses again. Johnson was sitting in his chair, bent over the checkerboard. He hated to treat his deputy so harshly, but if he hesitated, things wouldn't look believable.

"Evening, Sheriff," Johnson said, knowing the familiar sound of his boss's steps. Clinton's uppercut caught his right eye, knocking him off the crate and onto the stone floor. An involuntary curse of pain sprang from Johnson's lips as Clinton knelt down beside the man.

"I'm sorry," he said with deep affection. "You're a good man, Johnson. Please stay down and claim you were knocked out."

"Sheriff!" Sara cried, alarmed, as she rushed from her cell.

"Shhh, child," Uncle Hiram urged. "Let him finish."

"Sara," Clinton said as he stood, "we're leaving. Sam's in the car."

"What?"

"I'm taking y'all a long way from here. We'll figure the rest out later, but now we have to go," Clinton pleaded. He then squatted down and placed his hand on Johnson's cheek. "Johnson, in the morning, just tell the truth. Say that I was too much for you and—"

"Don't worry, Sheriff," Uncle Hiram interrupted as his face split into a grin. "I'll tell 'em ole Johnson fought like a wildcat, but you coldcocked him and locked him up with me."

Johnson's eye was already swelling shut, and Clinton hoped he hadn't caused any permanent damage. "Sheriff, I'll be a proud conspirator in this operation," Johnson said as Clinton pulled him to his feet.

As he locked Johnson in the cell with Uncle Hiram, Clinton said, "Your retirement paperwork is already sent, and it'll take about two months to process."

"Thank you, Sheriff," Johnson replied, looking through the bars. Clinton wanted to say more, but they needed to go.

"What about Uncle Hiram?" Sara asked, still in shock. "We can't leave him here." The question hung in the air for a moment.

"Yes, you can, child," the old man said, smiling as if he was sending a daughter off to be married. "They'd catch you quickly with me riding along. Go," he urged. "The sheriff will take good care of you. Don't you worry 'bout Uncle Hiram. I'll be all right."

Sara took his weathered hands. "Uncle Hiram, you're the only friend I've ever had. I'll always think of you and your kindness."

Hiram squeezed her hands tightly. "Go. Leave this place. We'll see each other again someday, just like you said." Tears welled in Sara's eyes as she followed Clinton through the jail. As their steps faded, Uncle Hiram looked at Johnson and smirked. "At least you could have remembered to bring the checkerboard. I sure hope there's better players in prison."

*****

Clinton opened the door and peered into the now thickening fog. Not seeing anyone, he led Sara to the car. She slid in next to Sam and closed the door as Clinton started walking to the driver's side. "Where are you going, Sheriff?" Blackstone said from behind.

Clinton tried spinning to his left while pulling his lead sap, but Blackstone's fist crashed into the side of his head. He lost his footing as the second blow caught his jaw. Sharp pain flooded his brain, and his vision began to blur.

"You caught me by surprise last time, Sheriff!" Blackstone raised his fist again, but Sara leaped onto his back and held on tightly with her left arm as she scratched at his eyes with her right hand. Blackstone made a quarter of a clockwise turn and backed up hard into the side of the car. Sara's breath rushed from her lungs, and she slid from his back.

In those few seconds, Clinton managed to regain his footing and struck the top of Blackstone's head viciously with the sap. He swung again with a roundhouse blow, catching the now buckling man on the right temple. Blackstone fell to the ground, unconscious. Clinton drew in sharp breaths, wondering if he had killed the man. Sara gulped in large volumes of air when her chest released. Clinton pulled her upright. "You okay?" he asked.

"Yeah," she answered, breathing raggedly. "He just knocked the wind out of me. What are we going to do?" she asked, now frightened.

"Take him with us a ways," he answered, pulling the handcuffs from his belt. Clinton secured Blackstone's hands, then gagged him tightly with his handkerchief. He opened the trunk of the car and removed a length of rope. After securely binding his legs, he and Sara dragged the man into the back seat.

"We'll find a place to drop him along the way," Clinton surmised. He started the car and crept along slowly with the lights off until they were out of sight of the last house. As they crossed the county line, his breathing returned to normal.

"You okay?" he asked Sara. "That was a hard blow."

"I'm all right, Sheriff. I'll just be a little sore."

"Well, I appreciate the help. I'm lucky I'm not lying in the dirt."

"Mama," Sam asked, wiggling closer, "where are we going?"

He had been so quiet and still that his sudden question startled Clinton. He shook his head, letting Sara know they needed to get rid of Blackstone first. She whispered into Sam's ear, "Mama will tell you later, baby."

After crossing two counties, Clinton pulled the car to the side of the road. He stepped out, opened the back door, and shone his flashlight into Blackstone's face. Clinton felt mildly relieved that those dark eyes were glaring back at him. He roughly dragged him from the car, cut the rope that bound his feet, but left his hands cuffed and his mouth gagged. As he and Sara drove away, Blackstone managed to stand and watch with blurred vision as their lights disappeared up the foggy highway.

"Why'd you do it, Sheriff?" Sara suddenly asked.

"Why did you leave with me?" he asked.

"You have everything to lose, and I have everything to gain," she said, her voice low and husky. He shrugged, hoping she'd drop the subject of his motives. Clinton was relieved when she asked the next question. "Where are we going?"

Clinton then realized that Sara couldn't read his mind. "To Montgomery to pick up my mother and her sister," he said. "We're taking them with us."

"Where after that?" she asked.

Clinton couldn't believe how scared he was, so frightened, that she wouldn't want to go along and would try to make it on her own. "Meridian, Mississippi." Suddenly his heart sank and fear welled, restricting his throat and causing his words to come out raspy and hoarse. "Sara, check the floor around your feet. There should be a cloth bag." Clinton held his breath until she located the sack.

"It's here, Sheriff," she answered, her voice full of curiosity.

"Here, take the flashlight," he said, turning the light on and handing it to her. "Look around the floor to make sure nothing spilled."

Sara did as asked. "What's in the bag?" she asked, no longer able to contain the question.

"Money." The word came out flat.

Sara's eyes grew wide as she opened the bag and peered inside. "That's a lot of cash! How?"

He tried so hard to answer coolly but couldn't. His voice cracked as if a young boy in the throes of puberty. "I stole it from Milton Marion's safe," he said. He then rushed on, finally finding the courage to give her an option. "You can have a good part of that if you want to take Sam and go your own way. I mean," he hurried, seeing her about to speak, "you don't have to stay with us." He found some relief in her next statement. Not that she directly stated her intentions, but her words gave him hope.

"Is Meridian where we'll hide?"

"No. After Meridian, we'll take a train to the Dallas–Fort Worth area. We'll stay there long enough to get new identities," he explained.

"How do we do that?"

After hearing the word *we* in her questions, Clinton relaxed and explained the process with enthusiasm. "We held a prisoner a while back for the state. Flimflam man he was. He forged checks and conned people out of their money with shady investments. You name it, he'd done it," Clinton recounted.

"He told me that when he finished cheating someone, he'd catch a train to the next large city and visit a cemetery. There, he'd find some poor soul that was close to his age and take his name. In most places with large populations, they keep much better records of births than we do. He'd go to the courthouse and get a new birth certificate and become that person until it didn't suit him anymore.

"We'll have to find a family..." Clinton stopped there, not wanting to talk about something so grim. "That's why I chose Dallas, because of its size. More chances of finding what we need."

"So we'll pretend to be man and wife?" Sara asked inquisitively.

Clinton stole a look and swore that she was needling him. "Yes," he pushed on, "but not in the strict sense. I mean, it'll be easier to fool people if we live together. Keep us from getting caught. And if that happens," he added nervously, "tell the authorities I forced you to go. Maybe they'll go easier on you."

"Don't think that'll work," she said. "Johnson and Uncle Hiram saw me fly out of there with you."

Clinton smiled briefly. "Uncle Hiram will fill Johnson in on what he needs to say before morning, and I can't think of a better person to spin that yarn." A tender laugh rolled from her lips, and Clinton enjoyed the sweet sound.

"Uncle Hiram knew what you were going to do, didn't he?"

"Yes," he admitted. "He loves you as a daughter. You know that, don't you?"

"I do," she said, suddenly saddened. "His kindness was gentle and sincere. I hate to think of him going to—"

"Try not to worry, Sara. He has a way of getting by. We need to stay focused on getting away for Sam's sake."

Thinking of Sam brightened her face. "You're right, Sheriff," she said. She leaned down and kissed Sam's cheek.

"I drove up the day before the trial and talked to my mother and aunt. They'll have everything we need for the trip."

"And your mother agreed to this plan knowing that we'd be wanted by the law?" she asked, her question tilting higher at the end.

"Both are living on little," he explained. "And neither have had anything but a poor existence."

"But you're leaving a wife to run off with a convicted bootlegger with an illegitimate child."

Clinton could understand how hard it was to conceive that any mother would understand such a situation. "She never liked Ruth anyway. Hated her would be closer to the truth. Once you meet her, it'll be easier to understand."

"Sheriff, I dreamed of finding a good husband one day. This isn't quite what I had in mind." The words stung Clinton for a moment until she started laughing. When the last chuckle melted away, Sara asked, "Is Dallas the final destination?"

"No. After Dallas, we'll move south to Corpus Christi. I thought with it being a port town, you know, more people wandering through. Besides, I've never seen the ocean." He instantly regretted his words.

"I've never been out of the county," she said wistfully. In a moment of spontaneity, Sara reached across the car and patted Clinton's shoulder gently. Overcome with emotion, she made no effort to choke back her tears. Her voice broke as she said, "Thank you for giving my boy a chance."

Chapter 25

At the old house, Sara watched as Clinton's mother and aunt packed the trunk while he refueled the car. She tried to help, but the tall, gaunt Georgia Barnes shushed her out of the way. "We ain't got time for proper introductions right now," Georgia said. "That'll come on the long ride, and I can't wait to get to know your boy," she commented, taking one hurried second to glance at the sleeping Sam.

Clinton put two more cans of gas in the trunk so they could make it to Meridian without a stop. Georgia, with her sister trailing, walked out of the house, neglecting to close the door. Clinton took the package from her hands, wiggled it into the last available space, and closed the trunk. "Let's go," he said.

Sara waited as the two older women piled into the rear seat before she took her place in the front. Clinton started the car as the last door closed, and then he pulled out of the drive. Sam grunted sleepily as Sara picked up his head and placed it in her lap. The women were silent as Clinton maneuvered the car through the streets of Montgomery. As they crossed the county line heading west, the sun peeked over the horizon, flooding the car with a shaft of light.

Clinton said, "It'll be a long sunrise with it behind us."

Georgia chimed in happily. "Damn glad it's behind us." Clinton cringed because of his mother's cursing. "Started to set fire to that old place just for fun," she said. "There wasn't much wood left. Hell, it was just termites holding hands. It would have been damn fun to watch the roaches and rats that tormented us run for their lives."

"You'll have to excuse Mother, Sara," Clinton apologized. "She curses sometimes when she's excited."

"She cusses all the time," Georgia's older sister added.

"Hush, you," Georgia shot at Beatrice. "It's time for me to see the boy," she said, sliding forward. "Lord, honey," she commented to Sara after seeing Sam, "that's a pretty boy. Love his hair." She reached over and stroked his head. "What color are his eyes?"

Clinton answered for Sara knowing how startling his mother could be. "They're deep green, just like his mother's."

"Don't let me scare you," Georgia said, locking eyes with Sara. "I'm just too damn old to bother with politeness."

"I'm not scared, ma'am," Sara replied. "I'd much rather you didn't pretend about anything."

"Sweetheart, we'll get along fine," Georgia said, giving Sara's shoulder a squeeze. Georgia's grayish-blue eyes radiated character as she lovingly stared at the sleeping Sam. Although her face showed hard years, it came with a delightful look of worldliness and knowing. Her gray hair was long, and it spilled out wildly from an old straw gardening hat.

"Can I look at him?" Beatrice asked shyly.

"Yes, ma'am," Sara said. Georgia slid back, and her sister moved forward.

The two women couldn't have been more different. Beatrice had a plump face that consisted of round cheeks and an extra chin. Her eyes were a cross between green and brown, depending on the amount of light at the given moment. Unlike her younger sister, Beatrice lacked any vestige of height, and that enhanced her plumpness.

"I wish he were awake," Beatrice said in a voice so tiny that it was reminiscent of a mama cat meowing for her kittens.

"Don't you wake him!" Georgia scolded.

"Who put you in charge of me?" Beatrice hissed.

"I did," Georgia replied with a smug smile, "'cause God made me bigger than you, and smarter too."

197

"Did not make you smarter," Beatrice replied sharply. "I always got better marks in school."

"Haw, girl, that's because the old schoolmaster felt sorry for you. He just gave you better scores than me to make you feel good."

"You're just jealous because he knew I was prettier than you."

"My, my, my," Georgia said, rolling her eyes. "I had a whole basketful of beaus chasing after me. They knew I was the prettiest girl in the county, not you."

"That ain't the way I remember it, sister. Once…"

As the two siblings sniped at each other, Clinton dryly said to Sara, "Maybe prison would have been quieter."

*****

An hour later, Sam wiggled, stretched, and opened his eyes. "Mama, I'm hungry."

"Find a place to pull over and I'll get the food," Georgia said. Clinton turned right onto a dirt road, then pulled off to the side under an oak tree.

Sam stood on his knees, cocked his head sideways, much as a curious puppy would, and asked, "Who are y'all?"

Georgia spoke first. "We've been sent by God to take care of you."

"Are you angels?" Sam asked innocently.

"Not by a long ways, child," Georgia answered, amused. "We're just two old women who need a little boy to love."

Sam cocked his head again. "You don't look old."

"Lord, child!" Georgia giggled. "Me and you gonna get along fine. I bet you must be hungry. How about a fried egg sandwich?"

"I like those."

"Clinton, open the trunk. I've got a basketful of food back there."

"What do you mean you have?'" Beatrice huffed. "I helped make and pack all the food."

"Hush, girl," Georgia scolded. "You don't have to pick on every word."

"Yes, I do. Every time I did something for Papa, you'd take the credit."

"Lord, Beatrice, do we have to go over that again?" Georgia called over her shoulder as Clinton opened the trunk. Georgia lifted the basket out. "Clinton, you want to spread a blanket out and eat on the ground?"

"We'd better eat as we drive, Mother."

"Son, you look tired. Let me get some coffee for you. It'll be cold, but it'll keep you awake."

Within minutes, they were heading west again with Georgia passing out food and jars of sweet tea. After Sam finished eating not one but two sandwiches, he turned around in the seat to investigate the sound of more paper being unwrapped. Suddenly another wonderful, sweet aroma drifted through the car.

"Look what I made for you, Sam," Beatrice said with twinkling eyes. "Fried peach tarts."

While Sam scrambled over the divide and into the back seat, Georgia squawked, "I like the way you're taking credit for that!"

"Hush," Beatrice said as Sam crawled into her lap. "He'll love me more than you, and you know—"

"I don't see why!"

"Because you were Papa's favorite. It's just rightful that Sam will love me best."

"Humph! When you get through eating that, Sam, I'll tell you a story. Her tarts are so damn chewy that your jaw will hurt. Now come on over here and sit with me." Sam wiggled from one lap to the other as Georgia shot Beatrice a sly smile. "Now, Sam," Georgia began, "it all started when Lester Card came into town riding a mule backward."

*****

Clinton fought heavy eyes as the sun began to shine in his face. He was grateful when he saw the sign announcing the town of Meridian. First, he located the train station and then turned around and found a roadside motel within walking distance. Pulling up front, he parked and, with a deep breath, entered the building. He saw a bored old man with a bald head and droopy gray mustache behind the counter, squinting at a newspaper. Without glancing up, the man asked, "What can I do for you?"

"Like a room, please."

"Be two bucks," the man stated, never diverting his attention from the paper.

Clinton handed the man two one-dollar bills. The man removed a key from a box and threw it on the counter. Leaving the office, Clinton hoped everyone else would treat them the same way: bored and indifferent.

*****

Clinton drove the car over the bumpy, uneven ground. He saw tufts of overgrown grass springing up between the stucco-covered buildings and noticed where some of the sidings had broken away, leaving patches of exposed gray concrete. Rust stains trailed down the walls from old and neglected gutters.

A musty smell wafted past his nose as he stepped across the threshold of the unit. The two beds were somewhat made. He guessed the man at the motel office was in charge of housekeeping. The rumpled attempt matched his personality. An old four-drawer dresser that sagged slightly sat against one wall. Two faded portraits—one a waterfall scene and the other a placid hunter petting his spotted bird dog—hung over the beds. Both, he noted, were slightly crooked.

Clinton crossed the room in several strides, curious as to where the back door led. The sliding dead bolt moved easier than he expected. He pushed the door open, then swept his hand along the frame to remove several spiderwebs. Peering outside, he took in a small courtyard, which held two weathered picnic tables, and a building that was the community bath. The hustle and bustle of the women broke the uneasy trance he found himself in as he stared at the scenery.

"Here, Clinton," Georgia said, pushing a new pair of tan work pants and a brown denim shirt at him. "You need to get out of that uniform. We'll take care of the rest. Go, son, and do what Mama says," Georgia urged. Clinton took the new clothes without a word and walked out the door, grateful to have his mother's help.

He returned shortly to find Beatrice napping on one of the beds, Sam chewing on another peach tart, and his mother sitting in a very unladylike fashion on the floor, carefully counting the money. Sara leaned over Georgia, silently counting along. Clinton sucked in his breath, momentarily lost in her beauty.

With a slight rush, Georgia said, "Seven thousand and three more bundles to go." Sara's gasp and his mother's words made him feel lightheaded. A few minutes later, Georgia tossed the last bill onto the stack with a flick of her wrist.

"Eleven thousand five hundred and twenty-two dollars," Georgia announced proudly, grinning like a dead hog lying in the summer sunshine. "Son," she said, "you need to walk on down to the station and get our tickets to Dallas."

Chapter 26

Clinton awoke from the nightmare. He was still running from Milton Marion and Ruth as they pursued him. In the vivid dream, their mouths poured smoke and fire as they said, "We'll find you wherever you go!" Sitting up, he scooted back and leaned against the wall. Trying to calm down, he sat up higher so he could see the beds from his perch on the floor. His mother and aunt in the bed closest to him were sound asleep. He looked at Sara, expecting to find her sleeping also, but instead, she was watching him.

"You all right?" she mouthed in the dim light. He nodded even though the dream had scared him. She quietly rose from her bed and padded across the floor, taking a seat beside him. "It's all right," she whispered. "I couldn't sleep either. We'll feel much better when we get on the train and get moving."

"I know," he agreed.

*****

Once the time came, Clinton woke Georgia, and she sprang from the bed with the nimbleness of a woman half her age. Reaching for her favorite straw hat, she plopped it on her head and began to issue orders.

"I'm gonna shave," Clinton said, just trying to stay busy.

"Nope," his mother announced. "You need to let your beard grow because it'll change the look of your face."

"It's solid white, Mama," Clinton argued. "No one will even notice I have a beard. It's so light."

"Mama knows best," Georgia quipped. "And here, son, I've got something else for you." She dug around in one of the bags and pulled out a pair of wire-rimmed glasses.

"I can't wear glasses, Mother," Clinton protested. "They'll make me dizzy."

"I cropped Sara's hair last night while you were getting rid of the car, and she didn't say a word, and here you are, complaining—"

"How do you like your new hair, Sara?" Clinton interrupted in an effort to ignore his mother.

"Fine," Sara said, running her hand over the top. "Never had it like this before."

"Why'd you cut it so short, Mother?"

Georgia let out an exasperated breath. "So a scarf can hide the color. Sara, go find me a damn good switch. I'll tan his little hide and make him mind his mama."

"Oh dear," Beatrice tittered. "Here we go again."

Sara felt the situation wash over her. Fascinated, she listened as Georgia fussed with her grown child while Beatrice nervously wrung her hands in the background. Sam seemed content just to watch the show. Standing in this tumbledown motel, an escaped convict not knowing what the next second would bring, she felt the strangest of emotions—pure happiness. She had often dreamed of being part of a family.

*****

The old mechanical clock made a distinct sound each time it clicked off another minute. Sara sat beside Clinton, wearing a blue scarf around her head, praying her hair was hidden. Sam sat in Georgia's lap as she quietly whispered another story in his ear. Beatrice sat beside them, interrupting her sister on occasion to add in bits of color and detail.

Sara's back stiffened and their whole group sat in awkward silence as a police officer entered the station. Sara watched as he strolled to the clerk's window, chatted for a minute, and then nonchalantly walked out. They all released their collectively held breath as the door closed behind him.

Finally, the porter cried, "All aboard for Dallas!" Clinton carried Sam in one arm and helped the women up the steps with the other. After finding their seats, Sara stared out the window with her body coiled tightly until the train began to move.

*****

A raw north wind rushed across the plains and entered Texas, ruffling Sara's skirt and sending chills up her spine. She pulled her overcoat tighter, wondering if she had ever been so cold. Clinton stood nearby, writing down the names from the gravestones.

An eerie chill ran up Sara's spine as she wondered if the family whose identity they were assuming would approve. She hoped they would. Clinton finished rechecking the spelling and dates again. Another day or so would be required to research the records and collect their new identities, and then they could head south. She longed for warm weather again.

*****

For two days, they sat in a dingy room and worked to teach Sam the importance of their new names. His memory proved to be much better than everyone else's.

"You and Mama," he repeated, "are Jack and Ann Miller. I'm Camden Miller, and my grandmother's name is Bristol Miller."

"What about me?" Beatrice asked, not wanting to be left out.

"You're my great-aunt Columbia Woods. But I am supposed to say Daddy, Mama, Grandmother, or Aunt Columbia. I only say your names if somebody asks."

"I don't think we'll have a problem with Sam," Clinton said to the group. "One of us might slip, but not this child."

*****

Sara felt drowsy as she watched the countryside roll by. The click and clack of the train created a melody in her mind. Clinton sat beside her, teaching Sam how to count to ten. But when some vivid color caught her attention, she would point it out to her child. Brown was outpacing everything else.

"One, two, three, four, five, six," Sam said. "I forget what comes next."

"I'm not going to help you this time," Clinton said. "You'll have to think of it—"

"Seven," Clinton heard Georgia whisper from the seat behind. "Seven, eight, nine, ten."

"Very good," Clinton said, but Sam's eyes darkened and grew serious. "Something on your mind?" he prompted.

"I know I'm not supposed to ask till I'm seven." Sam hesitated for a second. "But are you my daddy?"

Clinton looked at Sara, and she gave him a quick nod, agreeing. "I am now, son," he said, looking into the boy's serious eyes. "And forever, I will be."

Sara never turned to see the delight in her son's face. She blinked hard, trying to clear her eyes so no one would see her cry.

Chapter 27

Ronnie Meeker sat at his desk, stretched his arms, then propped his feet up. He admired his new boots and thought, *This is the first good day since the sheriff ran off.* Milton Marion had assumed that he was somehow responsible for the sheriff's actions. Ronnie could still hear Marion screaming, "Find his damn ass and arrest him, Meeker! The county has appointed you acting sheriff, and I'll crush your balls if you don't catch him!"

Meeker dropped his feet to the floor and opened a desk drawer. "Another fine present from the sheriff," he said before taking a long sip of Uncle Hiram's whiskey. "Yes, sir, it's a fine, fine day."

*****

When Fred entered the jail that fateful morning, he found an unconscious Johnson lying on the floor of the cell. "He ain't moved since he fought with the sheriff," Uncle Hiram lied convincingly. "That last blow, when the sheriff hit his eye, would have killed most men," he added.

"I'll go get the doc," Fred said, feeling Johnson's throat for a pulse.

At that moment, Johnson opened his good eye. The other was swollen completely shut and was a kaleidoscope of colors. He said slowly, "I'm all right. Just a mite shook up."

"If you can sit on your own," Fred said, "I'll run down to the freight station and send a wire—"

"Naw," Johnson interrupted. "Why don't we wait till Meeker gets here? He'll probably be the next sheriff. Mr. Marion's gonna be mighty pissed about this. I'd just as soon let Meeker…" He trailed off as Fred nodded in agreement. Whoever was left in charge was in for a great deal of punishment from Milton Marion.

After Meeker arrived, his first inclination was to alert other departments, but then he thought better of it. He remembered that the sheriff had kept him out of trouble with his wife. Delivering the news about the sheriff running away seemed easy compared to the howling that ensued after Milton Marion opened his safe and found that his money was missing. But as the next few days passed, the abuse Meeker suffered caused his spine to stiffen and his resolve to grow. He never sent the wire.

*****

Ronnie took another long drink, felt the wonderful burn, and thought about the exciting news that Fred had just delivered: "Mr. Marion is dead, Ronnie! His wife said he got up this morning still carrying on about the sheriff. Suddenly he turned beet red in the face, his eyes bugged out, and he fell over dead. She told the undertaker that he hit the floor like a sack of potatoes."

The phone rang, interrupting Ronnie's replay of the event. "Hello. Sheriff Ronnie Meeker speaking." He really enjoyed the sound of his new title.

"Yeah, Sheriff," the voice said. "I'm Officer Glen Fillmore over in Meridian, Mississippi. We found an abandoned car with y'all's marking on it. You wouldn't know why someone would leave it here, would you?"

Meeker drew a breath, smiled, then lied. "I don't know why that fellow we sold it to would up and leave it. Guess it broke down, or he just didn't want it anymore."

"Sheriff, it runs just fine," Fillmore said. "The chief wants to know what you want to do with it."

"Well, I don't rightly know," Ronnie replied, trying to think ahead. Then it came to him. "It'll cost us about as much as it's worth to send someone after it. Why don't y'all just keep it in case that fellow comes back?"

"Just a second, Sheriff," Fillmore said. Ronnie could hear men talking in the background. "Sheriff, the chief says that'd be fine."

"Good," Ronnie replied. "That'll be the best. Have a good day now."

Chapter 28

Sara helped Georgia and Beatrice down the steps of the train while Clinton and Sam went to find the rest of their luggage. "Lord, this sunshine feels good," Georgia commented. "I don't think my bones will be warm for a month. Never thought about Dallas being so far north."

Sara wandered away from the women and found a bulletin board filled with local notices. She unpinned a faded white patch of paper that advertised a house for rent and slipped it into her dress pocket. Clinton and Sam returned with their belongings, finding all the women glancing around at the bustle of the station.

"Son, stay with the ladies," Clinton said.

"Where you going?" Georgia asked Clinton.

"It's a large town, Mama," he replied. "But there'll be some old codger around here who can tell me the best place to stay. There's one in every town whose sole mission in life is to watch the comings and goings."

Clinton walked the long wooden platform, watching the crowd, and it didn't take long to find the person he needed. He sat in a wooden chair that was leaned back against the wall. A faded Confederate hat adorned his head. Patched jeans and cowboy boots completed the Texan look. As Clinton approached, the man eyed him warily.

"Excuse me, sir," Clinton asked. "Could you direct me to a boarding house or a hotel of some sort?"

The old man studied Clinton before answering. "You ain't a Yankee, are you? Don't like 'em, and won't help them none," he said haughtily.

Clinton smiled easily. "No, sir. Born in Dallas."

"You sound like a Texan," the old man replied with a squinted eye. "My granddaddy died at Bull Run," he said. "Won't help a Yankee with nothing except leaving town."

"Nope, don't blame you a bit," Clinton replied, hoping he didn't have to relive the war before the question was answered.

"Three blocks down there." The man pointed. "Fine boarding house run by a Christian woman named Mrs. Tuttle. Makes the finest biscuits in this state, clean, and a fair price too."

"I sure appreciate the information."

"I'll see you at dinner," the man said, "seeing how she's my baby sister."

The group covered the distance quickly, anxious to end the day. The clean and well-kept two-story structure came into view. After Clinton walked up the steps, he read aloud the handwritten sign on the door.

House is empty of guests at this time. Take any bedroom upstairs. Dinner is leftovers. Breakfast and lunch are served hot. Bath is downstairs. Help yourself after leaving three dollars on the kitchen table.

Mrs. Tuttle

*****

That night, they met Mrs. Tuttle. She was warm, charming, well-endowed, and carrying considerable girth. She served cold peas, fried cornbread, and milk on her dining room table. Her brother, Basil Simmons, ate his fill without adding a word to the conversation.

After he finished his portion, he abruptly stood up to leave. Mrs. Tuttle admonished him. "Basil, you've got food all over your beard." He stood still while she used a napkin to sweep the cornbread crumbs away. After Basil made his departure, Clinton gently but persistently peppered Mrs. Tuttle with questions about the area.

"Mrs. Tuttle," Sara asked, entering the conversation, "I found an advertisement at the train station for a rental house. Would you know where this is?"

"I sure do," she answered after looking at the paper. "That house is two blocks from the beach, and I know the man who owns it. He's a lot like me. With times so hard, he's having trouble finding tenants that can pay."

"I can understand," Clinton said. "I don't know when this Depression will lift."

"I do know that Mr. Long would really like to sell the place."

"You think so?" Clinton asked.

"Don't tell him I told you so," Mrs. Tuttle quickly said. "But if you like the house, I'd guess you could get it for a fair price."

"How do we find him?" Clinton asked. "All we have is the address."

"I'll tell Basil to stop by Mr. Long's house before he goes home and tell him you all want to meet, say, nine o'clock tomorrow?"

"That'd be wonderful," Clinton answered.

"It's a nice home, Mr. Miller, built well. I'd guess a man like you could fix any problem there might be," she added with a slight fluttering of her eyes. Sara stifled her smile as the older woman slyly flirted with Clinton. Georgia winked at Sara as Mrs. Tuttle started tittering again.

*****

The next morning, they all sat on the edge of the high wooden porch as Clinton talked to Mr. Long inside the house. Sara loved what she saw, but she didn't dare dream that something this wonderful would be her new home.

Clinton worked hard to concentrate on Mr. Long's words because his large Adam's apple bounced up and down as he talked.

"Now, Mr. Miller, if you make me a good offer, I might just sell you this place," Mr. Long said.

"How much?" Clinton asked.

Mr. Long lifted his head, seemingly doing the math in the air. "Two thousand is a fair price," he offered.

"I'll give you fifteen hundred cash, Mr. Long," Clinton countered, stroking his clean-shaven face. He'd raked the beard away that morning, despite his mother's protest.

"Mr. Miller," Mr. Long said with his Adam's apple bobbing, "let's shake hands on that."

"Before we do," Clinton replied, smiling, "I'd like to talk to my wife for a minute. I'm sure she'll want the place, but…" Clinton finished with a sly grin.

"Yeah, I know," Mr. Long agreed. "Missus and me have been married forty-two years. Take all the time you need."

*****

Clinton walked with Sara toward the beach to talk privately, and they were both overwhelmed by the beauty of the scene. The moment and their first good breath of salt air washed over them as gentle winter waves caressed the shore. Sara couldn't believe the bold move he proposed as she stared, transfixed, at the moving water. Never in any dream had she thought this possible.

"What if we have to run again?" Sara asked, worried.

"I know the possibilities," Clinton replied. "But I like this town. The people here are used to folks coming and going. Anywhere we go will carry a risk."

Sara brushed her short hair back and tilted her head. "I'd love to live here. Please do what you think is best."

"Mr. Long is waiting to drive me to the courthouse and change the deed," Clinton replied. "I'll be back shortly," he said, already on the move.

*****

Sam wouldn't be deterred, and neither Georgia nor Beatrice would tell him that exploring their new house took precedence over the ocean. Sara found herself standing on the front porch alone while the trio marched toward the beach. The screen door opened silently as she stepped over the threshold and into a dogtrot hall. A sense of elation ran up her spine, causing her face to tingle.

She lightly ran her fingertips across the plain tongue and groove wood of the wall. Strolling carefully, Sara eased to the rear of the house. As she opened the wooden door, a pleasant breeze funneled through the hall. Savoring and memorizing the wonderful sea smell, she turned around to explore the rest of the house.

Midway through the hall and to the right, she turned and opened another door. Sara could barely contain a squeal of delight. The kitchen was huge with ample sunlight bathing the room. Her wide eyes spied a huge sink with a hand pump for water. With excitement, she moved the handle up and down, producing, at first, a rusty stream of water and then a clear one.

Spinning on her heels, she turned to face the entire room and saw several wooden cabinets. She opened each, finding several pots and one frying pan left by a previous tenant. Sara laid each pan on the counter and then examined the stove. Reading out loud, she said, "A 1936 Hardwick gas range."

She walked back to the hall, almost tipping on her toes the way a cat would tread through wet grass. She opened the door opposite the kitchen, and a rush of happy words escaped as she viewed the room. The sagging single bed covered with a white sheet and battered oak dresser were like gold glittering in her eyes. *We'll give this to Georgia and Beatrice,* she thought after backing out of the room. The next door in the hall wouldn't budge. It was swelled shut. She jerked on the handle several times to no avail.

"Maybe I ought to wait for Clinton," she mused, all the while knowing she couldn't. Firmly grasping the handle and raising her right leg to use it as a brace, she exerted all the force she could muster. The door sprang open, sending her flying backward and landing very unladylike on her rump. She laughed, then climbed to her feet.

Her hands flew to her mouth, muffling a schoolgirl squeal. Sara reached and felt the rounded edge of the porcelain tub. She twisted a handle, but no water appeared. *That's fine,* she thought. *We can carry water from the kitchen.* She moved the handle back to its prior position, then took a moment to gaze at the indoor toilet and sink.

Turning to the left in front of the stairs, Sara saw the living room and made no effort to hide her growing emotion. The four windows stood tall and proud, giving her a fine view of the front and side of the house. She thought of a pretty couch she had once seen in a discarded catalog and dreamily thought of sitting on something so fine and sipping a glass of tea.

Sara backtracked, walking to the stairs. Her hand slid up the dusty banister as she anticipated what lay ahead. The first bedroom felt airy and comfortable while providing two simple cots that would supply her and Sam's needs. She strolled over to the window and could see a distant view of the ocean. *Days from now, I'll sit here and read a book or tell Sam a story as he is lying on his little bed.* The very thought of that pleasure brought moisture to her eyes.

With the warmest feeling ever, Sara opened the last door. She was assaulted by the brightness of the room. Four long windows matching the downstairs illuminated and enhanced the large cavern. She decided quickly that the room was Clinton's. He had made all this possible by the boldness and kindness of his nature. For the first time in her life, she felt what it was like to truly live.

*****

Sara was pumping the handle and rinsing the rag when she felt someone watching her. Turning, she found Clinton standing in the door, his face breaking into a smile as their eyes met.

"The house is ours!" he announced with pride.

"Oh, Clinton!" Sara exclaimed. "It's so grand! I never dreamed of—it's got an indoor bathroom!" she gushed.

He was overwhelmed by her pleasure, and he truly loved her for it. "I'll get the water turned on," he responded, holding back on what he really wanted to say. "And later, I'll pipe up city water to the kitchen, and we won't have to use the hand pump anymore."

Her face suddenly creased. "Can we afford to buy water?" she asked. "How much does it cost?" The concept was foreign to her.

"It's not that much," he said. "And yes," he added, smiling. "After paying Mr. Long, I mentioned that I was looking for a job. The city is building a seawall not too far from here, so he drove me by there, and guess what?"

"What?" she asked.

"The foreman is the son of a friend of Mr. Long's. He hired me, Sara," Clinton announced proudly. "I've got a job!"

"Really!" she squealed. "That quick!"

"Yep. I start tomorrow."

"What'll you be doing?" she asked, delighted that he seemed so happy.

"Pushing a wheelbarrow," he answered proudly.

"Oh, Clinton," she said, suddenly overcome with despondency. "You've given up so much for us." Her shoulders began slumping.

"No, I haven't, Sara," he said, his blue eyes pained. "I've gained so much more than I lost."

"I'm sorry," Sara said. "I just hate to think of you doing—"

"Believe me," he interrupted, "it's work I'll enjoy much more than being sheriff. I'm sure you saw the gas stove," Clinton said, determined to change the subject. "I'll have to get the tank filled. It's out back, but it'll sure be better than trying to find wood."

"You're spoiling me, you know?" she said demurely, realizing it was the first time she had ever flirted with a man.

"Where's Sam and everyone?" he asked, embarrassed by his reddening face.

"They took off to see the water. Sam's probably worn them out."

"Well, Mr. Long said there's a store about a mile west of here. We need to get some things if we're going to stay in our new house tonight. I'm getting hungry," Clinton said to cover his growing desire.

Chapter 29

Ronnie Meeker stood in front of the office, cinching his coat as a raw winter wind blew a few brown leaves down the street.

"I don't see why we have to put him in chains, Ronnie," Johnson said scornfully as he struggled to lead Uncle Hiram down the steps.

"That's what the regulations state," Meeker replied, but then he added, "What you do after you leave here is your business." The old deputy helped Uncle Hiram into the truck and closed the door. While he limped around to the driver's side, Meeker gave his last instructions. "Take him to the processing gate, Johnson. The warden said you can spend the night with one of the guards and drive home tomorrow." This would be his last act for the county. He could've retired a month ago, but he was unwilling to leave Uncle Hiram in someone else's care.

*****

On the outskirts of town, Johnson stopped the truck and unlocked Uncle Hiram's chains. As they drove, he tried several times to engage his friend in conversation, but Uncle Hiram made no effort to respond. Finally, he left the old man to his thoughts. Late that afternoon, they approached the many fallow fields of the State Farm, which awaited spring plowing.

"You scared, Uncle Hiram?" Johnson asked as the gray prison walls rose out of the landscape.

"Naw. I am an old man," Hiram replied, tugging his nose. "I'll find a way to get by."

"I'm sorry, Uncle Hiram," Johnson said, hotness building behind his eyes. "I can turn around and drive away," he suggested, "and say you escaped. We can drive to Mobile and put you on a bus."

Uncle Hiram snorted, breaking the tension. "They'd never believe that. Don't worry about me. I'll be fine." Johnson was already wondering if he would ever hear his singsong voice again. "Johnson, you know the swamp south of the flats, don't you?" Uncle Hiram asked.

"Sure do. Hunted there when I was young."

"Go to the north end of the flats," Uncle Hiram directed, "and walk across. Go due east for about two hundred yards, and you'll see a big oak tree with a split trunk. Turn north for a minute or so, and there'll be a big mound of sand sticking out of the swamp. I've got enough whiskey buried there to keep you going for a long while. Can't have you buying whiskey from someone else."

"Thank you, Uncle Hiram," Johnson responded, his throat now tightening. "I was wondering what I—"

"Don't try to drink it all at once," Uncle Hiram warned. "And you still ain't beat me at checkers," he added.

Johnson drove around the perimeter of the prison until he saw the Processing sign. The brakes on the truck protested as it came to a stop in front of the guard shack. A uniformed man walked from the building to Johnson's window.

"You from Roxboro?" he asked, giving Johnson a friendly grin.

"That'll be us," he answered.

"That Uncle Hiram?" the man asked. Johnson had expected this to be formal. Using Uncle Hiram's local name didn't fit. "You all just sit here, and I'll be right back," the man instructed. Johnson followed his movements back to the shack and saw him pick up a telephone. The guard strolled out again and engaged both in small talk about the weather.

A few minutes later, another uniformed man, this one younger and more authoritative, said, "Come with me." Uncle Hiram got out of the truck. Johnson did the same, meeting Uncle Hiram at the front of the truck. Uncle Hiram stuck out his weathered hand, but Johnson refused it. He wrapped the smaller man in his arms. "You'll be out in two years, and I'll be here to pick you up." Johnson pushed Uncle Hiram back but held on to his shoulders. "I'll be waiting. You can count on it." Johnson released him and watched as Uncle Hiram followed the guard away.

"Don't be mean to him," he implored to the remaining guard. The man snorted. "Don't worry."

*****

Officer Redstone rang the bell, alerting another guard to open the steel gate. Uncle Hiram backed up a step as the cold steel swung free. His mouth was dry as cotton as he walked through. The clanging of the gate made his hand involuntarily rise and rub the back of his neck.

"Can you read and write?" Justin Redstone asked as he shoved a paper in front of Uncle Hiram's nose.

"Yes, sir," Hiram replied, squinting slightly to read the words in the dim light.

"Just a list of rules here," Redstone said, taking the paper and laying it on a battered wooden desk. "Just sign it at the bottom where it's marked." Uncle Hiram sprawled his name. "Follow me," he commanded, heading back to the entry gate. As it opened, he said, "The warden wants to see you."

Uncle Hiram remained quiet as they drove through the State Farm, wondering what this was all about. The man didn't seem threatening; he placidly smoked and thumped the ashes out the window. Soon, the fields disappeared, and they came upon a row of houses. Streetlights lined the paved road, and each home was painted a clean white.

The officer turned into a drive of one of the houses and stopped. Three prisoners in black-and-white striped uniforms were trimming bushes and never turned from their task. "Come with me," the officer said, opening the truck door. Uncle Hiram double-timed following the man to the front door. He rapped on the door twice, and it opened shortly. A tidy-dressed, brown-haired woman greeted the officer in familiar and pleasant terms.

"Come in, Justin," she offered as if this was a common occurrence. She glanced at Uncle Hiram, gave him a half smile, then walked away. He froze in place, not knowing what to do.

"She means you too," the officer said. Uncle Hiram nervously glanced around the living room and saw that it was comfortably furnished and snug. "Cap'n White, I've brought him to you," Officer Redstone said loudly.

Uncle Hiram's eyes swung toward the door that was propped open, giving him a short view of the kitchen. The small man that now stood before him certainly didn't fit the image of a warden. He looked more like a politician.

His hair, which was parted neatly on the left, had traces of gray about the ears. The rest was dark as charcoal, matching the dress pants he wore. Black suspenders were buttoned at the waistline, and his tie held a neat but loosely tied knot. The white shirt he wore was double cuffed, and the diamond cufflinks winked at Uncle Hiram as Captain White extended his hand.

"I understand I'm to call you Uncle Hiram," Captain White said gently as their palms met.

"That's what everyone calls me," Uncle Hiram replied as he looked into the man's kind and slightly amused gray eyes.

"Well," White started, pointing toward the woman, who now shared a comfortable chair with a small boy in the corner of the living room, "this is my wife, Amelia, and my grandson James." Uncle Hiram nodded his greeting to the lady, then looked at the boy and saw that his right hand was covered in big, mean, nasty warts. "Sheriff Barnes gave me a call after you were arrested," the warden explained. "And he assured me that you had the ability to look warts off."

"Yes, sir," Uncle Hiram replied, not taking his eyes off the child. "I haven't failed yet."

"Well, if you'd be so kind," the warden asked, "would you help my grandson?"

"Yes, sir," Uncle Hiram replied. "Be pleased to." He looked about the room and saw a footstool. He moved it to the center and then took a seat facing the boy. "Come here, child," he softly commanded.

The boy's grandmother gave him a little nudge, and he walked shyly across the room. When he was close enough, Uncle Hiram reached and gathered him in his arms. He gently spun the boy around between his bony legs and held his tiny wrist.

"Now what Uncle Hiram's going to do," Hiram gently explained, "is I'll take a good look at those things and then touch them lightly as a feather. Won't hurt a bit." Uncle Hiram stared at the warts for a moment, then touched each one. He gave the boy a short hug and whispered, "If they ain't gone in a week or so, Uncle Hiram will visit you again."

"Uncle Hiram," the warden said, "I've got some kind of bug eating my turnip greens in my garden. There's enough light. You think you can take a look?" They walked into the backyard, and Captain White said, "Uncle Hiram, the sheriff assured me that you are a man of your word." There, he paused and focused on Hiram's eyes. "So if I never put you behind the prison walls, I have your word you won't run off and be an embarrassment to me?"

Uncle Hiram suddenly felt relief wash over him. He had always been a free man and had wondered if he would go crazy inside the prison. "It wouldn't do you any good," the warden warned sternly. "If you did, we'd catch you easily with the tracking dogs we have."

"Yes, sir," Uncle Hiram replied. "Know you have the best."

"The sheriff also said that you're the finest whiskey maker he's ever seen."

Uncle Hiram grinned. "Been working at it a long time."

"Well, what we're going to do is let you ply your trade on a smaller scale just for my and my friends' consumption."

"Yes, sir."

"You see, my wife is a little tempest. Comes from her mother's side of the family." Captain White stopped and returned Uncle Hiram's grin. "You know how funny women can be."

"Yes, sir. Sometimes, they right cantankerous," Uncle Hiram agreed.

"We have a little shack hidden in the woods of the State Farm. A few of us enjoy gathering once a week to have a few drinks and play a little poker. Justin here is going to take you there, and you give him a list of what you need to get things started. If this works out, the two years you spend with us will be pleasant."

"Yes, sir," Uncle Hiram replied, already thinking about what he needed.

Chapter 30

Clinton's amazement at Sara's ability to barter grew each passing day. She spent little, but she managed to fill their home with the necessary items for living. "You should have seen her, son," Georgia said, replaying Sara's actions at a fish market. "She gave the man pure hell when he told her the price. 'Dang,' she howled, 'the fish you're selling are so old they'll smell in two hours.'

"Clinton, the man grumbled under his breath, saying, 'Go to the docks and deal with the boat captains, lady.' She arched her back and laced him with a fiery reply: 'I will! Nobody going to charge me that much for stinking fish that's been sitting in the sun for days.' She found where the docks are, and I'll be damned if she didn't get what she wanted cheaper."

"Mother," Clinton replied, worried, "y'all don't need to go down there without me. Fishermen can be a tough crowd, and—"

"Don't worry," Georgia interrupted. "She bartered with the butt of your gun sticking out of her pocket. If someone tries to hurt her, they'll find their family jewels missing."

Clinton was grateful that the job site was within walking distance from their home. He also enjoyed the growing litany of recipes Sara developed. The house smelled of something wonderfully delicious every day. One day, he invited his new friend Jacob Peters home for lunch, hoping Sara wouldn't mind. He knew Sara took an immediate liking to the man when Jacob snatched off his hat and bowed slightly at the waist as they were introduced.

"I'm pleased to meet you, ma'am," he said softly, dragging out each syllable.

"The pleasure's mine, Mr. Peters," Sara responded.

"I'd be right pleased, ma'am, if you'd call me Jacob."

"Be proud to," Sara said. "Now we're informal here. I'll be back in a minute with a bucket of water so you and my husband can wash up. We eat on the porch when the weather is pretty."

Georgia, who loved talking to everyone, plopped down beside Jacob, learning that he was only twenty-four years old and from McAllister, Oklahoma. "Would you like something else, Jacob?" Georgia asked, already determined to fatten the young man up.

"No, ma'am," he replied. "I can't remember when I've eaten so well and much."

"Glad you enjoyed it," Sara said after taking a sip of tea. "You're welcome anytime."

"Ma'am," he asked, "I'd be right obliged if you'd let me pay you for the meal."

"Jacob, you're our guest," she said, shaking her head. "Come back anytime."

The next day, Clinton came home for lunch with Jacob in tow again. The man, after eating his fill, broached the previous day's subject. "Mrs. Miller, today, I'm not taking no for an answer," he said, setting his jaw.

"Jacob—" she started.

"Now hear me out," he interrupted. "Most of us working on the seawall aren't married, so we don't get any home cooking. I'm sorry, ma'am, but I spread the word on how good your food is. There's about ten, maybe fifteen, men who'd be happy to pay you if you see fit."

Sara looked at Clinton for guidance, but he shrugged his shoulders, leaving the decision up to her. The next day, he came home for lunch with Jacob and six other men. Sara and Georgia fed each one while Beatrice tittered and kept their glasses full. The following day, there were ten men. Sara seated several in the living room while the others filled the porch.

Georgia walked between them, offering another round of fresh hush puppies. After taking a bite, one man said, "I bet as good as these are, you probably make a mean biscuit too."

She pushed her straw hat back, and her eyes twinkled. "Come by tomorrow morning, and I'll hand you one out the kitchen window."

A grizzled, sweat-stained face stared back hopefully. "You wouldn't put a piece of bacon in it like my mama used to, would you?" Loneliness radiated from the man.

"I surely will, honey," she answered. "Tomorrow morning, come to the kitchen window."

Early the next day, the very same man stood outside, first in line. After taking a bite, he rolled his eyes in appreciation. The light, fluffy smell of baking that had been drifting from the kitchen almost overwhelmed him.

"Ma'am," he said, "it's as good as my mama's."

"That's 'cause it's made with love, honey," Georgia answered, patting his rough hand. "Now run along and let these fellers behind you get something to eat," she commanded. Soon, between the three of them, they were clearing fifteen and sometimes twenty dollars a week.

*****

The soft days of April were soon upon them, and their life felt settled in the port town. Sara enjoyed sitting on the beach each Sunday afternoon, watching the blue-green water while listening to Sam and Clinton play. It helped soothe the nagging worries that entered her mind unexpectedly. Milton Marion and the bad memories would surface at unusual times, but strangely, it was thinking of Uncle Hiram that bothered her the most. She wondered how she could ever fulfill her promise.

Billowy clouds floated over the water, casting an occasional shadow, as Sara watched Sam lead Clinton into another silly game. For each, she had taken old overalls and hemmed them at the knees.

Sara lost herself for a moment, admiring Clinton's strong shoulders and ropy, muscular legs; and she loved the fact that he relished the role of being a father. Sam was flourishing from Clinton's love. The time in the sun had turned Clinton's skin a golden brown, unlike Sam, who had only gained a few well-placed freckles on his nose. Suddenly Georgia jarred her from her thoughts.

"Honey, stop looking at him like that if you're not going to do anything about it." Sara had been caught staring, and her face flushed with embarrassment. "Sara, turn around and face me," Georgia said. Sara scooted around on the blanket, feeling the sand moving underneath her.

"I don't know what you're talking about," Sara said, trying to bluff her way out of the awkward situation.

Georgia dug around in her cloth bag and pulled out a metal flask. "Here. Take a sip, and then we'll talk," she urged, pushing the canister toward Sara. "Oh, don't look so disappointed in me," Georgia said, responding to the shocked look on Sara's face. "A little nip every now and then doesn't hurt."

"Yeah, a little nip doesn't hurt, but you snort," piped Beatrice.

"Ha!" Georgia sniped. "You're one to talk, girl!"

"Oh, shut up," Beatrice replied in a snit because she couldn't think of a better comeback.

"Sara, you going to take a drink?" Georgia asked. "If not, give it back to me." Both the women giggled as Sara took a small, tentative sip. "Damn," Georgia said to Beatrice, "she drinks like a Baptist. Surprised she didn't look up and down the beach, making sure no one could see her." Sara shuddered as the warm liquid slid down her throat, and an unfamiliar feeling flushed her face.

"Now," Georgia started, "my boy follows you around, walking in your very steps, and there's nothing he won't do for you, and what do you do?" Rolling her eyes, she added, "Leave him cold every night, sleeping alone."

"We're not really married," Sara said after taking another sip. "It wouldn't be right."

Georgia grew serious. "I understand that you're not married in the legal sense or in the sight of God, but I do believe our loving father will forgive you. Sara, you'll have to go to Clinton. He's too much of a gentleman to lay a hand on you."

Sara pondered Georgia's words as the surf pounded the beach. She heard Sam squeal with delight as Clinton chased him down the beach.

"Do you know what started all this?" Georgia asked gently.

"Sister—"

"Hush, Beatrice. She needs to know," Georgia scolded. The two sisters exchanged a silent glance. Georgia spoke smoothly, trying to take the edge off the raw truth. "He was trying to protect me from hurt, Sara. His father produced a child out of wedlock with another woman."

Georgia took a deep breath. "The mother was a colored woman that lived in the settlement. Milton Marion found this out. He wanted Sam, so he used the fact that Clinton has a colored half brother to blackmail him."

"I don't understand," Sara said, leaning against a gust of wind.

Georgia shook her head as if amazed by Sara's naive nature. "Milton Marion threatened that if he didn't find a way to take Sam from you, he'd reveal what my husband had done."

"You mean the only reason he arrested me and Uncle Hiram was for—"

"Sara," Georgia quickly interrupted, "in our short time together, I've come to love you. But you're a little slow to catch on. Clinton was under tremendous pressure trying to protect me," she explained. "He did it for his mother, and one day, Sam might have to do the same for you."

Sara slowly raised the flask to her lips, taking another sip, the burn now completely unnoticed. "Mr. Marion blackmailed Clinton just so he could take Sam, and he didn't think about what it would do to me?" she asked, an angry tilt creeping into her voice.

"Don't blame him, Sara. The situation proved most difficult," Georgia answered. "I'm not making excuses for his actions, but as a mother, you should understand."

"Did you know what your husband had done?"

Wistfully, Georgia said, "Turn around and look at Clinton." Sara saw him holding Sam above his head and spinning the boy around and around. "Have you ever seen a finer-looking man?"

Now with her tongue loosened by the whiskey, Sara admitted, "He's quite handsome."

"His daddy was the same," Georgia replied. "I was smitten with Stu from the first moment I laid eyes on him. And," she added sadly, "if he were here today, I'd gratefully forgive him. Just look at him, Sara. A man couldn't love a child more." Sara couldn't deny it. Clinton truly loved Sam. "That wasn't my husband's only indiscretion," Georgia admitted. "I knew of others but chose to turn my head. And I also made a decision never to tell Clinton that his father was a rounder."

"Why?" Sara asked curiously.

"Because he looked up to his daddy just the way a boy should."

"I understand that," Sara admitted. Her whole life, she had longed to have a father to guide her. "You never said if you knew about the other child," Sara said bluntly, now slightly tipsy.

Georgia corralled her hair and put her hat on as the Gulf wind grew stronger. "No, Sara, I didn't," she answered, her face twisted in disgust. "That was until that smug little bastard Milton Marion showed up in Montgomery the night you and Uncle Hiram were arrested."

"I thought that was what Clinton had been desperately trying to avoid?"

"It was, but Marion felt Clinton wouldn't follow through. He stood in the doorway of that cockroach-infested place and gleefully told me what a louse my dead husband was."

"Tell her what you called him, sister," Beatrice tittered, anxious to join the conversation.

"Hush, girl."

"No," Beatrice said. "You're always telling me to hush. It was really funny," she said, turning to Sara and ignoring Georgia. "Sister told him that his mama and daddy weren't married, and then she screamed that he was a sorry-ass Yankee carpetbagger. Then, Sara," she continued, her eyes growing bigger, "she grabbed a butcher knife and chased after him, screaming that she was gonna cut his heart out. She ran him around that big car a good three times, calling him names I didn't understand. I wrote them down, though."

"Beatrice, damn you."

"He finally gained enough ground and managed to get in his car. Sister stood there shaking the knife as he drove away."

"I'd have killed his ass if I had caught him," Georgia hissed. "I scolded Clinton for bending under the pressure," she stated. "I'm not that damn fragile. But how can you stay mad at a son who's only trying to protect you? And when he told me his plans for you, Beatrice and I were happy to agree. We knew he was in love with both of you. And I never liked that damn ugly girl he got trapped into marrying anyway. It's eating him up inside, Sara. He's afraid that if he tells you the truth, you'll take Sam and leave. He'll never touch you until the air is clear."

"Did he tell you that?"

"No, but he's my son," Georgia replied. "I can read his face every time he looks at you."

*****

Sara nervously lay on her bed, watching as Sam fell into a deep sleep. Feeling that he wouldn't wake, she slipped away to Clinton's room. She found him sitting up in bed, the room illuminated from a shaft of moonlight pouring through the long windows. Surprised by her presence, he unconsciously pulled the sheet up to cover his bare chest.

"Is something wrong?" he asked as Sara stood beside the bed, staring at him.

"No, nothing's wrong," she whispered. "I know what happened, and I don't care." Sara reached for the hem of her nightgown and pulled upward. She stood there naked in the moonlight for a moment before sliding into his bed.

Chapter 31

Sara turned her face to the wind, enjoying the gentle southern breeze, and Beatrice and Georgia were as content watching Clinton and Sam as they collected a bucket of periwinkles for the night's stew. But their enjoyment was shattered as a man half walked and half trotted from the west. He stopped in front of the ladies and then waved for Clinton and Sam to join.

"Have you heard the news?" he asked breathlessly as the two arrived.

"No. What's wrong?" Clinton asked as the man inhaled and shuddered.

"Pearl Harbor!" he responded on the exhale. "It's been attacked by the Japs! We're at war!"

*****

Sara awoke and found Clinton lying on his back with his forearm resting across his eyes. She laid her head on his chest, cherishing the sound of his heartbeat. She felt his arm surrounding her shoulders. Her eyes squeezed tightly shut, trying to force the tears away. They had been fighting so bitterly over the last month.

He was determined to fight for his country, and she had unabashedly pleaded, begged, and cajoled him not to. She had argued that they were living an assumed life, and the draft board couldn't find him. When that failed, she cried for nights, begging that she would fade away and die without him.

Her efforts were in vain, so she sank into desperation, threatening that if he left, she and Sam wouldn't be here when he returned. But his words tonight had chilled and robbed her of her last shred of resolve: "I can't look Sam in the eye," he had said, "and teach him to be a man if I'm not one myself."

Sara whispered as his strong arms now tightened around her body, pulling her face close to his. "I love you, so I'll wait forever and ever."

*****

Clinton jousted for a position on the crowded platform as loved ones gathered to say goodbye to sons, husbands, and brothers. He hugged his mother and aunt tightly, almost pulling them off their feet.

"Take care of them, Mother," Clinton whispered in Georgia's ear.

"I will," Georgia replied strongly before tenderly kissing his face.

Clinton picked Sam up and hugged him tightly to his chest. "You're the man of the house now, Sam. Take care of the ladies."

As always, the boy's perception ran far beyond his years. "I will, Daddy, I promise," he replied, trying hard not to cry. But it was too much for the child, so Georgia gathered him around her waist, allowing Sam to hide his tears.

Clinton then turned to Sara and kissed her deeply. "I'll send money as soon as I can," he promised after the embrace.

"Don't worry," she said, desperately trying to be strong and not collapse into a sobbing fool. Clinton stared into her eyes and tried to find the right words. Sara breathlessly whispered, "I know you love me, and I will always be yours, darling, always."

Clinton lined up with the others as the boarding call was announced. After walking up the steps, he found a place and watched his family until the train started its slow journey from the station. A moment later, a lined and hard-faced Gunny bounded down the aisle hollering, "Find a goddamn seat and keep your frigging ass in it." Clinton dived for the first available place, jostling the young man who sat watching the passing scenery. Clinton stared ahead obediently as the sergeant shoved several recruits who were slow to obey.

"Noah Christian," Clinton heard as the cursing voice moved away. He turned, taking in the full measure of the young boy. His doe-like black eyes blinked slowly as if asking him not to respond unkindly to his boyish appearance.

"You can't be old enough to serve," Clinton blurted, his mouth getting ahead of his brain.

"I'm from the hills of Carolina," Noah answered timidly. "We don't grow very tall there."

"Pleased to meet you," Clinton said, offering his hand and regretting his brash assessment of the boy.

Clinton and Noah clung together as the train filled at each stop with more and more young men. It wasn't long before several fights broke out, and they watched as marine police administered justice via nightsticks against young hardheads. "I'm scared," Noah admitted nervously. "I'm really only sixteen," he whispered. "I lied to get in."

The open countryside disappeared that night as the train moved closer to San Diego. At three in the morning, it came to its final stop. With much haste, the marine recruits were moved by bus to Camp Pendleton. Clinton and Noah both swallowed hard as their feet hit the ground and the gates of hell opened.

*****

Sara's eyes hungrily tore through Clinton's first letter. After her breathing slowed and she assured herself that he wasn't in immediate danger, she reread it, this time hearing his voice.

My dearest love,

I'm so sorry it's taken me this long to write. It's been quite an experience since I left you, and I've found that I know very little. Our drill instructor informs me of this each day. I must say, though, the brunt of discipline is directed toward many others who have never succumbed to higher authority.

My vocabulary has greatly increased with many words I didn't know existed, and most would cause a sermon on Sunday morning. I've made a good friend, Noah, a tough little mountain boy, and we watch out for each other as brothers would.

Sorry, but I must end this letter because time is growing short. In closing, my love, I must say that each night, I allow myself to miss you for just a few minutes. For if I didn't keep you and our son from my mind, I'd drive myself crazy.

At those times, I can feel your wonderful arms around me, and each gentle kiss is tucked deep into my heart. You are the very life and breath of me, and I love you more and more each day.

Your loving husband,
C.

PS: Please give everyone a hug and kiss for me and let them know how special they are.

Chapter 32

Sara worked the window as Georgia stirred the stew. Now they fed men who were too old to serve or couldn't for physical reasons. She had feared that after Pearl Harbor, their business would lessen, but an influx of strangers arrived seeking the new shipbuilding and petrochemical jobs. Instead of losing customers, they gained.

"Morning, Mr. Collier," Sara sang, passing a scrambled egg-stuffed biscuit out the window.

"It is a pretty one, Mrs. Miller," Mr. Collier replied, handing Sara the correct change.

Sara dropped the coins in the metal box and leaned out the window to take the next order. Her adrenaline dropped, but she quickly regained her composure and spoke. "Good morning, Sheriff," she chirped brightly.

"Ma'am," the sheriff replied, removing his cowboy hat and revealing a bald head. Sara guessed, from facial lines and the beer belly that protruded from his average frame, that he was sixty or so. His gray-blue eyes didn't portray any unkindness, just curiosity. "Ma'am, I've gotten a complaint that you're running a restaurant without a license."

"I'm sorry, sir," Sara apologized. "Why don't you come in, and we'll talk about what I need to do?"

"That'll be fine," he answered. Sara filled several more orders as Georgia, who had heard the exchange, met the sheriff at the front door. Sara finished and shut the window as Georgia led the sheriff to the kitchen.

"Sheriff Tillman," Georgia offered, "why don't you take a seat and let me get you a cup of coffee?" Sara noticed that Georgia had shed her straw hat and smoothed her hair.

"I believe I will, ma'am," he replied easily, his taste buds salivating for whatever smelled so rich and sweet in the kitchen.

"Would you like one too, Ann?" Georgia asked.

"Sure," Sara said, coolly taking a chair. She couldn't figure out where Beatrice and Sam were.

"Hmm, what's cooking in that large pot?" the sheriff hinted.

Georgia poured his coffee, then answered, "Boiled fish is what we have for breakfast. It saves on having to buy—"

"Boiled fish?" he asked with a slight frown. "I've never eaten fish cooked that way."

"Sheriff," Georgia said, "let me fix you a bowl. It's my daughter-in-law Ann's recipe. You've never had anything like it." Georgia scooped out the largest grouper steak and added a large cup of broth. "Try this, and then I have something else for you."

The sheriff picked up his spoon, dipped it, and then sipped the broth noisily. "Dang, that's tasty," he remarked. He spooned a healthy bite of fish, then chewed thoughtfully and swallowed.

"Sakes alive!" he murmured. "I detect a little onion, but there's a touch of something that allows it to bite back."

"You have a good palate, Sheriff," Sara commented.

"You're going to have to tell me," he said. "Can't figure—"

"Just a dash of chili pepper and a little lime," Sara answered.

"Here's something else," Georgia said, laying another plate on the table.

"That pound cake?" he asked.

"Naw, sugar, that's johnnycake, not as sweet as pound. Dunk a little piece in the broth."

Sheriff Tillman did as suggested and spooned it into his mouth. "Ladies," he gushed with genuine respect, "this is something special."

Georgia said, "An old Negro woman taught me how to make that."

"My, my, that tasted good, ladies," Sheriff Tillman exclaimed after he had eaten his fill.

"Do you want some more coffee?" Sara asked, beginning to rise.

"No, I'm fine." The perpetual smile he had worn while eating disappeared. "Ladies, what exactly is going on here?" he asked.

Sara answered, "My husband is serving in the Marines, so we're just trying to get by while he's gone. There's not much pay for a private in the Marine Corps."

"Got three boys, ma'am," he said, his face quickly turning soft. "One's a marine, and the other two are Army. One I ain't heard from in six months. I worry, but it's put his ma to bed."

"I'm sorry," both women replied.

"We're all making sacrifices, ladies," he wistfully stated. "I expect we haven't seen the worst yet."

"Yes, sir," Sara agreed. She read the paper and listened to the radio daily. "Things aren't going well, especially in the Pacific."

"About this situation," he said. "Before the war, the city controlled business licenses and such. But now because of manpower shortage, everything has shifted to the county. I barely have enough people to cover the law enforcement aspect, let alone check business licenses. This place looks clean to me, so there's no need to get some government worker involved that can't find his rear end with both hands. If you want to continue after the war, come to me, and I'll see that everything gets through the proper channels."

"We sure appreciate you understanding, Sheriff," Sara said, feeling much relieved.

"Be aware, ladies," he warned with an impish grin and a pat to his full stomach, "I'll be dropping by from time to time to check on things myself."

*****

Each day, Sara opened the mailbox with high anticipation and lowly disappointment if there was no letter. Today, she held her breath. It had been a month since she had heard from Clinton. She squealed with schoolgirl delight when she saw his familiar handwriting. Sara ripped the letter open and hungrily devoured his words.

My dearest, beautiful love,

Our first phase of training is coming to an end. Scuttlebutt has it—that's another new word I've learned. It means "rumor"—that as soon as we finish, we'll ship out to take Wake Island back from the Japs. I doubt it's true. A lot of talk flies around in what little idle time they give us.

And again, my love, the moments each night that I think about you and our family are the only thing that keeps me from insanity. I can feel your sweet kisses and warm breath as if you are lying beside me. Please tell Sam—and when I finish this letter, I'll write him one also—Mother, and Auntie how much I love and miss them.

Your loving husband, always and forever, sweet love of my life,
C.

Chapter 33

Blackstone Shelton tilted the bottle, draining the rest of his beer. He sat in silence, figuring that he could spend two weeks in Corpus Christi before signing on another ship. Deciding that food outweighed another beer, he spun around on the stool and stood. "Is there somewhere a man can get a good meal?" he asked loudly.

The bartender, a tattooed old salt whose time had passed, answered, "Yeah, about half a mile up the beach. There's a couple of ladies that serve good food. If you see the docks, you've gone too far."

*****

The harsh sunlight caused Blackstone to squint his eyes as he walked. The sun began to warm his body, but the frozen water of the North Atlantic would never leave his mind. He would have to go back. The merchant marine union wages were just too good. His deal with Roxboro vanished a day after Milton Marion died. "We've decided to put the contract up for bid," the group of commissioners had said. *Bastards*, he thought. *You wouldn't have dared if Marion were alive.* He lost the contract and quickly became an outcast.

The worn path inland was marked by a man sitting in the sand, enjoying a fried fish sandwich. "Where'd you get that food?" Blackstone asked.

The nearly toothless man answered without looking up. "Couple blocks up there."

"Thanks," he replied, not feeling the pleasantry. As Blackstone caught sight of the house, his mind excitedly triggered. Something was familiar about the redheaded woman, and he quickly ducked into the shadow of another home.

Blackstone rubbed his aching knuckles, now realizing that his quest for revenge would be fulfilled. Hate welled in his wretched soul as Sara moved about the porch, serving customers. He had often dreamed that the score would be settled. His passion was so consuming that, at each port, he spent the majority of his time wandering about for that one in a million chance.

His desire crested when he remembered the embarrassment of being left handcuffed on the side of the road. Adding to his hatred was the likely chance that a German torpedo could cause the gray Atlantic water to swallow him. He had the perfect physical disability to dodge service. He had no arches, and his left foot was one size larger than the right. He could have stayed warm and gotten rich in Roxboro if not for the two of them. Leaning against the house, he wondered where the sheriff was.

Blackstone nonchalantly strolled back to the beach. By late afternoon, he had concluded that the house he had used to observe Sara was vacant. He returned after dark, hiding and watching their patterns. The next day, a loose-lipped local said that Clinton was off to war. After another night, he had concluded that they were all alone and unprotected. *How much of Marion's money do they still have?* he thought. *Tomorrow night, I'll know.*

His urge for lust and revenge surged as Sara stood in the bedroom window before extinguishing the light. *Patience,* he prodded himself. *Give her a couple of hours to fall into a deep sleep.* Finally, Blackstone rose and crept toward the house. He gingerly put his weight on each step and then stood on the front porch. He peered through the screen door and saw that the heavy wooden door was open. He grasped the metal handle of the screen door but found it locked.

Blackstone opened his knife, stuck the blade through the thin wire, and used it as a fulcrum to unlock the simple hook and eye latch. He waited several seconds, but hearing no one stirring, he stepped inside. He approached the stairs, cautious as a cat stalking a bird. He climbed slowly and carefully upward. At the landing, he stood for a minute, hoping to make Sara quietly surrender to his demands. If she didn't, he would just adjust his plans as things unfolded.

After two more cautious steps, he grasped the door handle. The knob turned easily, and he pushed the door open inch by inch. After gaining enough room to slip through, he entered with his knife ready and eased toward the bed.

From behind the door, Sara slowly extended her arm. As the gun met flesh, she pulled the trigger. The old cotton shirt wrapped around the barrel hid the flash and muffled the sound. As the second shot struck, Blackstone's legs quivered and gave way.

Days before, Sam's new gift had alerted Georgia to the problem. She had given him a collapsing telescope so Sam could keep the Gulf safe from Nazi submarines. It had proven itself more than useful. Being an inquisitive woman, Georgia climbed to the second story to make sure it worked properly. The man she spied watching their home looked too familiar.

*****

"It's him," she informed Sara, "that dark, curly hair and arrogant stance are sure giveaways. He was watching us, and it's just luck he didn't see me."

Sara's legs were suddenly jelly-filled. "How could he," she stuttered, "all the way from Roxboro, find us here?"

"Just bad luck, I suppose." Georgia shrugged. "The war, maybe. Who the hell knows?"

"He'll call the law, won't he?" Sara asked, looking as though she would faint.

"For all you've been through, you still don't know much," Georgia stated bluntly. "He will want you, money, or a combination of both! Characters like him don't go to the authorities."

"What can we do?" Sara asked, her voice shaking, but Georgia ignored her question.

"My guess is," Georgia replied, thinking out loud, "he'll try to slip in on you at night. Be more dramatic—"

Sara interrupted. "What can we—"

"We take advantage of the fact that we know he's here."

"And do what?"

"I'll kill him if you won't! He's not ruining Sam's—"

"Damn him to hell. He's not hurting Sam," Sara said, suddenly catching fire. "I'll see him dead!"

"That's my girl," Georgia returned coolly.

*****

With her body shaking, Sara pulled a quilt off the bed and laid it beside Blackstone. Georgia thumped up the stairs, entering the room butcher knife first.

"You think I'd miss?" Sara asked dryly.

"No, but I wasn't taking any chances." Georgia crossed the room and looked out each window. Only one house close to them was occupied.

"How loud were the shots?" Sara asked.

"Like a broom handle falling to the floor," Georgia replied. "The widow Ely's house is still dark, and she's really the only one to worry about. Let's get him on the blanket before he bleeds out completely." With their combined strength, the two rolled Blackstone over onto the quilt. "You start digging, girl, and I'll clean the blood up," Georgia commanded. "And, Sara, make sure it's deep enough so a dog can't smell the body."

Sara shuddered slightly at the instruction. "Sam?"

"Slept right through it," Georgia said, cracking a smile. "And except for Beatrice wetting her pants, everything's fine."

*****

Grateful for the lack of moonlight, Sara pushed the shovel into the soft sand. They had argued about where to bury the body. "Hell, Sara," Georgia had insisted, "if it's under the kitchen window, every customer will walk right over it and pack the sand. Besides, we'll be shielded from prying eyes there."

It took three hours before Sara was satisfied with the grave. She scampered out of the deep hole and rested for a minute. Her arms and legs were on fire, and huge blisters covered her palms. After taking a deep breath, she pushed herself up and walked to the front steps.

The two ladies were waiting there, and Georgia whispered, "Hold the screen door." The quilt had proved effective for sliding his body down the stairs. Now with Sara helping, the process of moving Blackstone was easier. Sara used the shovel as the two old women pushed sand with their hands. The burial went quickly, and soon, the three were stomping the sand tight. When they finished, Sara swept the area clean of their footprints.

The fatigue of past sleepless nights dragged at their tired bodies as they washed the blood, sweat, and dirt away. Sara gathered their dirty clothes and carried them to the fireplace. As the fat lighter flamed, Georgia and Beatrice joined her. Georgia held out the familiar flask, and Sara didn't hesitate. She took a long pull, then passed it to Beatrice, who took a short sip, snorted, and whispered more fiercely than they could have ever imagined. "To hell with that son of a bitch."

Two days later, Sara opened the mailbox, longing for the man she loved. She had prayed for hours on end for deliverance from the things that she had done. "Please, God," she begged after seeing his letter, "let him come home on leave. I need him so desperately, just to touch him and draw strength from his presence. I ask this in Jesus Christ's holy name, amen."

My dearest love,

Our training is done, and we are shipping out. I don't know when I'll be able to write again or where I am going. Please do not worry for my safety. I am surrounded by the greatest fighting men in the world.

I can only say, over and over again, that I love you more with every beat of my heart. The memory of your love, touch, and tenderness will keep me alive and well. Kiss everyone for me.

Love,
C.

Chapter 34

October 24, 1942

Dusk was settling over the jungle as Clinton and Noah studied the rugged terrain. Young Noah's face poured sweat, washing away little tracks of dirt. Clinton saw him shake involuntarily and was grateful that he hadn't been bitten by the jungle bug. Slapping at another mosquito, he thought, *Not from the lack of opportunity, though.*

As Noah watched their line of fire, Clinton opened his canteen and took a drink of scarce water. He replaced the top as Lieutenant Colonel Chesty Puller approached. Clinton tapped Noah, and they watched as their commanding officer worked his way down the line, encouraging his marines. The colonel squatted next to their muddy foxhole and produced a sweaty candy bar from his pocket. "Thought you boys might like some pogey bait," he said.

Clinton looked into his craggy face, wondering where the hell he had found such. They hadn't eaten in two days. A rifle cracked, and dirt kicked up at the colonel's feet. "You might want to be a little more careful," Clinton said. "Damn snipers are all over the place."

Chesty Puller studied the two exhausted faces. This point in the line was where he knew the Japanese would push the hardest. "Hell, son"—he chuckled—"damn Japs couldn't hit a bull in the ass with a bass fiddle." Not giving them any time to laugh, he asked, "You boys got enough ammo?"

"Yep," both replied.

"Grenades?" Clinton shook his head, wishing for more. They were the most effective tools in night fighting. "We're the only thing between them and Henderson Field, boys," Puller said. "If we don't hold, we all die. Give the bastards hell!" he urged as he moved away.

Clinton peeled the soggy, sweat-soaked paper from the candy bar, then broke it in half, giving Noah the larger piece. Both stared into the jungle as darkness fell. Clinton cursed bitterly when the sky let go a tropical downpour that gave cover to the Japanese who were beginning to probe the line. Noah's fever-ridden eyes caught movement, and he squeezed his trigger. Clinton followed, and now two Japanese soldiers wriggled and screamed in pain not twenty feet in front of their position. Moments later, three more enemies advanced up the muddy slope. Clinton and Noah fired in unison.

Heavy firing flashed up and down the line, and dying screams pierced the air. Clinton hastily wiped the sweat from his eyes and then quickly sighted his rifle as more enemy advanced. Twice, as the battle raged, he crawled from their hole, shoving dead Japanese down the hill to keep their line of fire clear.

With wet, slippery hands, Noah tried to jam another magazine into his M1 Garand. Failing on the first try, precious seconds were lost. Clinton shot two of the four Japanese soldiers now overrunning their position, and the third, he thrust with his bayonet. Noah screamed as he grappled in hand-to-hand combat with the enemy. Clinton dropped his rifle, pulled his long KA-BAR knife, and repeatedly stabbed the Japanese soldier. As Noah struggled to regain his footing, Clinton threw the dying man from their foxhole. He grabbed his rifle, firing from the hip, as another wave pushed forward.

Dawn broke over the battlefield, revealing a hazy fog mixed with gun smoke and the misery of war. As word came down the line that they were being relieved, Clinton and Noah wearily crawled from their position. They slung their rifles, leaned on each other for support, and slogged through the mud to the rear. They had been on Guadalcanal since the initial invasion, and both were astounded to still be alive.

Chapter 35

"Got a telegram for you," the young man said, peering through the screen door.

Sara's pulse quickened, and her hands trembled as she opened the envelope. "He's coming home!" she screamed, her heart now beating again. "He's coming home on leave!" She looked up and found the boy gone, and she couldn't blame him. So many messages contained the words, "The secretary of war desires me to express his deepest regret…"

*****

"Here, honey, put this on," Georgia said, holding out a lipstick. Sara frowned and shook her head. "It'll give you a little more color," Georgia urged.

"I don't know," Sara replied, resisting but really wanting to try it.

"Damn it," Georgia cursed. "If I have to wrestle you down and—"

Sara smiled at Georgia's determination to win the battle. "I will if you leave the straw hat at home," Sara teased impishly. It was so old and beaten that it wouldn't even make good stuffing for a mouse's house.

"What's wrong with my hat?" Georgia shot back defensively. "It's one of the rare presents my husband gave me. I'm kinda attached to it."

Sara sighed deeply, wishing she had left the subject alone. "Help me, Georgia," she said. "I've never used lipstick before."

"Neither have I, honey," Georgia replied. "But it can't be that damn hard."

"What if he thinks I'm becoming brash?" Sara asked, suddenly worrying.

"Sara," Georgia bluntly said, "he's been gone a long time, and all he wants to do is come home and get naked with you."

"Georgia!"

"Well, it's the damn truth!"

*****

Sara felt the vibration of the train long before it made the final curve and came into sight. Breathlessly, she waited as the train hissed to a stop. People began to disembark, and she stared at the windows, trying to see Clinton. Passenger after passenger greeted loved ones and then quickly disappeared.

Wearing her feelings openly, Sara fearfully asked Georgia, "You think he missed his train? Should we check the telegraph office?"

"No, he's here, honey," Georgia said, weeping at the sight of her son. "He's helping someone."

Sara saw Clinton backing slowly down the steps in front of a frail soldier awkwardly trying to navigate on crutches. His left pant leg was folded and pinned back to compensate for his missing limb. "There he is," a female voice cried happily behind her. "There's my baby!" Clinton stepped back as the mother clutched her son in a deep embrace. His faint voice sailed sweetly in the air: "I'm home, Mama."

Sara was shocked at Clinton's appearance. His once bronze skin was now yellow, and his eyes were hollow and haunted. His uniform fell loosely from his shoulders as if it was a size too big. "Here I am," she cried, surging forward as Clinton turned to the sound of her voice. He wrapped his arms around her, picked her up, and buried his face in her neck. They clung to each other, neither wanting to ever let go.

"Daddy!" Sam pleaded, now clinging to Clinton's leg.

Clinton released Sara and picked Sam up, embracing the child with a tight hug. "My, you've grown, Sam," he said after setting the boy down. "How old are you now?" He couldn't remember.

Sam ignored the question and asked excitedly, "How many Japs did you kill for me?"

Clinton avoided the question by asking another. "Did you take good care of the ladies like I asked?"

"Yes, sir," Sam answered proudly, brandishing a salute he had practiced for days.

"Good," Clinton said after giving him another hug. "I knew I could count on you." Clinton then reached for his mother. "You're getting younger, Mama," he exclaimed.

"Your son keeps me going," she said, grateful that God had answered her countless prayers.

Clinton then leaned down, hugged Beatrice, and whispered in her ear. "You been keeping them straight? I know how difficult Mama can be," he teased.

"Ain't a chance in hell with that impossible woman," Beatrice answered. "But I do my best."

*****

Sara lay with her head on Clinton's chest, content to hear his heartbeat and feel the rise and fall of his body.

"Noah's going to be here the last two days," Clinton softly whispered into the night air. "I tried to convince him to come sooner, but he wanted to give us more time to ourselves. I hope you didn't mind me inviting—"

"A friend of yours is always welcome."

"He hasn't got much family," Clinton said, feeling as if he needed to explain. "His mama died young. Daddy a drunk. He probably hadn't eaten three meals in the same day till he joined the corps."

WHERE THE COTTON ONCE GREW

"It's okay, darling."

"He's like a little brother."

Sara felt his breathing grow deep and his body relax. Hours later, she awoke with a fearful start as Clinton thrashed, fighting with an invisible enemy. Sara ducked under his swinging arms, clutched his chest, and called out loudly to him, "It's me, honey! It's your Sara!"

Clinton's eyes flew open, drenched in fear. He calmed after feeling her arms around him. Hours later, she finally talked him back to sleep.

*****

Noah stood nervously after shaking hands with Clinton. Sara took the initiative and hugged the young man after sensing his uneasiness. "Noah, my husband holds you in high regard. Welcome to our family." That night, Sara realized there was an unspoken bond between the two men that she would never understand.

They all made several attempts at feeding them, but their well-intended efforts failed. Instead, Clinton and Noah chose to sit on the porch and share a bottle of whiskey under a declining moon. Sara felt ashamed, but she listened at the window to their slurred and haunted voices.

"You knows it buddy. I ain't coming back next time."

"Yes, you are," Clinton slobbered. "Ain't a nip that can take you."

"Bullshit. Marine, you the toughest son of a bitch I've ever seen. Got that Jap off me."

"Just helping out. You's...going...to..."

"I was gone, buddy. He had me." Sara heard Noah start to cry mournfully.

"Naw...you's fine. Hell, if it whuttin' fer you, I be rotting in that damn jungle. Time after time, you..."

*****

249

The rare, cool, overcast day of Corpus Christi added to the misery of the farewell.

"Noah," Sara said, trying to be strong, "after this is over, come back here to settle. It would mean a lot to us." She wondered for a second if he was going to cry.

"I'd like that," Noah said. "It's really nice here."

"It's settled, then," Georgia chimed, grabbing him for another hug. She hadn't wasted any time adopting Noah. "You will write me."

"What about me?" Beatrice interrupted.

"I meant the both of us, sister," Georgia fumed. "Must you pick on every…"

Sara clung to Clinton until the final boarding call. He kissed her lightly once more, then turned and walked away.

Chapter 36

Sara awoke from a fitful sleep, then swallowed hard, trying to remove the tackiness in her throat. The September air was heavy and thick, making it difficult to breathe.

"Honey," Georgia softly said as she slipped into the room, "I can feel it. Clinton's in battle."

"I know," Sara responded faintly as Georgia sat on the bed. "That won't help," she murmured as a flask was pushed in her direction.

"It can't hurt," Georgia said knowing that neither would sleep.

*****

As the LVT churned through the water, Clinton saw the smoky island of Peleliu coming closer. He wondered how any enemy could be alive after the three days of shelling. *It's a miracle*, he thought, *that me and the kid are still together. Most of the men are new.*

Clinton grabbed Noah by the arm, pulling him so close that their helmets collided. "Stay behind me on the beach!" he commanded. Noah's face was ashen, and his eyes were frightfully round, and so were all the others'. His response was a fearful nod. *God, he's just a kid*, Clinton thought as the LVT slammed into the shoreline.

As the ramp dropped, bullets buzzed like angry hornets through the salty air. The cruel reality of a beachfront assault filled Clinton's eyes. The marines were pinned behind a coral wall, and the Japanese defenders were chewing them apart. Dead men washed in the waves, and the water responded by turning a crimson red.

Clinton felt warm urine running down his leg as he dived into the sand. He and Noah crawled forward as others fell and died. Over the sounds of battle, Clinton heard the repeated screams for a corpsman's help. They took cover behind a disabled tank, grateful for its protection.

"Move forward, marine," an officer shouted roughly, grabbing Noah by the collar, yanking him upright and dragging him toward the wall. Clinton scrambled to follow until a deadly volley of rounds struck the two men. He dropped to the dirt and crawled frantically to his friend.

A machine gun raked the ground around Clinton as he covered Noah's body with his own. With a high-pitched wail, he screamed over and over again, "Corpsman! Corpsman!"

The ragged young man, his face and hands already painted red, dropped to his knees beside Clinton. "Move so I can check him." Clinton rolled away, and the corpsman felt for Noah's pulse. He shook his head, glanced at the officer, and moved on to other cries. Mindless of his own death as withering fire danced all around, Clinton hugged Noah's lifeless body tightly and began to sob.

"Move forward, damn you," an officer screamed while trying to wrap the bloody stump of his missing hand. Clinton stared at the man through a blue haze, no longer hearing the sounds of battle.

The captain slapped him sharply across his face with his remaining hand. "You can't win the damn war sitting there, marine!" he roared as if he, too, had lost his mind.

Clinton fought for control, forcing his legs to move. As he lurched forward, following others, a horrific stinging sensation tore through his body. *Sara*, he thought as the grayness came, *my beautiful Sara.*

*****

Sara's hands trembled as she lowered the coffee cup from her lips. She looked at Georgia, then at Beatrice, hoping the knock at the door was just in her mind.

"Do you want me to answer?" Georgia asked as the rapping continued.

"No."

"I'll go with you," Georgia said as Sara stood. Beatrice turned back to her coffee, but she couldn't find the strength to raise the cup. An ill wind had filled their home, and no one could rest. Even Sam, in his perpetual state of being a little boy, had become infected.

Sara heard Georgia's soft prayer as she opened the yellow telegram. With trembling hands, she read the following:

> WESTERN UNION
> T28 31 Govt=wx Washington D.C.
>
> 16 1022 am
> 243 Bonn Rd Sept 16, 1944
> Corpus Christi Texas
>
> Regret to inform you your husband Private First Class Jack Miller was seriously wounded in action on Sept 15, 1944 on Peleiu period You will be advised as reports of condition are received period
>
> =ULIO THE ADJUANT GENERAL

"He's alive, Georgia," Sara whispered, all her strength now gone. "Thank God, he's still alive."

Chapter 37

A light and airy breeze blew through the kitchen as Sheriff Tillman spooned the last piece of johnnycake in his mouth, then took another sip of coffee. "As always, your food is the best I've ever eaten."

"It's always a pleasure to have you," Sara replied honestly. He had become a staple in their home, and she looked forward to each visit.

"You still turning down my offer, Mr. Miller?" the sheriff asked Clinton. For the last month, he had constantly offered work.

"Yes, sir," Clinton replied, scratching his chin. "I'll find something, but I don't think I'm cut out for law enforcement."

Each time Sara looked at Clinton, she cherished his very sight. She had come so close to losing him. His outward scars would always show, but he was gaining weight, and his color was returning. Most wouldn't guess that for a solid year, he barely clung to life. His service had cost him a kidney; shattered his right femur, leaving him with a slight limp; and left a fragment of a bullet in his liver.

She knew, though, that the greatest scars were within. The war had cost him Noah and countless other buddies and left him wondering why he lived when so many others died. His lack of employment hadn't given her any worry yet.

"How's your wife?" Sara asked, hoping the sheriff wouldn't mention the job again.

"She has good and bad days. It helps some that Rector's home now." Rector Tillman returned from the European theater two months earlier, but his two brothers were in overseas graves. "The loss of our boys touched her deeply," he said sadly. "She still sets them a place at the table. We tried talking to her—"

"If it gives her some peace," Sara said, "I can't see the harm." She could suddenly see Lilly sitting and rocking all night long.

"Well, I didn't come here to burden my friends," Sheriff Tillman said, slapping his knee. "Remember when I first talked to you about the business license?"

"Yes," Sara answered. "That was your first visit."

"Since the war is over, things are changing, and I won't be in charge much longer. Best we do something about your situation."

"What can we do, Sheriff?" Clinton asked.

"I'd love for you to stay here, but you'll have to spend a lot of money to turn this into a proper restaurant. But there's a nice little place not far from here that's for sale."

"I don't know," Sara said, frowning. "How much would—"

"Drop that worried look, girl," Sheriff Tillman said in a fatherly tone. "The owner will give you a good deal."

"Think so?" Clinton asked, unsure about possibilities.

"No doubt," Sheriff Tillman answered, his face smug. "I did a little homework after he made a few complaints about you stealing his customers. Found two outstanding warrants, and he's suddenly motivated to sell his restaurant and move on."

"How much?" Clinton asked bluntly.

"Two thousand dollars, cash money."

Sara looked at Clinton for guidance, but he was looking at her. "What does that include?" she asked.

"The building, a complete kitchen, and every table, chair, spoon, knife, fork, and napkin that you'll need. Come on," the sheriff urged as he stood. "Let's go over there right now and take a look."

"Sheriff, how can I ever thank you for the kindness you've shown?" Sara suddenly asked, wondering why he had given her a pass these last four years.

"I always longed for a daughter," he humbly admitted. "And when I saw you the first time, I just took you as my own. Hope you don't mind," he said softly with a bowed head. "I just like looking out for you."

"No," she answered, tears springing in her eyes as she hugged the old man tightly. "In fact, I'm right proud."

Chapter 38

Ruth Marion worried about the swollen bump on her chin as heavy rain pelted against the kitchen window. Clair had died two months earlier, and now Ruth cursed under her breath about the mildewed old home. She thought back to the week after her father died, and her anger grew.

She had assumed that with the boy gone, everything would be hers. In fact, she had purposely ignored Clinton's many late nights at the jail, hoping that he would run away with the girl. It was the best way to get Sam out of the picture. But the shock of finding that the money, properties, and bank were all left to Clair increased her bitterness. She had fumed as everything was sold to Milton's wealthy friends.

*****

"We're moving to Savannah," Clair announced as the money transfer was completed.

"Damn you, Mother," Ruth shouted hysterically. "I'm not moving!"

"Well, if you stay in Roxboro," Clair replied calmly, "how will you live?"

"What do you mean?" Ruth shouted. "I deserve at least half the money!"

"You're not mature enough," Clair said dryly.

"What do you mean?" Ruth asked, her face tight.

"Unless you come with me, you don't get an allowance."

"I'm not a child!"

"Think of it as a salary. You'll get paid to cook and clean for me."

"You mean I'm your servant?" Ruth asked bitterly.

"You can do it my way," Clair said with a brief smile, "or after my death, all the money will go to the poor."

"You wouldn't dare!"

"Every penny, Ruth," she stated flatly. "If you want an inheritance, you'll do what I say."

*****

Ruth's mind wandered to Clair's deathbed confession, and her face began to burn.

*****

"It's time you know everything," Clair said quietly as Ruth hovered, wondering how much money was left.

"What is it, Mother?" Ruth asked, sick of playing the dutiful daughter.

"Your father," Clair said, her voice barely audible, "went to Roxboro to take the place of his mean, nasty old grandfather, but let me start from the beginning." Ruth took a wet rag and wiped away the saliva clinging to the corner of Clair's mouth. "Aunt Shiva, Milton's great aunt, reared your father in New Jersey. What happened to his parents or why she and Milton didn't live in Roxboro was something they wouldn't talk about."

"New Jersey—"

Clair interrupted, her face pinched in pain. "I need a little sip of water." Ruth held her question, poured a cup, and then held it to Clair's thin lips. She took a drink. "Milton's grandfather didn't care for him, but the aunt kept lobbying on his behalf. There wasn't anyone else to receive the inheritance, but the mean old man was unpredictable."

"You've made it clear that you didn't like—"

"He worked people to death just to make another dollar. I don't doubt he insisted on gold dollars in his funeral suit thinking he could bribe his way out of hell."

"Go on, Mother," Ruth said, exasperated.

"The old aunt became distraught as the years passed, and she gained no firm commitment for Milton, so she started writing letters of praise about his business skills."

"What kind of—"

"He had a dental practice," Clair answered. "His aunt stretched the truth—"

"He never said anything about being raised in Jersey," Ruth said. "I thought North Carolina."

"That was my family, and he told everyone what he wanted them to believe." Ruth wiped a bead of sweat from her own lip. "You didn't know that he was married once before either."

"What do you mean? He married twice?" Ruth asked with arched eyebrows.

"It didn't last," Clair stated. "You were two months old when she packed up and ran away."

I've been betrayed by everyone, Ruth thought, the blood draining from her face at the shocking news. *My own mother and father... Clinton running off with that whore!* Ruth saw the bemused look on Clair's face and wanted to smother her. "And you just pretended to be my mother all these years?" she asked, her eyes narrow slits.

"There's a reason," Clair explained. "The day after your mother abandoned Milton, he received a telegram. It said, 'If you're worthy of my money, come to Roxboro and show me.' Milton was in a pickle because if he showed up wifeless, he'd have to explain why. In those days, men that couldn't control their wives were considered weak."

"How did you get involved?" Ruth asked suspiciously. "I thought you were from North Carolina."

Clair gave a raspy laugh. "My folks were long on social graces, breeding, and putting on airs but short on cash. I came along late, so by the time I was sixteen, they were getting along in years."

"I don't need to hear your whole family—"

"I'm an old, dying woman," Clair responded. "Be patient."

"I'm waiting."

"I had fallen in love with a sharecropper's son. Oh, how I adored him," Clair confessed. "And Clinton was made in the very image of Joseph!" The words stung Ruth so hard her back arched. "My parents didn't approve, because of his lowly station in life, and I underestimated their determination to keep me from my lover.

"Oh, don't look so shocked," Clair said, reacting to Ruth's expression of disdain. "We felt deeply for each other. It wasn't some silly crush. The next thing I knew, I was being rushed to the train station. My widowed aunt Salem had married a Yankee, so they shipped me north. Mama and Daddy figured, with me being away, I would get over him. You can imagine the fury I—"

"No, I can't," Ruth replied smugly, wanting her words to hurt.

"Clinton left," Clair sparred, "because you never showed him one ounce of kindness. He was a gentle, loving person, but you were a tyrant like your father. No man could live and hold up his head—"

"I'm tired of you taking up for him," Ruth said, her eyes glowing.

"I'm sure you are," Clair responded knowingly. "After two weeks there, I received a letter from a cousin saying that Joseph left town after Daddy spun him a tale about me courting another man. Needless to say, I was infuriated. My aunt thought differently than my parents. High breeding was fine, but it didn't pay the bills. She'd been kept informed by Milton's great aunt about his expected inheritance, but when Milton was faced with going to Roxboro wifeless, they concocted a plan.

"Your father's desperation played on my feelings. He promised that if I'd help, when the old man died, he'd pay me a large sum. The offer of money and family revenge was appealing, so we left the next day. At first, things were pleasant while your father worked day and night to appease his grandfather. Milton hired a maid to take care of you, and that left me free to shop, visit with whoever I pleased, and do nothing but enjoy myself.

"Two years later, that old goat died, and your father inherited everything. My anger toward my parents was fading, and Milton agreed to support them. One night, after getting a divorce on the sly, he asked me to marry. I agreed, seeing no need to change my pleasant life. Falling in love with money is very easy.

"Milton wanted a son, and two years later, I was pregnant. Oh," Clair said, beginning to weep, "how it saddens me to think about Trace. He was the spitting image of the old man, and somehow, I always knew he was destined to leave in a horrible way."

Ruth's temper overcame her disgust, and she lashed out. "How can you say that about your own son?"

"Because it's the truth," Clair said sadly. "He was cruel and got what he deserved! May God have mercy—"

"I ought to smother you," Ruth sneered, the urge almost overpowering.

Clair fearlessly laid down the gauntlet. "Go ahead. You'll only shorten my pain."

"Are you going to finish?" Ruth asked, now desperate to leave the room.

Clair obliged. "After your brother was born, Milton became more ruthless and cunning, falling in love with his absolute control. His attitude toward me changed, but I fought back with my best weapon. He'd created a fable about his family, and I threatened to tell. I stood toe to toe with him to his dying day."

"How did you get him to leave you everything?"

"That's all you really care about, isn't it?"

"Just answer the question! How did you push me out of the way? Daddy could have given me a share. Then I wouldn't have been forced to live like this."

"I'll never tell," Clair replied, growing weaker, "just because you want to know so badly. But I will tell you why we moved here. It's because this is where I found my Joseph. He'd never married, so we were free to resume our love affair. The trips I made over the last years, he accompanied me."

"Damn you!"

"Don't worry, Ruth, there's plenty of money left. But while I could, I spent lavishly on that dear man. Think what you want about me. I've already made my peace with God."

"He must not have loved you, because he isn't here now. I am," Ruth said, hoping her words hurt.

"I'm a vain woman," Clair admitted. "I'd never allow him to see me in this state. Oh, this damn cancer," she said, her strength gone. "There just wasn't enough time."

Ruth drew a short breath, sickened by the admission and the stench of the hot room. Clair's raspy exhale traveled through the thick, humid air as Ruth closed the door, leaving her to suffer alone until death finally called.

*****

As Clinton's picture stared back, Ruth's mood grew darker. She had already justified her lust for revenge; he was simply the only person left.

Rubin Scott knocked while using his free hand to hold his raincoat closed. He ignored Ruth's audible gasp as she looked into his burned face. The pale, grafted skin coupled with his lack of ears always caused even the most polite person to stare.

"I understand you have a job for me," Rubin said, breaking Ruth's trance.

"I do. Come in," Ruth said. After hanging his raincoat, she led him to the kitchen. "Would you like something to drink?" she offered in a friendly tone, hoping he would take the case all others had declined.

"No, ma'am," he replied.

Not wasting any time, she laid Clinton's picture in front of him. "I want you to find him," she stated flatly. He studied the photograph as Ruth gave her version of the story. "I'm told you're the best," she lied knowing he was her last hope. "And I want him punished."

"You do realize there's a great possibility he's already dead," he stated.

"How could that be?" she asked. She hadn't considered the possibility. *Hope the bastard is dead,* she thought. *And that whore too!*

"He could be lying in a grave overseas or at the bottom of the ocean," Rubin pointed out.

With contempt, she replied, "He wouldn't be the type. He'd find a way to dodge service, and I want to know where he is."

"I don't come cheap," he flatly stated. "This might take six months, a year, or I may never find him."

"I've got money to pay," she said, beginning an ugly glare. "But don't think you can cheat me. I want detailed reports on the expenses."

"Agreed," Rubin replied as he stood up to leave, taking the photograph and the few personal papers that she had of Clinton.

Chapter 39

Clinton opened the cash register and began to count the day's take. After tallying the total, he removed a beer from the cooler. He took a long swallow and felt a wave of weariness. All their regular customers had come to their third-anniversary celebration. The last couple had just left, and he had sent Sara home after promising to follow her closing ritual.

Sara and her constant companion, the retired sheriff Tillman, had decided it was time to open another restaurant on the west side of town. The old lawman had sniffed out a steal, and they were in the process of refurbishing. Clinton smiled for a moment thinking about how the old sheriff loved and protected Sara.

As he thought deeper, a reoccurring worry surfaced. She couldn't let go of the fact that there wasn't a safe way to fulfill her promise to Uncle Hiram. He also knew that Danny played a part in her late-night restlessness, and he felt powerless to help. A light rapping broke his thoughts, and Clinton walked to the door. After lifting the Closed sign and peering through the glass, he saw a scarred and disfigured face staring back.

"We're closed," Clinton said loudly.

"I just need a minute," Rubin Scott lied. "I'm closing my place, and I've got some equipment to sell cheap."

Clinton hesitated at first, then relented, because the man wore the familiar sign of a veteran. "Come in," he said, stepping aside so

Rubin could enter. "Have a seat, and I'll be with you in a moment." Rubin sat at the nearest table and admired the old fishing nets that decorated the walls as Clinton finished the bank deposit.

A slow, morbid fear began to rise in Clinton's soul as he stuffed the cash into a bank bag. Sheriff Tillman hadn't spoken of any other restaurant in town closing. *And he would know*, he thought. He slowly reached for his pistol under the counter. Milton Marion entered his mind as he pointed the revolver at the man.

"You can put that away," Rubin said calmly while holding his suit coat open to show he was unarmed. "I mean you no harm."

"What do you want?" Clinton asked, his eyes wary and body tensed. "You're not selling anything."

"Correct," Rubin answered honestly. "But I do bring great news from Clair Marion." Clinton felt his knees go weak. "I assure you that if you'll kindly stop pointing that .38 at me and let me buy a beer, I'll tell you wonderful news."

"Sit here," Clinton commanded sternly while pointing at a barstool. Rubin walked to the bar and sat down. Clinton stuffed the gun in his beltline before opening the beer. *If killing him is necessary, then so be it.*

Rubin Scott took an appreciative drink. "I won't prolong the agony, because Clair wouldn't have wanted it that way. She thought a lot of you."

"How so?" Clinton asked, totally confused. "Milton—"

"He died not long after you left," Rubin announced.

"He's dead!" Clinton exclaimed, finding it impossible to hide his relief. "How?"

"Heart attack," Rubin answered dryly. "Guess he couldn't stand parting with any of his money. Ruth wasn't in the will, so Clair got everything," he added, giving Clinton details through the sale of Marion's interests.

"But what—"

"After coming home from war," Rubin interrupted, "I couldn't resume my job as a police officer for obvious reasons. Instead, I hung out a shingle as a private detective in Savannah, and that's how I met Clair. Did you know that's where she and Ruth—of course, you didn't," Rubin said, answering his own question. "She walked into my office one day and told me this rich story about the trial and you running away with a prisoner. She knew that after she died, Ruth would desire revenge, so she wanted to ensure your freedom."

"Why?" Clinton asked quizzically.

Rubin Scott grinned. "You reminded her of an old beau."

"Huh?" Clinton grunted, but then he thought about all the strange looks and winks that Clair had given him.

"She thought you deserved better in life and wanted a plan in place."

"What kinda plan?" Clinton asked, still leery about this strange story.

"She had me pay every private eye within three hundred miles of Savannah just in case Ruth contacted them. I've got twenty-three signed agreements in my safe."

"How much did that cost?" Clinton asked, truly astounded.

"A lot." Rubin chuckled. "Hell, Sheriff," he added, "she even insisted that we pay for an agreement with the Pinkerton Agency."

"No shi…" Clinton stopped short.

"She spared no expense for you."

Clinton wanted to believe him but was cautious. "But just because I reminded her—"

"It's deeper than that," Rubin explained. "We got to be great friends, and often, before she got sick, we talked."

"Sick?"

"She's dead," Rubin stated flatly. "This was set up ahead of time. I'd guess she had a premonition. She felt guilty about what Trace did and also about not protecting Sara and the boy from Milton Marion. Sometimes," he explained, "people need to clear their conscience. You've seen it on the battlefield."

"I'd have never thought," Clinton said, shaking his head in disbelief. "Just how can you ensure my freedom? You found me!"

Rubin took on a business tone and explained, "Ruth gave me a picture and what little personal information she had. I guessed correctly that you joined the war effort. It pays to have foxhole buddies, and I leaned on one that works in the War Department. He gave me unlimited access, and I pored through all the photographs of different units, trying to match your face."

"You've got to be kidding," Clinton exclaimed, nearly dropping his beer. "There are millions, and the pictures aren't that good."

Rubin smiled before answering. "I made a wild guess where you would try to hide. Texas was my first, because of the state's size. California was my second. That narrowed my search somewhat. I was just lucky," he admitted. "It was a vague shot, but your height helped in the search. I looked at thousands of photos before spotting you and matching the paperwork. But it really wasn't necessary."

"Why go to all that trouble, then?"

"My own satisfaction," Rubin said with a shrug of his shoulders. "After my friend led me through the official process of a veteran dying, we assembled every piece of paperwork, down to notification of the family, service records, and death benefits. The package that's in your real name looks and smells official. She was delighted to find you dead and downright gleeful to receive your government life insurance. As of five days ago, Ruth thinks you died in Northern Africa." Rubin remained silent as Clinton absorbed the news.

"What about Sara and Sam?" Clinton asked, concerned again. "Do you think she'll try to find—"

"No," Rubin answered decisively. "People who feel superior to the masses are the easiest to con. Just to pad the bill, I spun a tale on how I tracked them down also. Included in this information was a newspaper article on Sara and Sam's terrible automobile accident in San Diego. I collaborated the article with death certificates. Sir," Rubin said, smiling as widely as his face would allow, "I skinned that woman down to the bone."

Clinton was euphoric. "What do I owe you? You didn't have to find me and tell me this."

"Nothing," Rubin replied. "I was enthralled with the story and wanted to meet you. But most of all, I enjoyed screwing Ruth."

Chapter 40

"Clinton," Sara said, the moonlight bathing their bedroom, "Sam's twenty now."

"So?" Clinton asked sleepily after rolling over and pulling Sara close.

"He can take care of himself if something happens. I'm not waiting any longer. Uncle Hiram was my friend, and I'm going to see him."

"Sara," he replied, not wanting to hurt her, "you know that after all these years, he's already passed away."

"I know," she sadly agreed. "But that makes no difference. I made a promise."

*****

Clinton insisted that Sam take a preliminary scouting trip to Roxboro for Sara's safety, and he undertook the mission with the enthusiasm of an OSS agent sneaking into Nazi Germany. He found Johnny still living there and gathered the history his mother requested. His report started out with a comical account of how Uncle Hiram never saw the inside of a prison. As Sara laughed, years of guilt melted away.

"You could have told me what you'd done long ago," Sara said, scolding Clinton.

"I didn't know for sure that the warden would believe me," Clinton replied.

"I get the only husband that can't lie to make me feel better," she retorted, throwing her hands in the air.

"There's nothing much left," Sam said, "except a gas station, one branch bank from Meadville, a restaurant, and the old court-house, which is falling apart."

Sara could sense, as Sam paused to sip his iced tea, that much more foreboding news was coming. She went over the details as he drove her toward the Roxboro county line. The one that hurt the most was Danny's death. His body lay in France, and she had already vowed to visit her brother. Somewhere deep in her soul, she had always hoped they could somehow become family.

Sara stared at the many fields where cotton once grew as she remembered the rest. Mr. Ewell, whom she would never consider her father, was dead. Kind old Johnson, gone also. She was surprised to learn that Ronnie Meeker died a heroic death and posthumously received the Medal of Honor. Victor Turlock was in Fort Leavenworth prison, serving a life sentence for deserting his men under fire.

"You okay, Mama?" Sam asked, noticing Sara's vacant look.

"Just a little nervous," she replied, brushing a stray hair away. "Many bad memories are here."

"We can turn around if—"

"No, son," Sara replied, patting his leg. "It's all right."

Soon, Uncle Hiram's home came into view. The rough exterior remained, but the yard now grew luscious green grass and was trimmed with blooming azaleas of red, pink, and yellow. Looking to the rear of the home, Sara saw two large wooden barns.

"Remember, Mama, Johnny is a veterinarian," Sam said as he tapped the horn. "That's so he can hear us at the barn," he quickly uttered after Sara gave him a sharp look. "You want to wait on the porch?" She agreed and opened the door. Minutes later, Johnny climbed the steps and offered Sara his hand. She refused the greeting and instead wrapped him in a tight hug.

"You look just like your daddy," she whispered in his ear.

"I don't know if that's a compliment or not, Ms. Sara," Johnny lightly replied.

"It is, Johnny," she insisted, holding on to his arms and taking a better look. "He was a kind and generous man."

"I agree, Ms. Sara," he replied, but with raised eyebrows, he added, "He was also a character."

"Please call me Sara," she urged, releasing her grip.

"All right," he agreed. "Come in and let me fix you two something to drink."

Sara glanced around the house and saw that it looked more modern now with newer furniture and pictures on the walls. Where there were once bare floors, rugs now covered the wood planking. The kitchen table remained the same, she noticed, as she took a seat.

"What would y'all like?" Johnny asked.

"You wouldn't have a taste of Uncle Hiram's finest, would you?" Sara hopefully asked.

"Yes," Johnny admitted. "I make a little for family and friends." He brought out a bottle and poured a small amount into three glasses. Sara gave him a look, and he added another generous portion to hers.

"Mother, it's only nine in the morning," Sam scolded.

"Little nip won't hurt, dear," Sara said, tipping her glass. *How many times did I hear that?* she thought. Georgia and Beatrice had lived rich, full lives in Texas, and she would always miss them. They had fussed, fought, and loved to the very end. Sara took another sip and then asked in a hushed voice, "Tell me about Mr. Ewell's last years."

Johnny hesitated until Sara gave him a wanting look. "After you left, he would stop a stranger on the street to confess his sins. After Danny died, I guess he decided it was God's punishment for what he'd done. He became listless, lost interest in his land, and just faded away."

Sara didn't show any emotion until Johnny spoke again. "Sara, there's something you should know." She eyed Sam, and he sheepishly looked away. "Mr. Ewell sold his land to me before he died," Johnny revealed, "with instructions to give you the money if I ever saw you again."

Tears sprang from her green eyes, and she made no attempt to stop the flow. "Give it to charity," she cried, unable to contain herself. Johnny looked at Sam and found him nodding in agreement. Both sat patiently waiting for Sara to regain control. As her tears ebbed, Sam passed her his handkerchief. She dabbed her eyes dry, then spoke in a throaty voice. "Johnny, Uncle Hiram was my only friend during a very dark time. If you would, give us directions so I can visit his grave."

"Sara," he said, "the difficulty involved to bury Daddy on the property was great. But after filling out tons of paperwork, Washington finally relented. His plot is out back. I'll take you there." Johnny held Sara's arm as he walked her down the rear steps. The day was warm, and the sun felt wonderful on her face.

"I'll get the flowers," Sam said, walking away. Sara waited with Johnny, his comforting touch never leaving her arm. Sam soon returned, and they resumed their walk. They came to a small clearing, and Sara saw the wooden fence of the cemetery.

Johnny stopped Sara for a moment and softly said, "You didn't ask, so I need to tell you that I buried Mr. Ewell here also. Daddy wanted it that way."

Sara felt slightly embarrassed at first, but she shook off the feeling. Uncle Hiram had given her so much more. Johnny released her arm as Sam handed her the flowers. They stayed behind knowing she wanted to be alone. She opened the gate and walked through. Paying no mind to the dew, she knelt in the grass beside his grave. After placing the flowers, she brushed a sandy rabbit track from the gray slab.

Sara lightly touched the simple inscription—"Uncle Hiram"—then leaned down, placing her cheek against the sunlit stone. "I came back, Uncle Hiram," she whispered as her tears began to flow. "Just like you asked."

About the Author

Stephen Harris started life as a farmer and a cattleman's son and listening to all the tall tales of the South. It wasn't long before he became adept and was spinning his own yarns as a child. His father once remarked, "Son, you'd rather climb a tree and tell a lie than stand on the ground and tell the truth."

After spending his early years with horses, cattle, and dirt, he moved on to becoming a professional pilot. The love for telling stories never left him, though. Several novelettes were produced, and countless humorous stories were written just for fun. Finally, with the insistence of family and friends, he sat down and wrote a full-length novel about his beloved South.

Stephen Harris resides in Central Alabama with his wife, daughters, sons-in-law, a gang of grandchildren and also, last but not least, Piper the wonder dog.

CPSIA information can be obtained
at www.ICGtesting.com
Printed in the USA
LVHW101434260422
717283LV00011B/33